THE
SEVENTH
SONS

A SYCAMORE MOON NOVEL

DOMINO FINN

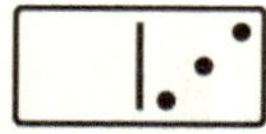

Published by Blood & Treasure, Los Angeles
Second Edition

Cover by James T. Egan of Bookfly Design LLC.

Print ISBN: 978-0-692-31706-8

DominoFinn.com

"***Supernatural* meets *Sons of Anarchy.*** Detective Maxim Dwyer is a man on a mission and nothing is going to stop him from finding his missing wife—not shape-shifting hard cases, outlaw bikers, or government cover-ups. Finn's *Seventh Sons* is a story you're not going to want to put down."

- James A. Hunter, Author of Strange Magic (Yancy Lazarus Series)

The Seventh Sons

Part 1 - The Sighting

i.

"If you really want proof of werewolves, just put me in a room with a heavy door that locks and sit with me for twenty minutes."

The man in the hospital bed tugged his left wrist. The handcuffs clinked securely against the bed's aluminum frame.

Detective Maxim Dwyer scratched his three-day beard and considered the prisoner. He pulled his cell phone from his jacket and pressed the awkward button on the side. The screen flashed 2:45 a.m. and he returned it to his pocket with a sigh.

"Forget I asked," said Maxim. "I didn't arrest you because of local superstitions. I want to know what happened in Sycamore Lodge earlier tonight."

The man glanced at the other two prisoners in the room.

This wasn't a conventional hospital. It was a limited clinic that sat atop the marshal's office, and the only care provider in Sanctuary. The small town wasn't entirely isolated in the woods—it was only thirty minutes west of Flagstaff and its first class facilities—but it was quaint enough that the city services were crammed into a few buildings on Main Street. The fire department was staffed with emergency responders who had treated the prisoners at the scene, and this upstairs clinic had doctors who could handle most common treatments.

This was a special room. A secure room. It had four bunks, two guards posted outside, and a mesh of wired glass that served as the single fixed window. The only light, from a table lamp, cast a warm glow on the prisoners.

Four beds, four bikers, thought Maxim. Except one of the beds was empty. It wouldn't be filled tonight.

A wiry blonde woman lay with a fresh cast on one arm and cuffs on the other. A rough-looking Indian man, also cuffed, had a cast on his leg. Neither had ID and both were sleeping, whether the result of drink or medication, Maxim wasn't sure.

The third prisoner was the anomaly. He carried identification with a given name of Diego de la Torre. Twenty-seven-year-old Hispanic male, Michigan license. They had all crashed their motorcycles. The other two bikers had been lucky to only sustain minor lacerations and broken bones. Diego had been luckier still; somehow, he was mostly unscathed.

He was also the only one of the three who was currently coherent.

"You can't keep me here, Detective," murmured the man in a vaguely South American accent.

Maxim grinned. "From where I'm standing, that's exactly what I can do."

Diego's eyes narrowed.

"No, I get it," said Maxim, putting his hand up before the prisoner could argue. "Your motorcycle club is above the law, is that right?"

"That's not what I mean."

"Then what? Is this a bad time for you, with the full moon and all?"

Maxim chuckled. The grotesque rumors shadowed the motorcycle club. They were the reason for its peculiar reputation. Whispers of beasts were not uncommon among the criminals who frequented his jail, but this went further. Even some of the veteran officers in the station had similar wild claims. Word was, these bikers were wild animals inside.

Maxim wasn't so sure about that. It wasn't that he discounted the supernatural outright—rather, he thought of himself as an open-minded skeptic. Wait for proof, even look for it, but don't believe something based entirely on talk or supposition. After all, his job was about following evidence.

"I know you don't believe," said Diego. "But I know you want to. Why else would you ask me about it?"

The detective shook his head dismissively. He didn't

know why he'd asked. It was a throwaway question before he went home for the night.

"Just curious."

Diego nodded. "That is my offer then. I can show you proof if you take me to a separate room."

It had already been a long night, and the prospect sounded more tiring than exciting. But again, Maxim thought about following the evidence. If a suspect offered to show him a wolf, how could he refuse?

"I can just wait here to get that proof," replied the detective. He spun around with his hands in the air. "In fact, maybe I should get the video camera from the interrogation room downstairs for your big moment."

"You have a small cell where you can lock me to the table," rasped Diego, less a question than a statement. He gritted his teeth as if he'd made a decision. "Fine, let's go there."

"That room isn't for tourists, Diego. I've got to fill out paperwork if I take you there. It's a pain in the ass." Maxim wasn't lying, either. It meant the difference between leaving in twenty minutes or an hour, at least—not that he had any reason to make it home. Maxim caught himself rubbing his silver wedding ring with his left thumb, and then forced the thought out of his mind.

As always, the detective was willing to put the work in if he knew it would yield results. The department guaranteed overtime, but more importantly, Maxim had a reputation to maintain.

Going home on time was never his priority, but it didn't

hurt to play coy.

"Trust me," Maxim asserted, "you and your friends will see the interrogation room in the morning when one of you flips on the others. My shift is over, and I'm on my way out." The detective took a step backwards and lifted his cheeks in a playful smirk. "Although, if you're willing to transform for me, I could give you a few extra minutes."

Diego rubbed his free hand through his wavy black hair. He was balmy and distraught and appeared to be looking around the room for a means to escape. Fat chance in this situation, lycanthrope or not.

Maxim continued backing up into the open doorway.

"This is a serious matter," insisted the prisoner, glancing at his unconscious friends. He lowered his voice to a whisper. "I'm taking a risk trusting you. You're a police detective. Don't tell me you haven't seen or heard anything suspicious. Strange signs, unexplained disappearances?"

The detective stopped hard as if he'd walked into a wall. His eyes instinctively moved once again to his wedding band. Diego's plea hit too close to home. Maxim eyed the doorway to see if anyone else had heard.

"What do you know about disappearances?" demanded Maxim abruptly.

The prisoner shook his head. "Only signs. Trends."

Maxim clenched his jaw. He wouldn't let Diego control the interrogation. "I need you to understand the position you're in. I have better things to do than stay here and talk all night." The detective told the same lie often and well. The truth was the best thing going for Maxim was his career and his reputation as a closer. "However, if you want to tell me what happened in that roadhouse tonight, then I can find time for you."

The biker grimaced as he faced Maxim's stern countenance. "Fine," he relented. "You take me down there so I can confess. Then I'll give you your proof." Diego paused as he examined the analog clock hanging on the far wall, silently counting. "But only if we go now."

Maxim smiled. Everyone had buttons to push, and he was good at finding them. This was just another night in the office. But as he looked into the solemn face of the man in bed, with pupils wide and almost pure black in the dim light, something didn't feel right.

ii.

Three Hours Earlier

Before the vocals had a chance to start, Maxim switched the station. His wife loved that song, and she was the last thing he wanted to think about now.

He leaned back in his faded green sedan. The headrest scratched his head where the fake leather had cracked. It was a familiar feeling, and not entirely uncomfortable. Sitting in his car for long periods of time was part of the job.

These days, working was the only thing keeping him going. Even at night, when he was technically off the clock, when there was nothing going on, he desperately needed the distraction. But his world was filled with reminders.

A song. A memory. A glimmer of the full moon reflecting off his silver wedding band.

It was funny, he thought. As much as he avoided thinking about Lola, he still wore the ring. He supposed it was his last shred of duty. Like a string tied to his pinky, it was a reminder he told himself he needed. Even if it cut off his circulation. Even if it strangled him.

Finally, after two years of hitting the bottle pretty hard, the detective needed something else. So he sat outside the roadhouse and waited. For what, he wasn't sure.

Was it resolve? Courage? Or was it just the bitterness of not knowing?

Maxim had only been a detective for a few years, but he'd taken to the job, heart and soul. Understanding all the angles was in his blood now. And he knew, however smoothly the twelve years of his career had gone, the Sanctuary Marshal's Office was letting something slip by.

Sanctuary was a small town situated in an Arizona forest. Colloquially, the greater area was known as Sycamore: vast wilds of mountain highlands, thick greens, even open desert. It was a jumbled tapestry of landscapes, mostly free from human intervention, not untouched but unchanged. It was wild, as were its sparse inhabitants.

Sanctuary was on the edge of that, with a front row seat

to the beauty. And the danger.

The Sanctuary Marshal's Office enjoyed its outsider status. The department preferred to handle business internally, in its own way, and that's what had recently piqued Maxim's ire.

He wasn't supposed to be here, outside Sycamore Lodge.

The biker roadhouse was a cesspit of tough guys and cheap beer and was known for the occasional brawl. It was only when matters crossed the line that the police even took notice. This was reinforced by the standing order from the marshal himself: no one was to interfere with members of the local motorcycle club, the Seventh Sons.

With them, a singular kind of discretion was paramount.

The Seventh Sons didn't live or operate within town limits, but they were staples of Sanctuary nonetheless. They usually just passed through to commiserate and drink and fight at Sycamore Lodge. The roadhouse was far enough isolated that the noise and hooliganism weren't major concerns for the citizens or the department, and the club historically enjoyed a lot of leeway.

Tonight, it was finally time to put pressure on them. So Detective Maxim Dwyer sat alone in his parked car, under the moonlight, and watched the raucous crowd inside and out.

A voice came over the police band. "Still a whole lot of nothing out here, sir." It was Gutierrez, the rookie Maxim had posted on the only road out of town.

Maxim picked up the handset and replied. "I know. I got eyes on some of the club members at the Lodge. Are you set?"

"Stop sticks are ready to deploy if needed. You sure about this, though? I don't think we're supposed to be keeping tabs on the Seventh Sons."

"Just follow orders, rookie. You won't catch the heat. The sergeant said he didn't need you tonight, so you're all mine. Let me know if you see any other club members pass you by. Otherwise, let's keep the radio clear."

"10-4, boss."

Maxim dropped the handset and sighed. Everything about the Sons was untouchable, from their shady dealings to the otherworldly rumors that had the citizens spooked. Police departments doling out special treatment was a harsh reality of life, but why let a motorcycle club benefit?

It didn't make sense, and Maxim refused to be a drone any longer. The only thing he had was his job, and he didn't know what would happen if it stopped making sense.

Eventually, Maxim's patience paid off.

A commotion broke out in the heart of the roadhouse. It spread like a wave and spilled into the patio. The intense crowd made it difficult to source the problem, but the screams were urgent. Maxim skipped out of his car without bothering to turn it off.

As he pushed his way through the revelers, several bikers fled the ruckus.

"Marshal's office!" screamed Maxim, holding up his badge. His right hand rested on the Glock at his belt. "Stop!"

He was sure he was heard above the noise, but the men

ignored him. Maxim tried to cut through the panicking people, but their activity was too frantic to contain. As he shuffled one way, they shuffled the other, and the tide was difficult to overcome. By the time Maxim reached the lodge doorway, he lost sight of the bikers.

Fortunately, the hardened patrons of the bar settled down. The live band stopped strumming their instruments and the screams died down. A circle formed in front of the stage, revealing a bloodied stone floor.

That's when Maxim heard the motorcycles rev up outside. He saw the four bikers again, rolling into the street with their headlights switched off. The detective cursed and raced back to his car. His foot was on the gas and the tires kicked up dirt before he closed the door.

"10-31," he called into the radio. "This is it." Maxim flicked his lights and siren on.

The motorcycles were difficult to keep up with. With their lights off, the detective had to rely on the ever further flashes of their brake reflectors. Maxim was considering his options when one of the bikes slid onto its side in a flurry of dirt.

He skidded his vehicle to a halt and sprang out of the car.

"Hands up!" he commanded, drawing his weapon.

As he closed on the suspect, his urgency melted away.

"What the?"

A moment of thought was all Maxim needed. He holstered his firearm, marched back to his car, and picked up the radio. This wasn't about snooping on the motorcycle club anymore. Standard procedure no longer applied.

Maxim couldn't let the Seventh Sons leave town.

"Deploy the spikes, Gutierrez. Take them down."

iii.

Spike stripes were designed with a single purpose: to stop vehicles by shredding their tires. As a tactical surprise, in the dark with their headlights off, the bikers didn't stand a chance.

Now, with their injuries stabilized, nothing was stopping Maxim from getting answers.

"Gutierrez!" he called out.

A young man in pressed blues entered the clinic room. He was a bit short, but the stocky sort, and combined with his crew cut gave him the appearance of a marine-turned-officer. The reality was that Gutierrez had never served and didn't quite have the needed discipline. He was a bit of a joker, really. And tonight, of all nights, he'd decided to wear a triangle goatee with some kind of handlebar mustache.

"What is it, Detective?"

"Let's take this one down to the box." Maxim motioned lazily at Diego as he moved into the hallway and turned halfway around, waiting for them to take the lead.

As he stood there, the detective's eyes scanned the rest of

the short hall behind him. Recessed lights lined the ceiling, creating a bath of sterile illumination. An empty front desk with a sign-in sheet, a branching hallway for a wide service elevator and a set of bathrooms, and three other rooms with closed doors filled out the floor. Straight ahead, in the direction he motioned Gutierrez to go in, was an always-open pair of double doors and the staircase down to the marshal's office.

At this time of night, after the doctors had gone home, the clinic's skeleton crew amounted to a single nurse. Tonight it was Renee. Maxim smiled. He liked her the most because she always kept their conversations flowing, no matter his troubles. For the moment, however, she must have been attending another patient somewhere. Renee was nowhere in sight.

Too bad. Maxim again caught himself spinning the silver band around his finger. He immediately felt guilty.

The detective's eyes moved to the other rookie guarding the ward. He sat across the doorway with his back against the wall, which would normally afford a great view of the prisoners—except he was playing a video game on a portable console.

"Kent, keep an eye on the other two, and let me know if they wake up and start talking." The officer didn't look up or cease his finger tapping, but he gave a quick nod of acknowledgment.

Gutierrez pushed the prisoner ahead of him as they passed through the doorway. Like the other suspects, Diego wore only a loose hospital gown. He had some bandages on his right forearm and hip to account for minor road rash and some bruising on his shoulders and knees. Because the floor was cold, the man had been allowed to keep his worn, yellowed socks on. Although the holes in the toes created a comical appearance, Maxim didn't want to take the situation lightly.

"Listen, Diego. I won't tolerate any surprises." The detective brushed his right jacket back and placed his hand on his gun holster, more a signal of readiness than a threat. As the two shuffled by him, Maxim shook his head and addressed the rookie. "And, Gutierrez. Shave that damn mustache."

"Sorry, boss," the uniform chuckled, "but I don't think there's enough hair here to glue to your bald head." He laughed and pushed the prisoner into the stairwell, wearing a stupid grin the whole way.

The detective sighed and rubbed both hands on his head, checking to see if Kent had noticed the quip. Ever since Maxim had shaved his hair close to his scalp, the rookie had been on him about it. So what if his hair was receding a bit? He surely wasn't going bald at thirty-two.

Still, something had been bothering him, and he refused to call it an early mid-life crisis. As gifted as he was, he hadn't managed to recover his wife after she disappeared two years earlier. Living without her created a void inside him that he was just beginning to comprehend. However easily work had come to him thus far in Sanctuary, there remained the nagging feeling that he needed to understand more. This determination, whether through carelessness or curiosity, brought him to consider the bikers an aberrant type of thorn.

In truth, Diego had him hooked the second he mentioned disappearances.

Trailing them downstairs, Maxim hit the ground floor, turned into the police lobby, and entered the marshal's office. It was a large room littered with desks and outdated computers and had the old kind of fluorescent bulbs that buzzed. The far wall was exposed brick, and the ceiling tiles were still stained from the years when smoking was legal in government buildings. The only two officers in the room besides the rookie were Hitchens and Cole, two veterans who were as much a relic in these times as the office itself.

"Get out of the way, black," said Gutierrez to Hitchens as he passed him by.

"You keep calling me black and I'm gonna file racial discrimination charges on your ass." Hitchens tried to scowl but couldn't hide his smirk. "Fucking spic."

Maxim shook his head. If Gutierrez was an instigator, the two veterans were stock cartoon caricatures: Hitchens was heavy and bossy and loud and Cole was tall and muscled and reserved. The humorous moment did not last long.

"Dwyer, what in the hell do you think you're doing?" Hitchens always spoke plainly. He didn't care if it got him into trouble, and it often did, but Maxim appreciated that nuance about the man. He was overweight and in his fifties but still dependable in most situations.

This wasn't one of them.

"The marshal is going to flip his lid when he finds MC

members in our jail!"

Barney Hitchens was the patrol sergeant, so he was accustomed to getting his way. He didn't hold rank over the Criminal Investigation Unit but the marshal certainly did, and the marshal would not be happy that Maxim had chosen to observe and interfere with the bikers at Sycamore Lodge tonight. None of the police were cleared by the brass to monitor the club, and Hitchens and Cole, perhaps concerned with their pensions, never bent that rule. The two uniforms had responded to the motorcycle accident, but they wanted no part of locking up the Seventh Sons.

"Someone needs to account for the dead man, Hitchens. What else could I do?"

The grizzled officer was only half sympathetic. Gutierrez escorted the prisoner to the interrogation room and Hitchens watched them with uncertain eyes. "You should have just left it alone, that's what. And on a full moon, no less."

And there was the real reason no one interfered. Fear.

This was a small department and the veterans could get away with just about anything—but they were flat out afraid of the motorcycle club. Hitchens was bull-headed and coarse, but his superstitious nature had those qualities beat. Too many long nights in the woods, Maxim supposed.

Still, maybe the timing of the full moon had influenced Maxim's decision to watch the bikers on this particular night. The veterans had reasons for their beliefs; if Maxim was to be convinced as well, tonight was a promising candidate.

Cole, ever diplomatic, attempted to ease the tension. He was a decade older than the sergeant, but that didn't stop the taller man from hitting the gym and showing up his friend. "Just make sure when the marshal reads your report that it doesn't involve us, 'cause we're not here."

Officer Cole wasn't as abrasive as his counterpart, but his message was the same. For someone in such prime physical condition, Maxim thought it curious that he was afraid of the wolf stories too.

"You got it," was all Maxim could get in before they marched toward the exit.

Hitchens, without looking back, left one last piece of his mind. "Make sure you know what you're doing." The two veterans left the marshal's office for the night.

So it was to be a skeleton crew downstairs as well, then. Their gray hair may have been evidence of wisdom or cowardice, but neither rubbed off on Maxim.

iv.

The detective entered the small interrogation room as Gutierrez locked Diego's left arm to the reinforced steel bar on the table.

"And his right arm too."

Maxim wasn't sure that he believed in werewolves, and

he knew the man's right arm was bruised, but it wouldn't be said that he taunted the unknown. He gave Gutierrez his set of cuffs to keep Diego comfortable with stretching room and then slid a plastic chair across the dirty linoleum tiles to the front of the table opposite Diego. Maxim considered the empty chair for a moment.

"Don't worry, Detective Dwyer, I won't bite." Diego spoke plainly between the thin mustache and goatee circling his lips. "I can guarantee your safety if you can guarantee mine."

He looked calm in his seat, leaning forward on the table with his hands clasped together. For a man banged up in an accident and wearing nothing but tube socks and a hospital gown, he seemed strangely put together. He had a confident, strong jaw, a decent tan, and aside from his frazzled black hair, he was well groomed.

The rookie grabbed a camcorder leaning against the corner wall and unfolded the tripod. "Don't tell me you buy into all this dog talk, sir." Gutierrez positioned the camera to get a good view of Diego in the limited light, putting his hands up to block out a shot like a director might frame a scene. "Although this video could make the front page of Reddit if this guy did something crazy!"

Diego contemplated the young man with the waning patience of a father, eyes again appearing black as night. "You live in the middle of these beautiful woods, just south of the Grand Canyon, yet your computers..." he said, trailing off as if his amusement were enough explanation.

Gutierrez raised his eyebrows. "Don't pretend like

you're too good for Facebook, bro. When you take pictures of your giant hole in the ground, you gotta post them somewhere."

The prisoner blinked slowly and said, "I don't like to carry my cell phone on me."

The rookie scrunched his eyebrows together. "Why not? It's called a mobile phone because you're supposed to take it with you."

It may have been the harsh yellow bulbs recessed in the low ceiling, but Maxim had no need for jokes or philosophical discussion at this late hour. He just stood there and gave Gutierrez an unwavering stare that conveyed the state of his sense of humor until the rookie retreated from the boxy room, closing the door behind him. Maxim's gaze traveled from the video camera, making sure it was on, to the suspect, seated calmly and leaning on the table, and finally to his vacant chair. With everything in place, the detective gave a heavy sigh and melted into the seat.

"How's my bike?" Diego's slight Hispanic accent was well-integrated and hard to place.

"It's fine," Maxim replied. He wasn't very familiar with motorcycles, but he did note the conditions of the accident vehicles for his report. "You laid it down and scratched it up but it's good to go."

The door opened meekly and Gutierrez popped his head in. "Yo, that's another thing. Do you think I can ride that bike one day? It is dope."

"Gutierrez!" Maxim glared and the rookie disappeared again.

Diego could not hide his smile. "It's a beautiful machine, isn't it? A brand new Triumph Scrambler. It really stands out from the pack."

That was something else the detective had noticed. The other club members opted for old Harleys.

"Okay, let's start this off. This is Detective Maxim Dwyer," he recited in monotone, looking back at the camera although barely concerned if he was actually within frame, "interviewing suspect one in the Sycamore Lodge stabbing." The detective nonchalantly turned to his companion and leaned in. "Please state your name, for the record."

The prisoner's face brightened ever so slightly, as if the game were afoot. Maxim recognized the sign as either deceptive or playful, thinking Diego didn't realize the magnitude of trouble he was in. Did he think he could just walk away from all of this?

The man answered with a proud flair, exaggerating his accent as the name rolled off his tongue. "Diego de la Torre, sir." The prisoner even bowed his head slightly, like he was the star in his own play.

Maxim rested his back against the inflexible chair and put his right foot on his knee. Where was he to start?

"You've previously mentioned arriving at Sycamore Lodge at about ten o'clock. Is that correct?"

"That is."

"And what were you doing there?"

"Oh," Diego said, shaking his head as if the reason were unclear. "I suppose the same as everybody else."

"Meaning you were looking for trouble?"

Diego chuckled. "Trouble, perhaps, but not the sort you're interested in."

Maxim studied the man's body language. Diego had appeared very frayed before, and back in the clinic, he'd had an insistence about him, almost like some of the drug addicts the detective had occasionally arrested. But locked up down here, the prisoner was the perfect model of composure. Maxim hoped this change in demeanor didn't reflect a shift in the man's desire to be forthcoming.

"According to eyewitnesses, the two we've got upstairs were drinking for hours before you showed up. They both exceeded the legal limit of alcohol in their blood, but you tested completely negative."

"Maybe I don't drink," posited the suspect.

"They say it's hard to trust a man who doesn't drink—"

"Would you trust me more if I admitted to lying about it?"

Maxim sighed as he watched the upturned corners of Diego's mouth open into a wide grin. Not only was the suspect wasting the detective's time, but he was having fun doing it. Maxim should have known this wasn't going to be an automatic confession.

"Diego, I would trust you more if you didn't hide behind clever banter. You told me you wanted to confess. So what is it exactly that you have to say to me?"

The suspect had no immediate answer. He looked at the bare walls, examining all four of them. Maxim closed his eyes and rubbed them as he realized what Diego was searching for. The detective reached into his jacket's breast pocket and placed his phone face up on the table. "Five minutes till three."

"Then we still have about ten minutes."

"Good. How about we drop the werewolf thing until then and keep talking about the case?"

Diego's lips covered his large teeth as they closed to form an inquisitive pout. "Aren't you at all intrigued?"

Maxim didn't blink. "If this is all you want to offer me, then I'll lock you back to your bed and head home."

The prisoner's black eyes drilled into the detective's face. Maxim's abiding stare was all that returned. After a moment, the steadfast will of the officer proved stronger. Diego couldn't hide his agitation briefly and pulled his head down to his hands so he could brush his hair back.

"Fine, Detective Dwyer, ask your questions."

Now they were getting somewhere.

"What was the fight in the bar about?"

"Some guys were having a conversation when they were interrupted. I heard shouting over the music. The place erupted and people started punching people." Diego looked straight into Maxim's eyes earnestly. "I wasn't involved. I just wanted to get out of there."

"Wrong place, wrong time, huh?" The detective snickered. "Listen, I'll believe the werewolf thing before I buy that story. All of you sped down the road into the woods in complete darkness to elude me. Everything that involves one Seventh Son involves them all, and you were right in the middle of it."

"So that's it. You think I'm in their gang?"

Maxim stopped himself before he asked his next question. He'd thought the biker would at least afford him that much. The motorcycle club wasn't allowed to wear jackets or other gang paraphernalia within Sanctuary town limits. Because of the department's operational procedures, they didn't have a definitive list of all the members.

Still, Diego's ID was from out of state. While these bikers came from any number of places, it was possible he was telling the truth. Maxim would track the man's credit cards in the morning to be sure, but for the moment he would humor him. He saw where this was going.

"What are you telling me, that you don't know the other bikers at all?"

Diego flashed his hands out with a magician's flourish, as if something had disappeared. By Maxim's account, it was his leverage.

"That is what I'm telling you, Detective. I don't live in Sanctuary. Haven't been here longer than two nights. You can check with the Motel 6."

Maxim cocked his head to regroup his thoughts. A stranger from out of town on a different kind of motorcycle —maybe these pieces were part of the same puzzle.

"So, if you didn't know any of the others," Maxim spoke deliberately, making sure to lay his trap perfectly, "why did you chase them out of the bar?"

"I wasn't chasing anybody."

"So why didn't you pull over when I lit you up?"

"What did you expect me to do? You can't prosecute me for not stopping while being chased by two gang members!"

"Ah!" Maxim crossed his arms over his chest in a practiced motion. "So you were involved then?"

Diego paused, realizing he'd given more information than he had intended. He let out a measured breath and looked down at the cell phone sitting on the table. The screen was off.

"I don't know, Detective. They thought I stabbed their friend, perhaps."

This was the path that Maxim wanted to venture down. The fight didn't matter, the DUIs would be charged—all Maxim really cared about was finding out who stabbed the fourth biker. The lodge could keep its scofflaw clientele, but the detective was determined to prevent any more incidents from spilling into the streets.

"Who attacked the victim?"

"I told you I didn't see it happen, Detective." Diego's repetition of the formal title meant he was regulating his dialog, being careful about every word he revealed. "You're the Sanctuary resident. You know how petulant those bikers are. We got into words because I spilled some beer on someone. But the stabbing happened later."

"So what are you saying, Diego? A fight breaks out, you don't see anything, but you get chased from the bar for no real reason?"

"That's what I am saying, yes."

"You and the two bikers?"

Diego's eyes darted to the side as he searched for meaning to the clarification. He appeared to be aggravated by his confusion and let out a stern reply. "Yes."

"And what about the fourth man—the one who was stabbed? Why was he chasing you?"

Diego gawked at Maxim incredulously. "He made it outside?"

"The stabbing victim was the last one outside. He was on his motorcycle a few hundred feet until he collapsed, leaving you three ahead. By the time I got to him, he was dead."

"Son of a bitch."

"That's right." Maxim reiterated the question to emphasize how ridiculous it sounded. "So this man, the victim who got stabbed, also incorrectly identified you as his attacker and gave you chase?"

The suspect's cuffs rattled against the steel bar as he pulled his hands to lean back. Diego looked up at the ceiling and slowly shook his head in wonder. "I don't know. I didn't think that dude was getting up."

Maxim had caught the man off guard and hoped to leave him scrambling to regain his footing. People were usually more honest when they weren't in control. A nudge here, a shove there, and Diego would slip up. He'd already practically admitted to witnessing the stabbing.

"You see, Diego, there's something that confuses me. I keep going over it again and again in my head." Maxim stood up and flipped his chair around, holding the plastic back in front of him as he straddled it and sat down again, assuming a more aggressive posture.

"The three of you were ahead of me when you crashed. Those two upstairs, they sustained broken bones and got cut up pretty bad.

"But you..." Maxim stressed the words as the prisoner once again focused on him, unsure of where he was being led. Maxim thought it a good sign that he commanded the man's attention and let the words hang in the air for a moment longer before continuing. "Besides a few minor scrapes not even worth mentioning, you were miraculously unharmed in the accident."

Diego leaned forward and reached for the detective's phone, fumbling to turn it on, frustration slowly marring his cool. Maxim stared into the man's eyes with a fierce intensity, enjoying the hunt. As the screen lit up and illuminated the prisoner's face with cold light, the detective didn't waver his gaze. After a moment, Maxim grabbed his phone from Diego's hands and put it back into his pocket without even looking at it.

Maxim wouldn't be seeing any werewolves tonight. He knew what this was about now—the prisoner was stalling for time.

"If those bikers were chasing you, then you would've been the first to hit the spikes and go down. Do you know why you didn't get hurt in the accident, Diego?"

The man scowled as he got angry at Maxim's inference. He stood up and pushed forward against the chains defiantly. Still, despite the hostile display, Diego made no move to attack the detective. Nor, noticeably, had any words escaped his lips to defend himself.

Not to be outdone by dramatics, Maxim jumped backwards out of his seat and kicked his chair to the side. It skipped against the tiles and bounced harmlessly off the two way mirror, ringing loudly through what Maxim knew was the entire first floor. Maxim stepped forward to meet Diego's stance.

"The reason you didn't hit the spikes, Diego, is because you were behind the other two bikers on the road!" The man's eyes pressed into a cold stare as Maxim kept pounding on the point. "You saw them hit the strips and wipe out, so you laid your bike down to avoid the accident! You were chasing them, Diego. That's why your bike was okay! That's why the tires weren't shredded! That's why you weren't hurt!"

Diego rocked from side to side nervously. Maxim didn't let up.

"You stabbed the man, Diego, didn't you? And you attacked the other two. That's why they ran from you."

"Damn it, Maxim!" Diego lashed out as if he was familiar, even comfortable, with conflict. "What do you think is going on here?" The man's shoulders heaved up and down as he panted hard. He was getting worked up again, either because of the adrenaline of the interrogation or because all the events of the night were finally catching up with him. "What do you think is happening in Sycamore?"

The two men stared at each other in silence. Maxim was unsure how to respond, but he was done with the supernatural theories. Seeing was believing—not stories, not talk.

The detective thought he heard some murmuring on the other side of the window, but he threw his hand up to signal them to stop any interference. Maxim was a little more heated than he wanted to be but he was still in control. He didn't want any interruptions now.

Instead, he slowly walked to the door and leaned his back against it to hold it closed. With a sly smile on his lips, Maxim simply stared at the harried prisoner.

For some time Diego de la Torre, in his hospital gown and tube socks, was a figure of resolute determination. But Maxim waited and the man's heaving slowed, his posture softened, and he eventually sucked his lips into his mouth and shook his head.

"Maxim," he said in a muzzled voice, "we're going about this the wrong way." Diego reclaimed his seat and ended the standoff. The resigned man touched the tips of his fingers together as he pondered his next words. Maxim stood up straight, off the door, eager for what came next.

"You might have your theories about what went down tonight, but you need to understand that these people, all of them, are very dangerous."

Maxim brushed his wedding band with his other hand. "Now you've finally said something I do believe."

Diego continued in a somber tone. "How can a man judge what actions are appropriate without knowing the truth?"

The detective put his hands on his hips and sighed sympathetically. "Our actions come back to haunt us, Diego." Although Maxim was trying to gain the man's trust, he almost believed in what he said. "In a way, all I really do is make sure karma holds up. We need to, all of us, be accountable for the things we do."

Diego stared down at the table, subdued. This was the moment, Maxim thought, for the truth to come out. The prisoner opened his mouth and stopped midway through, mulling over his next words carefully. He wiped the hair on his lips and swallowed hard. Maxim began pacing around the room in a circle as he watched the man come to terms with his current situation.

"What do you know of the supernatural, Maxim?"

The detective rolled his eyes as he stepped around the table. He expected a confession. "I don't."

Diego raised his head and said, "Sycamore has a problem with werewolves."

Maxim slowed to a stop behind the sitting prisoner. He leaned his head down and whispered into Diego's ears, "You're the one with the werewolf problem."

Diego blinked. "And what does that mean?"

Already prepared for the question, Maxim had his cell phone in his hand. He turned the screen on and gently placed it on the table in front of the suspect. Diego glanced down as 3:19 a.m. illuminated the glass for several seconds before reverting to black.

"It looks to me like we've gone far over your twenty minutes. If there was a shred of sincerity in you, shouldn't you be transformed by now?"

Diego appeared slightly confused, scrutinizing the blank screen. "It should have been now," he stuttered, "but planetary alignment varies from—"

"Enough with the stalling! I haven't seen a werewolf in thirty-two years, and that's not changing tonight."

Maxim hovered over Diego's back and the man turned his head awkwardly to face him. "If you don't believe me, then what are we doing here?"

The detective's open hand quickly struck the table, his silver ring making a loud thump on the cheap wood. "The confession, Diego! You said if I took you down to the interrogation room you would give me a confession!"

The suspect turned to face forward again, leaning back comfortably in his chair. "Yeah, I said that," Diego started slowly, "but if I admitted to committing a crime, then you'd put me in prison."

"That," said Maxim as he circled the table, standing where his chair used to be, "is precisely the point."

Diego pressed his closed fist into the table softly to stress the matter. "Unless I'm not guilty of anything."

Maxim crossed his arms. "Then why say you're going to confess?"

V.

Suddenly, muffled gunshots shattered the peace of the night.

Maxim instinctively squatted down for cover, looking left to right, but it was hard to pinpoint the source of the shots. The interrogation room was sound resistant and at the end of a hallway, so most noise funneled from that direction anyway.

As the startled detective reached for his firearm, he backed into the corner and got an encompassing view of the door, the window, and Diego de la Torre all at once. The prisoner sat quietly stern, hands in fists, looking both calm yet ready to strike at any instant.

The detective pointed his Glock 22 at Diego.

"Those were police discharges," Maxim said. "What are they firing at?"

The prisoner did not waver under the gun but his voice did ease up to sound more soothing. "Do not shoot me, Maxim."

A cacophony of metal thrashed above and wild footsteps scampered overhead. Maxim's experienced hands did not falter.

"If anyone comes for you, to try to break you out, I will make sure you don't step a single foot outside this room." The barrel of his pistol aimed squarely at the prisoner's center mass.

Diego raised both of his arms carefully, empty palms facing the detective. This time there was no magic trick. The prisoner was still calm under pressure but at least appeared to be taking the threat seriously.

"Maxim."

Suddenly the door swung open with a heavy urgency. Both men quickly turned to face the intruder. It was Gutierrez, except instead of his usual lackadaisical grin, he wore an expression of pure panic.

"Sir! The prisoners upstairs, they're escaping!"

"Shit!" Maxim quickly stood up straight, pointed his gun at the ground, and tried to regain his composure. A sideways glance at Diego confirmed he was sitting attentively in his chair, still safely chained to the table.

Gutierrez, however, was spooked. Without Hitchens and Cole, he needed a senior officer to lead him through this. "Where's your weapon, rookie?"

"What?" he said, confused by the question. "Right here." Gutierrez pointed at the gun holstered to his waist.

"Well get that firearm into your hand and cover my back!"

Diego stopped him as they took a step to the door. "Maxim, I said I would guarantee your safety. I can only do that if you stay here with me!"

Gutierrez stared at the prisoner with uncertain eyes and looked to Maxim.

"I have an officer up there, Diego."

"Then at least uncuff me. Let me go up there with you. I can help."

The rookie ran his eyes between both men. He had a skeptical expression but not one of disapproval.

Maxim, however, knew that winging things in these situations got people hurt or killed. There was a right way and a wrong way to do things, and he needed to set the example if no one else would.

"That's not happening."

The detective shoved Gutierrez out of the interrogation room with him, slammed the door shut, and locked Diego de la Torre in with the company of a table, two plastic chairs, and a video camera.

Upstairs, a quick series of pistol discharges rang out.

The two policemen sprinted through the main office. Seeing no other officers in sight, they continued up the stairs to the clinic. Maxim took the lead, only slowing near the top of the steps, pointing his gun forward towards the double doors. The rookie behind him did as he had been trained and stayed a few steps back on the opposite wall, occasionally making sure no one was behind them.

"Sir, if we get through this, I swear I'll shave my face!" Gutierrez shook his head nervously. "I really don't want to die with this stupid gringo mustache!"

At the threshold of the clinic, Maxim surveyed the scene and slowly advanced. The light in the hallway was nearly blinding after emerging from the duskiness below. The reception desk was still empty, and Kent's chair, once leaning against the wall supporting the officer, was lying on its side in the same spot. Next to it on the floor was his handheld device, still playing a chiptune.

He couldn't see anything else, but Maxim heard coarse breathing from within the hospital room.

The detective signaled Gutierrez to stop and inched to the left side of the hallway, opposite the open door. Maxim stepped to the left once, then again, and again until the innards of the bedroom were revealed to him.

It was dark inside but there was enough ambient light to see. Three of the beds had been thrown around the room. The two that had held the prisoners were bent in haphazard twists and had their aluminum bars broken off. The clay table lamp was shattered, its pieces strewn about the floor, and Maxim noticed crumbled pieces of plaster casts interspersed with the debris.

Kent was in the far corner, sitting against the wall, holding his neck and spitting out ragged breaths. Renee, the clinic nurse, was also present, kneeling down, attending to his wound.

Above the two of them, what was left of the glass in the window framed a jagged portrait of bent wire and open air. Both prisoners were gone.

"Not possible," hissed Maxim in a state of bewilderment. He stepped forward with his weapon raised and heard the crunch of clay under his feet until he reached the window. The gap in the ripped wire mesh was wide enough to afford egress to the prisoners.

The concrete plaza in front of the building was a twenty foot drop below. From there it was only a short distance to the street. One of the faux-antique light posts made of plastic resin had been snapped in half; its illuminated dome, still lit, rested on the sidewalk. Further yet, lying aflutter in the middle of the wide road, was a hospital gown.

Maxim projected a path past the well-lit town square and jerky movement caught his eye. Racing up the cross street in the distant darkness, he saw two large blurs retreat behind a building. Then the small town of Sanctuary, partially illuminated by the elemental light of the full moon, returned to its normal lull.

Maxim cursed to himself as he turned away, still

incredulous at what had just occurred. He had seen it with his own eyes. How was that possible?

Kent spoke up, suddenly forcing the detective to return to the present moment. "I got some shots in them, sir." He sounded weak.

Maxim put his free hand up, motioning for silence from the wounded officer. "Don't strain yourself. Is he going to be okay, Renee?"

The nurse was strangely cool considering the crimson on her hands. "I'll need to call the doctor back for stitches but it looks minor."

Relief swept over Maxim as he allowed himself to breathe out. He holstered his weapon and nodded at Gutierrez, who was standing in the doorway, to do the same. With his right hand, the detective leaned down and patted Kent on the shoulder. He was unsure of what to say. He had questions but now wasn't the time. Gutierrez pulled a phone from his pocket and dialed the doctor.

For a moment, the world around Maxim was frozen. It was a surreal experience as the truth dawned on him. He wasn't sure if Sanctuary felt larger or smaller, but somehow it seemed as if he was standing in the middle of a giant car crash. Then something tugged at him, reminding him that he was the only thing not in motion.

Suddenly the detective remembered Diego locked up downstairs and had a sinking feeling. Maxim broke out into a sprint and dashed by Gutierrez, past Kent's toppled chair, through the double doors, and down the steps.

After the recent commotion, all Maxim could think

about was how empty the police station seemed by comparison. He rushed through the large office and into the back hallway, fumbling with his keys. The seconds ticked by in slow motion as the lock turned and Maxim sprung the interrogation room door open.

Not sure what to expect, he burst in, his hand resting on the butt of the pistol on his belt.

Diego de la Torre sat upright with a reserved stillness, wearing an amused expression on his face, his hands firmly secured to the table.

"Maxim. Good to see you are still alive."

The detective let out a nervous chortle, relieved that Diego was still in custody. "What the hell happened up there?"

The prisoner looked at Maxim with admonishment. "Really, what have we been talking about this last half hour?"

The detective's breaths still came quickly. As he waited to recover himself, he stared at Diego and envied his composure. "And what about you?" said the detective, exasperated.

"Well," he began nonchalantly, as if this were routine, "I told you I would give you proof of werewolves, and I also said that I would guarantee your safety. But most importantly," said Diego, a smile crossing his lips, "I made sure I wasn't anywhere near those two when they turned. In case you haven't picked up on it yet, we aren't on friendly terms."

Maxim could not ignore the man's smug satisfaction. But

how could he be angry? Yes, he had been manipulated, but Diego's actions probably ended up saving both their lives.

Gutierrez walked up to the open door of the interrogation room, scratching the back of his head. "The doctor is on his way, and Kent looks like he'll be good."

Diego interjected. "If anyone has been bitten, make sure they get a full rabies vaccine regimen." Both officers looked at each other with furrowed brows.

"What is it you do exactly, Diego?" asked the detective. "Are you chasing these wolves then?" The prisoner sat silently as he pondered the questions. "Did you stab that man?"

"Why, Detective Dwyer, I was not involved in that incident in any way." Diego, mixing his accent with a hint of playful wit, continued. "I'd read that biking through these lush woods was a majestic experience, and after a long day of exploration, I figured I would stop at a dive bar and meet some of the local color."

The prisoner stared deadpan at the two officers. Maxim knew what was happening. He had seen this before. Without the other two prisoners to question, Diego's account of victimhood would be unchallenged. What's more, with the other bikers actually having attacked Kent and escaping police custody, that scenario even appeared likely. If Diego's records came back verifying that he didn't live in Sanctuary, and without proof of him having committed any crimes, he would likely be set loose without charges.

The thing was, Maxim wasn't sure if that bothered him

anymore. He now knew that the rumors about the werewolves had some foundation. He had proof the Seventh Sons were dangerous. It was hard to fault Diego if he had somehow drawn their ire. The man would need to spend the night here, probably, but would almost surely be released in the morning.

Diego de la Torre was a free man, and he knew it.

"Maxim, when can I pick up my bike?"

The detective's left hand cupped his temples as he tried to knead away the stress.

"Just tell me this first. The man that died..." The detective was going to ask a question, but he got tripped up by the phrasing. What could he ask that Diego would actually answer truthfully?

"He was one of them," the prisoner jumped in with, seeming to actually confide in the officers. "And very dangerous."

Without removing his hand from his face, Maxim closed his eyes. "Get him out of here, Gutierrez."

As the prisoner was unlocked from the table and shuffled out, Detective Maxim Dwyer took a few extra moments to compose himself. How could he have been so blind? But the reflection of light on his wedding band energized him with renewed purpose. There was more going on in Sanctuary than he had allowed himself to acknowledge and it had taken a stranger to show that to him.

With a calloused sigh that indicated the weight of the work ahead, Maxim reached over to the video camera and hit the stop button. This one would get erased.

Part 2 - The Pack

i.

Two days ago, Diego de la Torre had killed a man. The death hadn't been part of the plan, but in retrospect, that had been primarily due to the fact that there had been no plan at all. Sometimes, the biker reasoned, when all sensible avenues have been exhausted, risk was the only remaining recourse. At least, that was his justification as he returned to the scene of the crime.

Sycamore Lodge stood boldly against the relentless Arizona sun. The isolated roadhouse was an old fashioned mix of stone and wood and belligerence, the kind of place where nobody had any upstanding business. Near enough to fall within Sanctuary town limits yet deep enough in the Sycamore woods to retain its wild identity, the bar attracted a diverse population of outsiders. As such, it had become a popular haunt for the local motorcycle gang.

The biker pressed his gloved hand against the door and took a breath. Last time he was here, that night, a raucous crowd had filled the patio and the doors had been kept open for easy passage and a cool breeze. Tempers, however, had remained high. Perhaps now, at this early time of day, the heat would suppress the more vile nature of the bar's occupants.

Diego was wearing his full leathers now. His heavy black jacket was armored with inner metal plates, and he had steel-toe long boots with padded knees under his black leather pants. Everything he wore was a dark, matte shade of black that purposefully absorbed all traces of light. Running along the right side of the outfit were heavy scuffs from when he had slid off his bike. Diego grimaced as he pushed open the heavy door. After being released from police custody, it had taken him all of yesterday to sleep the soreness off. But that had been time enough.

The daylight had trouble penetrating indoors despite the large windows lining the wall. Diego waited for his eyes to adjust to his dim surroundings after pulling off his sunglasses. They were cheap and plastic, just bought this morning to replace the ones he had smashed in the accident. If only all mistakes were so easily corrected.

Diego squinted his black eyes and Sycamore Lodge fell into focus. The main room had a long bar and wooden cocktail tables and cushioned chairs. Antler sconces emanated red light and cast shadows like fingers reaching out of hell. The raised wood floor rung hollow under

Diego's heavy boots and seemed to interrupt the quiet murmur of the patrons.

Good, he thought, only a few tables of guests, and no one at the bar. Diego released the door to take off his gloves and it slammed shut behind him.

The right side of the establishment had a step down to an inlaid stone floor. As with the patio, the tread of heavy feet had worn down any finish that may have once existed, and the floor held the look of grit that was inherent in the desert. This alcove culminated with an empty stage that was really nothing more than a raised platform. Live music would surely return with the dusk, but for now the absence of activity was welcome.

A darkened stain was still visible on the stones where Diego had stabbed the man. According to police, the victim had managed to leave the roadhouse and die off-premises, but that didn't change that the act had happened here, and while nobody who frequented this building would dare tell the police what they saw, the few who knew what happened would certainly hold Diego personally accountable.

The biker didn't know much about the dead man. He had been massive, threatening, and drunk. He was also a werewolf.

Werewolves were much stronger than normal people, even in human form. A fist fight could be deadly if the wolf wasn't controlling itself. Entering this situation without a weapon would have been stupid, but the best strategy involved only talk. Besides, Diego liked to think that he had a way with words.

The biker stood in place as his eyes swept across everyone in the bar. Brown glasses, pink lipstick, jean shorts, baseball cap—he needed to be careful since any number of them could be wolves, even the pretty girl bartending. It was much easier to detect werewolves in the hours before they turned, but the full moon, along with first impressions, had already passed.

Mind your own business, bro.

His sister's words invaded his thoughts and brushed away his caution. Angelica was only twenty-two. At five years his junior, Diego had always taken responsibility for keeping her safe. She didn't generally like his meddling, but they came up in a bad neighborhood and she often made even worse choices. And this last time, with this last guy, Diego had made the mistake of letting him take her away.

He brushed his wavy black hair back and put his sunglasses on his forehead. Diego's right hand reached to his left wrist and patted the leather jacket sleeve, feeling the silver knife strapped beneath. Then he stepped up to the bar.

Diego took the farthest stool to the left, trying to keep as few people behind him as possible.

Mind your own business, bro.

She usually said it half-jokingly, even when she knew he had saved her ass. And Diego had tried. But somehow Angelica had finally gotten herself into real trouble.

ii.

"You're new in Sanctuary, ain't ya?"

Diego smelled cinnamon and looked up at the bartender. She had a milky complexion and long, dyed-red hair. She looked like a model with her high cheekbones and thin eyebrows. She wore bright blue jeans and a spiked black corset that clung tightly to her big hips and accentuated her breasts. Topping off her wardrobe were silk gloves running to her elbows and a choke collar loosely hanging from her neck.

"I've only been here a few days," Diego answered, "but I feel that I've been productive with my time so far."

"Oh yeah?" she asked playfully. "What have you been up to?"

"Looking for a girl."

She leaned her chest forward as she rested her elbows on the bar. "Isn't everybody?" Diego raised his eyebrows and chuckled. "What are you having?" she asked.

"Do you have a spicy Bloody Mary mix?"

"Everything's spicy here." The bartender grabbed a tall glass and filled it with a scoopful of ice and rested it and the pitcher of tomato juice in front of her. Then she picked up a clear bottle from the shelf behind her. "How about a Grey Goose?"

Diego shook his head and pointed. "Just that."

The voluptuous woman traced Diego's finger to the shelf but appeared confused. "Just the well?"

"No, just the Bloody Mary mix."

She laughed for a second then stopped, realizing he wasn't joking. "It..." she started, jutting her chin to the side, "I don't think that's in the system."

The biker smiled. "That's fine. Just charge me for the full drink."

The cute girl shrugged in acquiescence. "I'm Melody, by the way." The bartender poured the mixer and placed the glass in front of Diego. "What's your name?"

He slightly bowed his head to the side. "Diego de la Torre, madam."

"De la Torre?" she asked, her eyes lighting up. "What is that, Mexican?"

"Not that I know of." Diego sipped his drink. It was a good, peppery mix.

"Oh, man of mystery, huh? That means this girl you're looking for ought to be quite mysterious herself."

Without seeing any other immediate leads, Diego figured the bartender was the best person to start with.

"Her name's Angelica. Curly black hair, skin darker than mine. She came out this way with a guy from the motorcycle gang."

Melody threw her head back and let out a robust laugh.

Diego wasn't sure what was funny. "The Seventh Sons, do you know them?"

The bartender kept laughing and waved her hands to excuse herself.

"It's not like that," Diego said. "She's my sister."

"No, no, I'm sorry," said Melody, finally taking a breath. "That's not it. Why, did you think I was jealous?"

The girl really was determined to flirt. This was one of the few times where that insistence frustrated him. "What am I missing?"

Melody pressed her body against the bar and touched her glove to his hand. He felt the tension leave him as he looked into her pale green eyes. Her face was the most serene and welcoming thing he could imagine. Then her gaze snapped to a fixed point behind him, and just for an instant, he recognized fear.

iii.

"You've got some balls coming back in here."

Diego turned at the sound of the familiar voice. Somehow, the exact man he was hoping to avoid was standing at the front door.

"Gaston."

The man, who was in his mid-twenties, was tall, towering above most, yet he still seemed to have a wide build. He was clean-shaven down to his shaped sideburns, but he wore his cropped hair in wild spikes in all directions, longer at the top to form a messy fauxhawk, dark brown with blond highlights. Gaston wore several earrings; they were liberally hung on both ears and ran up the side cartilage. His broad forehead and eyebrows cast his eyes in shadow, but Diego knew what they were hiding.

Gaston aggressively strutted towards him. "I owe you a little something for Steve."

Diego presumed that was the name of the man he had killed. "You know the rules, Gaston. If a dog bites, you have to put it down."

Melody stepped back away from the bar and watched the two intensely. The sound of chair legs abruptly sliding on wood pierced the air as an older couple near the opposite wall stood up to leave. Gaston looked back and forth at the crowd as if to decide what he could get away with. It didn't matter. In this bar, the presence of witnesses was not going to protect Diego. That was for sure.

"Listen," Diego said, putting his hand up as a sign of peace, "I'm not here to fight, just to talk. Just like last time."

"Last time you got a little stabby."

"Granted, but you weren't being very helpful either."

Gaston's eyes glanced at the bartender and then back to Diego. The tall man turned his head and spit on the floor in a show of contempt.

Diego couldn't resist rubbing his fur the wrong way. "Not unless my sister was in hell and you were directing me to her." What was it about the cocksure, tough guy image that so easily baited him?

The bartender giggled, fascinated more by the tension than the words. Gaston roared at her. "You could go to hell too, Melody!"

"Oh, real tough guy," she responded, toying with him. "Just because I have a collar doesn't mean I'm wearing a leash, you know."

Interesting, Diego thought. There's some history between these two.

"Gaston," he restarted, determined not to escalate things further, "if you had just told me where Angelica was instead of going to the back with that party girl, then I would've been out of your hair." Indeed, the biker gang seemed more interested in toying with him than telling him what he wanted to know. Diego had to make it clear that he was serious as many times as it took for them to listen.

"You think 'cause we hung out a few times with your sister back in Detroit that I owe you anything?" Gaston clapped dirt off his gloves dismissively. "I don't care what that bitch is up to. She was just along for the ride."

"That's bullshit! She fell in love with you. You practically kidnapped her."

Now it was Melody's turn to laugh at Diego. "Gaston?" she spat. "Ha! The only girls he can impress are the ones who use more hairspray than he does."

The man shoved strong fingers at the bartender. "Melody, one day you're gonna learn your place in this MC."

Diego turned to look at the girl in shock. So she was one of them, another Seventh Son. Melody just gave him a sideways wink as she addressed Gaston. "Yeah, yeah. You're all talk."

"Well maybe it's time to change that, huh?" Gaston took a step towards and turned his attention to Diego. "You wanna talk? Let's talk outside back."

Diego was still sitting on the stool with his back to the bar, facing Gaston. Again, just like last time, the man was being unreasonable. Diego watched as three truckers shuffled out of the lodge. The witnesses were fast disappearing.

Mind your own business, bro.

Diego shook his head. It didn't have to be this difficult. He looked at the red lights, the metalwork on the shelves, the animal heads on the walls, and sighed. "You know, Gaston, over the years I've discovered that there are really only two types of werewolves."

The tall man stood his ground and stared on. Diego heard Gaston's leather glove stretching as he balled his hand into a fist, eyes still in shadow.

"The first type," Diego continued, "are the loners. Some poor dude realizes he's different and either lives a long peaceful life as a hermit or goes wild and gets put down. You see that a lot."

Diego paused as he sipped more of his tomato juice. Melody and Gaston were a captive audience and idly waited for the rest.

"The second type of werewolf is more complicated. They decide to group up and live in a pack. They have others help watch their backs. These kinds of wolves usually withdraw and live amongst themselves. They know that they are stronger together. Harder to take down."

"You're damn right," said Gaston, exchanging a look with Melody. If Diego wasn't sure before, he was now. Not only was she in their gang, but she was one of them.

"But the thing about the pack, you see," said Diego, spinning the ice in his glass, "is that it exists to protect the whole. Just like that loner can step out of line, so can the pack member."

Gaston smiled. Behind him, an older woman in a cowboy hat approached.

"Except, usually," said Diego, finishing his point, "when a pack problem is corrected, it happens from within."

Gaston stood tall in silence for a moment. Melody let out a small gasp. Diego leaned to the side to get a better view of the woman watching. And that's when Gaston struck.

A right fist hurled towards Diego's face. He put his hand up to block the shot. The blow slammed Diego's arm into his own head, and he couldn't counter the overwhelming strength of the werewolf. He was knocked off the seat and landed hard on his back. A cocktail glass shattered inches from his face.

The big man kicked hard with his boots. Diego winced in pain as he reached under his sleeve and touched the silver knife with his fingertips. This dog was getting rabid.

iv.

The woman in the cowboy hat pulled Gaston back. "You boys cut this out!"

Diego eyed Gaston and was amazed that he was listening, moving behind her. This same woman had been sitting at a back table eating the whole time. How much had she heard?

Diego kept his hand on the blade under his sleeve.

He couldn't place her age, maybe fifty, but time had treated her well. Her clothes were simple, just a light pink tank top and faded blue jeans with black cowboy boots. She had long, light brown hair under her hat, some of it graying but all of it teased out as if it were still the eighties. Her sweet face was punctuated by bright, pink-violet lipstick.

Gaston appealed to her. "This is the guy that killed Steve, Mom."

"I know who it is," she snapped back, "and he's right. Steve was an asshole who liked to fight and finally went and got himself killed."

The woman spoke with a strong southern melody that almost sounded sweet even when stern.

Gaston's face burned as his voice hit a grave note. "He called you Mom, just like the rest of us."

Diego didn't think the two looked related but lumping the dead man into the same family was a stretch. Steve was Mexican.

Diego sat up slowly, leaving the silver strapped to his arm and wiping tomato juice off his face. "You're in charge of this gang, I take it?"

"It's a motorcycle club, honey." The woman turned to Melody. "Get Mr. Torre—de la To—Get Mr. Diego another drink, will you?"

The bartender smiled. "You sure he didn't have too much?" She began filling a glass with ice anyway.

Diego rubbed the bump on his head and saw that he wasn't bleeding. His body was sore, though. The last few days had been rough and being kicked didn't help.

He grabbed his sunglasses from the floor and stood up with a slight whimper. As he tried to put them back on his forehead, he noticed that one of the arms was broken and a lens had fallen out. Diego rolled his eyes and tossed them to the ground.

As he returned to his seat, the bartender placed a fresh glass in front of him. Gaston paced back and forth and then threw his arms up. "Wait, so we're just gonna let him sit in here like nothing happened?"

"Shut up, Gaston," said Melody in an almost musical yet certainly annoyed voice.

"Well," he stepped back a few feet with an indignant expression on his face, "I seem to be outnumbered by pussy."

"Don't forget to count yourself." Diego's eyes flashed. "It's a common mistake."

The tall man looked like he was going to go at it again, but it was the older woman who spoke up.

"Boy, what are you doing in this town? You can plainly see your sister ain't anywhere near here."

The answer caught Diego off guard. Finally, somebody was being straight with him. "What happened to her?"

Melody jumped in. "Sanctuary wasn't really her cup of tea."

Mom shook her head. "It was more than that. That girl wanted to be in the MC, but she didn't want to prospect. She wanted everything handed to her. I told her it wasn't a good fit and she moved on."

"What?" Diego felt the frustration coming back to him. He couldn't stand the thought of having to track her to a different town. "Well, where did she go?"

"Heads up, Mom," Gaston called out. He was looking out the front window. "Police." Diego saw a dark green car pull up.

"Well, great." Mom took her hat off, placed it on the bar, and fixed her hair. "He's probably just here for one of his drinking spells, but the both of you better get out the back all the same."

"I'm working, Mom," Melody pleaded.

"Shush now. Go back to the clubhouse."

She sucked her teeth and hissed through her lips, but Melody obeyed.

Gaston, on the other hand, walked slowly, pressing his boots hard into the wood floor as he stepped up to Diego. He cleared his throat in a measured manner and cracked his knuckles. "I think it goes without saying what happens if I see you again." Gaston cracked Diego's sunglasses under his foot. "If you were any kind of smart, you'd listen to Mom and disappear." Then the tall biker walked backwards towards the front door.

"I said, out the back," Mom insisted. Gaston just stood in place, grinning his big teeth at the woman in defiance. Then the front door opened.

Detective Maxim Dwyer stepped inside, draped in the same black suit he'd been wearing the last time, only now he had a white panama hat on as well. It had a medium brim and an indented crown with brown trim. It didn't really match the rest of the outfit.

Gaston turned and purposely positioned himself in the detective's path. Maxim just stopped, cocked his head, and sneered at the man. Diego chuckled. He'd been the subject of that same stare before.

After a moment, Gaston just shrugged and walked around the man, leaving Sycamore Lodge. Then Maxim took off his hat and greeted Mom.

"Hello, Deborah. I'm glad I caught you."

Her cheeks almost exploded as a large smile crossed her face. "So good to see you, Maxim! You're here a little early today. And it's Debbie, hon."

The detective's eyes locked on Diego and had a slightly puzzled expression, like he was wondering what the biker was doing here. Maxim nodded his head slightly. "Noticed your Scrambler parked outside."

Once again, Diego leaned his back against the wooden bar. "Nice hat."

Deborah threw her hands up and acted shocked. "Well, I don't know where this bartender went off to, but I'm sure she wouldn't mind if you poured yourself one."

"Not this time," said Maxim quickly. "I'm here concerning the death of Esteban Varela. He was a member of your club, was he not?"

"Call him Steve, honey. This ain't Mexico."

"He was one of yours, wasn't he?"

Diego saw fear or apathy reflected from the other Sanctuary officers, but Maxim was different. Something was driving him. Two days ago he was investigating a murder and now maybe the wolves who had escaped, but something told Diego that the detective was chasing something altogether different.

Mom turned around and walked to the bar, putting her painted nails on the edge. "Yes. It was terrible what happened to that boy. Tell me," she started, "where are you with that investigation?" Her eyes looked a strange shade of orange in the red light, and they traveled from her hands to Diego's face. "Did you ever find the murder weapon?"

Diego quickly glanced at Maxim, who was suspiciously watching them both. The biker instinctively wanted to cover the knife in his sleeve with his other arm but didn't want to make any telling movements. The detective was too observant. It was well enough hidden where it was.

"Unfortunately, Debbie, we've had no luck sweeping the area and no one we interviewed here that night saw anything." Maxim looked around at the few stragglers still in the bar like he was condemning them. "Any idea why that might be?"

Whatever third parties remained in Sycamore Lodge started to finish up.

Deborah turned to the detective and took his hat from his hand, playing up her southern charm. "Well you know how small town folk are. They don't always trust authority."

Diego picked up his new glass as he sat watching and couldn't help chiming in. "I suspect it depends on the authority."

Maxim ignored the comment. "And what about the man and the woman who escaped custody? Do you have any idea where they are now?"

Mom twirled the detective's hat in her hand methodically. "Well, you know I wasn't here that night, but I'm told they were drifters, not associated with the MC. No one at the clubhouse knows anything about them."

Maxim nodded knowingly. He looked like he expected these answers. But Diego wondered about the gang's operations and cut in again. "Where exactly is your clubhouse, Mom?"

Deborah pursed her violet-pink lips and crow's feet hugged her experienced eyes. "Dear," the woman started, impatiently, "I ain't your mommy and my clubhouse is deep in the woods of Sycamore." Deborah looked straight at the biker. "Your sister ain't there, and I don't know where she is."

She turned to the detective and put her hand around Maxim's tie, brushing off some lint. "And more importantly, it's outside your jurisdiction, sugar. So don't go getting yourself into trouble."

The woman pulled off the sweet act pretty well, but nobody got into her position without being able to bite, and she was starting to bare her teeth. Deborah placed Maxim's hat gently back atop his head and said, "Y'all are just gonna need to trust me."

Diego put his drink down when he noticed his hand was shaking in anger. His sister was somewhere else and he needed to be there. Maybe that place was the Seventh Sons clubhouse or maybe there was something there that would lead him to her, but what was damn sure was that this woman's smug disregard wasn't helping him.

The biker softly slid from his barstool as he controlled his breaths. He felt the need to act, but what was he to do with a police officer present?

Instead, the detective broke in.

"You know what? I've changed my mind."

Maxim walked around Mom and slipped behind the bar. He grabbed himself a Maker's 46 from the top cabinet, placed it next to the biker's tomato juice, and filled a rocks glass halfway. Maxim stared at the drink and slid it in little circles along the wooden surface, swirling the liquid within.

"Sister, huh?" he said without even looking up. Then Maxim brought the glass to his lips and swallowed it in one gulp.

Diego hadn't mentioned Angelica to Maxim the last time they'd met. Maybe he should have, but he didn't want the motive of a kidnapped sister entering the cop's judgment. The detective had still suspected Diego's guilt, even though it couldn't be proved, but there was no sense adding an alibi to his arsenal.

"Ms. Holton," said Maxim, his tone more gruff, "I

already got reamed for doing my job by the marshal yesterday afternoon. If you have any concerns for me, I'll ask that you leave them to him."

He poured himself another round and held the bottle up to the biker. Diego, still standing, put his hand on top of his glass. Maxim shrugged.

"Secondly," he continued, "concerning my jurisdiction, it is true that the reach of the marshal's office does not cover all of Sycamore and that your clubhouse is far outside of Sanctuary, but this lodge is in my town. And, at this moment, you are right in the thick of it."

Deborah fumed but held her false grin well. "Your town, is it?" Deborah crossed her arms over her chest. "I suppose you aren't aware that Sycamore Lodge existed here long before your town sprang up?"

Maxim sighed. "That was well before your time, Deborah."

"Well, thank you for noticing," she said defiantly. "It's true just the same. This lodge was an outpost in the nineteenth century for the surveying of Beale Wagon Road. The trail was ordered by the president himself, and he appointed his friend, Edward Fitzgerald Beale, to build it. Water, flat ground, a straight shot—it was the best path west for hundreds of miles before Route 66 and the Interstate ran across the more tenable land to the south."

The detective blinked back his obvious boredom. "I'm not in the mood for one of your history lectures. Is all of this leading somewhere?"

Deborah glared at him. "The point is that this building

has been here for a long time, and it has outlasted many masters. Through the boom times to the founding of Sanctuary to the isolation of the highways, this bar has withstood. All of Sycamore, really. And the Seventh Sons ain't no different."

"You're from Alabama, Deborah. You didn't have anything to do with the club twenty years ago."

"Maxim," she said, "I feel sorry for you. It's tradition and family that give meaning to life."

The detective tilted his head in a careless gesture. "You're not going to make me arrest you, are you?"

Deborah's eyes narrowed. "What do you think you're doing?"

"Just filling in blanks. I'd like to start with you coming down to the marshal's office and answering some questions for me. You'd be a big help in the investigation." Maxim assumed an exaggerated expression of concern. "And of course, with your friend being the victim, I'm sure you'd like to assist in any way possible."

Deborah had a look on her face like she was properly dumbfounded. The woman was definitely more surprised than upset by Maxim's insistence.

Diego watched them both intently as he sat down again. He had learned that the detective was not a werewolf the other night when he didn't turn, but he hadn't been sure how friendly he was with the gang. Because of their potentially illegal operations, motorcycle clubs often bought out the authorities, after all.

Instead, Maxim looked to be crossing an invisible line.

Diego recalled an older police sergeant complaining to Maxim about the prisoners the night they were arrested. If the detective was indeed prioritizing justice over procedure, then perhaps he was someone who could be trusted.

The roadhouse was now empty except for the three of them. Maxim was holding his second bourbon, and this time he sipped from it. Deborah paced a few steps away and came back as she mulled over his proposal. Diego thought it was obvious to everybody that the gang was up to no good. The real question was how deep Maxim wanted to dig.

"I really miss your Lola," said Deborah with soft words. "She often spoke of your stubbornness." Diego perked up at this revelation. "Sometimes she even thought it was a good thing."

It suddenly became apparent to Diego just how small of a town he was in. Everybody in Sanctuary seemed to have deep ties.

"I know you like to tell yourself that your drinking got heavier after your wife disappeared, Detective." Mom rapped her fingernails on the bar. "Truth is, you were always a hopeless drunk."

Diego watched as Maxim spun a silver ring around his finger with one hand and killed off his drink with the other. "Thanks for your cooperation, Debbie."

The detective walked out from behind the bar and headed for the front door. Deborah went to the table with her plate of unfinished fried chicken and picked up a gold-sequined purse. The woman pulled out a compact and casually reapplied her pink lipstick as Maxim waited. Then she returned to the bar and placed her cowboy hat back on her head, facing the biker.

"I didn't like your sister, Diego. She was a princess and riled my people up." Deborah's orange eyes glistened. "Gaston was in over his head. Angelica wasn't cute on him. She was here for the power... and I told her to get out."

The woman walked out through the door that Maxim was holding open for her. She paused in the warm air, pulled a pair of large sunglasses from her purse, and put them on. Taking the opportunity to get another word in, she turned around and the sun reflected off her silver lenses.

"Y'all are just two boys looking for two girls. There ain't nothing special about that."

She continued outside and left Maxim standing a moment longer. He looked back at Diego. "I didn't know you were missing somebody..."

The biker watched the detective as he failed to finish his thought. Maxim, also, was looking for someone. That's why he was pushing people who didn't like to be pushed. Diego had to respect that, even if the man was poking at wolves.

He gave a small nod to return the sentiment, and Maxim walked out the door.

V.

Diego de la Torre sat alone in the roadhouse. The rays of the sun peeking through the windows were longer now. In time, they would fade and the shadows would take over, welcoming a new throng of drinkers yelling above live country music. But before all of that happened, Diego had Sycamore Lodge all to himself and his thoughts.

The quiet should have been more soothing.

It hadn't been easy tracking Gaston to Sanctuary but it had been straightforward. He belonged to a gang with some notoriety. He was a loudmouth. Whatever obstacles Diego had encountered along the way, he'd always had a trail to follow.

But now his sister might be on her own. Or she could be missing, like the detective's wife. In one way or another, Angelica was still lost out there, and she needed him.

Without finishing his drink, Diego stood up and placed his wallet on the bar as he counted a few bills. The brown leather wallet was well-worn. Through the yellowed plastic ID window, he saw an old picture of himself under the words "United States Public Health Service Commissioned Corps." He folded the wallet back up and returned it to his back pocket. That wasn't him anymore.

On the counter, next to the money he'd laid out, was the Maker's 46 that Maxim had taken from the cabinet. Diego gave it a long look and then slid his fingers across the hardwood, nudging the bottle off the bar. The glass shattered as it hit the floor.

The biker walked out to the patio and put his hands up to shield his eyes from the glare. He would need to buy another pair of sunglasses. Jumping off the stone porch into the sand, Diego welcomed the heat of the sun and walked up to his Triumph, the lone bike outside Sycamore Lodge.

This was true freedom, outside, on the road.

As he was putting his riding gloves back on, Diego heard a Harley engine rev up from behind the bar. He turned his head and saw Melody slowly pulling up beside him.

He chuckled. Guess she didn't make it back to the clubhouse yet.

She didn't ride with a helmet or other gear, but then again, she didn't need the protection. Her magenta hair whipped her face as the wind picked up. Diego looked down her body and traced over her shapely legs straddling the large bike. It was a heavy hog with scratches and dirt and replacement parts—a far cry from her meticulous wardrobe.

Melody stopped her bike right next to him. "Have you ever considered that what you're looking for doesn't exist?"

The woods were thick here and there were no other buildings in sight. Even the winding road disappeared into them. One direction headed back into town, and the other into the wild, some degree closer to his answers.

"Is it true what Deborah said, that she's gone?"

Melody returned a smirk. "Mom can seem scary at times but she's a sweetie. And Gaston, don't you worry about that dummy. Angie knew how to handle him."

Angie? His sister hated that nickname. Angelica was much prettier. Why wouldn't she want to use her full name?

"She knew you'd come for her, you know," the girl continued. Melody's green eyes almost looked sad. Her chest heaved in her corset as she reached out and handed him a sealed envelope. "She wanted you to have this."

Diego grabbed the letter. It was unmarked except for a single "D."

Melody planted her foot in the sand and leaned over from her bike, into Diego. She pressed her lips against his and closed her beautiful eyes. Diego wrapped his arms around her and the two shared an embrace.

When she pulled away, she left her soft hand on his cheek, rubbing his trimmed goatee with her thumb. "Your sister was a better kisser."

A stunned Diego watched as Melody righted her bike and walked it forward a few feet. Her pale cheeks blushed slightly, and she gave him one last wink and rode away.

The biker wiped his mouth with his glove as he watched her full figure disappearing around a turn, no doubt heading back to the clubhouse.

Diego ripped open the envelope and unfolded the single paper within. On it was the handwriting of his sister: "Mind your own business, bro."

The biker shook his head; he couldn't help but form a slanted smile with his lips. Where did that leave him?

With a quick look around to make sure no one was watching, Diego withdrew the silver blade from his sleeve and slid it into a special casing in the exhaust on his bike. When it snapped into place, it looked like a part of the engine, indistinguishable as a separate piece, much less a weapon.

The biker pulled his full-face helmet over his head. Despite the rest of his outfit being a matte black, this piece was a flat gold color that clashed with the shaded lens. He couldn't be completely devoid of style, after all.

Diego jumped onto his Scrambler and wondered where to go next. The bike kicked into gear and threw dirt into the air, and he sped down the asphalt. A new breeze picked up and sailed into the trees, carrying his sister's letter with it.

Part 3 - The Hunter

i.

Some days started better than others. In the present circumstances, Maxim had barely taken his jacket off and already Sergeant Hitchens was lecturing him.

"Let me explain something to you, Dwyer, for your own benefit."

The detective resigned himself to a sigh. He couldn't proceed with his work until he got this over with. He walked over to his desk and sat in his swivel chair.

The Sanctuary Marshal's Office was a small department. The main room was an open space that had desks for all nine officers. The high walls were lined with skylight windows, but the dirty glass and fluorescent lights bequeathed a musty air of the seventies.

It was likely that the other two shift officers were out on

patrol because Barney Hitchens was Maxim's sole companion this morning. While it was customary to speak above the irregular humming of the old air conditioner, such an impersonal gesture wasn't the style of the fatherly veteran.

"Hitchens, did I ever tell you that you were like the black uncle I never had?"

"Thank the Lord for that. I try to get Gutierrez to heed my advice but that boy isn't right in the head. I saw you finally convinced him to shave his face!"

The officer grabbed the padded chair on the side of Maxim's desk and pulled it away to account for his large girth. "Hell," the old man started as he plopped down in the chair facing the detective, "if I was really your uncle I would've whooped your ass a long time ago."

Besides the sergeant's longtime friends, most officers working for Barney Hitchens found him to be unnecessarily abrasive. For Maxim, it was the opposite. The fact that the detective's Criminal Investigation Unit didn't answer to the patrol sergeant certainly helped avoid friction, but there was more to it than that. Enemies cajoled; friends complained.

Many times this friendship materialized in the form of advice.

"When someone," he began, enjoying his soapbox, "let's say the marshal, for instance, tells you not to do something, and you go ahead and do that thing anyway—well, you're at least supposed to pretend that you didn't know better."

Hitchens, of course, was referring to Maxim's investigation into the Seventh Sons Motorcycle Club. Until three nights ago, the rumors of local werewolves were unfounded in the detective's eyes. Finally, after twelve years on the job, Maxim had seen the proof that he'd needed. Two bikers that had been in his custody transformed and escaped under the full moon. For Maxim, that changed everything.

However, one vital thing that did not change was the marshal's advisement to stay out of club affairs. The detective had ignored the mandate yesterday and brought the Seventh Sons president in for questioning.

Maxim sighed again and shook his mouse back and forth to wake his computer up. "She came in to talk to me of her own free will, Hitchens. She wanted to help find the killer —"

"Son," he snapped, "don't use that fool excuse on me!" Hitchens looked at the detective with wounded eyes. "And you'd better think twice before telling that to the marshal, now. He's not as cordial as I am."

Maxim couldn't hide his smirk. It was true that Deborah didn't exactly volunteer to come to the station. The outlaw club was brash and anti-authority, and its members equated helping the police with betrayal. Based in the unincorporated Arizona wild of Sycamore, the Seventh Sons had mostly managed to avoid run-ins with Sanctuary police. But recent infractions, particularly the murder at Sycamore Lodge, warranted a breach of terms—at least in Maxim's eyes.

"She was friends with my wife, Hitchens."

"Mmm hmm," he acknowledged, dismissing the

sentiment. "And you think she's not friends with the marshal too? I'm just telling you to watch your back around her because she's watching hers. And if it's in a corner, she will bite you."

Maxim opened his drawer and shuffled through a stack of notes. He didn't doubt what the sergeant said but thought his worrying was overprotective. Maxim wasn't pushing anybody too far, at least not yet. His hand locked onto the paper he was looking for.

"It's funny," Maxim mused, allowing his thoughts to take him off course. "Lola and I got into fights all the time, so of course Deborah always despised me. But after my wife disappeared, Deborah treated me better, almost like she felt sorry for me."

"Is that what this is all about? Lola again?"

Maxim slammed his desk drawer shut. When his wife had disappeared, he did everything he could not to unravel.

"You know," said Maxim, "I moved to this town with her to become a police officer."

Hitchens nodded slowly. "Twelve years is a long time."

"And I'm good at it," continued Maxim. "But that didn't help Lola..."

Maxim had remained professional and focused on work without her, making sure not to take any actions that could be considered personal. Over the last two years, he had done things the way they were supposed to be done. And still, in the end, it hadn't gotten him what he needed.

As was often the case of late, Maxim stared wistfully at the silver wedding band he wore. Could he truly say that he had lived up to the commitment it promised?

Hitchens shook his head and went limp, relaxing back into his chair. "You did all a man could do, son."

Maxim simply turned the ring around his finger and watched the etched symbol complete a revolution.

"You did interviews, swept the area, checked neighboring towns, put out statewide and national alerts—"

"None of that worked." Maxim closed his eyes as he remembered the pressure he had been under. "A year in to being a detective and it was the first big case that I couldn't break. I was so concerned with being a good cop that I didn't think to be a good husband."

"But Maxim," said the sergeant softly, "you're a good person. Following procedure is just part of that. It's all this," he said, motioning at the paper in Maxim's hand, "that is going to destroy everything you've worked for."

Hitchens was too afraid of riling the wolves up. He was an old-timer who no longer took risks because the only thing he considered was what he could lose. But he did sound convincing.

"And it still won't get you Lola back," he added.

Lola. Maxim didn't delude himself—he knew they had been having problems. Things hadn't been perfect, but the hope of better times, the chance to right wrongs, was no longer afforded to him. It was almost enough to make a man lose himself.

Maxim kept his head down. "Is it weird that I still feel like an outsider in my own town? Without her, I have no sense of permanence. I have no real ties to Sanctuary."

Hitchens had no answer.

The droning air conditioner only served to remind Maxim of what little effect it was having. Beads of sweat invaded his buttoned white shirt. He needed to get his mind focused on work.

The detective opened his eyes and stared at the list of names on the paper in his hand. Maybe they were suspects, maybe they were wolves; the main thing was that they were a list of people to find and interview. While this new path he was on was actively discouraged, for the first time since Lola went missing, he felt free of invisible chains.

Maxim handed the paper to the sergeant. "This is a full list of the Seventh Sons membership."

Hitchens raised his eyebrows and counted down the names. "She humored you, you know that?" Maxim watched the man's eyes as he scanned the list, seeing if there was any recognition, but Hitchens didn't seem surprised by anything he saw. "Still, can't say I'm not impressed you got her to do that much."

A muffled discourse from the marshal's office interrupted the men. That's when Maxim noticed that the door was closed, and he looked to the sergeant with an inquisitive glance.

"Don't ask," said Hitchens, "because I'm willing to bet that your turn is next. Still, you should see the piece of work that he's talking to in there."

The back wall of the main office was made up of heavy brick and was the original boundary of the building; the small office and interrogation room had been added in more recent years. There was a window next to the door pane, but the old glass was yellowed with age, and the door was not meant to be transparent. Maxim stubbornly eyed the cloudy silhouettes as he always did, but he could never glean what transpired within.

The sergeant explained. "The prissiest, whitest Indian girl I've ever seen walks up in here like she owns the place, doesn't even look at me, storms in his office, and slams the door. They've been in there for over an hour now."

Maxim raised his eyebrows. "You don't think they're going at it, do you?" The detective swiveled his chair around to face Hitchens and said, "You might have to arrest her for sexual conduct with a minor."

Hitchens erupted into laughter and covered his mouth to muffle his mirth. Instead, the man succeeded in making awkward hissing noises as the air escaped his lips. "Now you leave that boy alone. He's not all that bad."

"Not that bad?" asked Maxim. "Mayor Boyd appoints his son as Marshal Boyd when he's half your age, and you think that's fair?"

The sergeant shook his head back and forth slowly despite Maxim's reasoning. "Your problem is you think you have a say in these things. Trust me, you don't want that job."

"I didn't say that I wanted it, just that I could do it better. But what about you? You've been here longer than anyone except for Cole."

The sergeant leaned in to whisper. "No way would I want to juggle the things that are thrown his way. That boy is probably nose-deep in government ass right now." The man made a ring with his fingers and fitted them around his lips to get the point across, then reclined with a boisterous smile. "Although, I might not mind it with this particular government ass. You'll see. You should take a shot at her when she comes out. Might do you some good."

Great, another dating conversation from the guys at the station. Women were complicated enough on their own. He didn't care to get them tangled into his work. Not now.

Maxim sat quietly, spinning his wedding band around his finger, waiting to see if Hitchens had anything else. It was a lonely moment, and Maxim felt like he was fighting against the world with every decision.

The sergeant, likely sensing the detective's outward isolation, threw the list of names to the desk. "Our couple isn't on here, huh?"

He was talking about the werewolves who escaped custody the other night. They didn't have IDs on them and were in the wind before they were identified. But they knew something and had to be found. That's why Diego, the third man arrested, had given them chase.

"I've verified that everyone on that list is not one of the fugitives. I've been told that they aren't in the motorcycle club and have fled town."

The officer knocked on Maxim's desk for good luck. "Don't worry. We'll find them." The heavy man slowly lifted his weight as he stood up. "You can't just take a shot at one of us and get away with it."

Maxim nodded. No one can attack police officers. That

steadfast rule applied even to werewolves. Any violation needed a swift response, otherwise the department appeared vulnerable. Maxim was glad that Hitchens felt the same way.

"Have you heard from Kent?"

The veteran's face brightened. "The stitches in his neck aren't pretty, but they've kept his head on."

Maxim winced. It was grim imagery but the truth was nowhere near as serious as it sounded. The wound was, by all accounts, superficial. As Diego had suggested, the detective had made sure that Kent got his rabies treatment, but Maxim was still nervous about his condition. He wouldn't be able to forgive himself if something happened to the kid.

Hitchens sucked his teeth to make a sound of disapproval. "Honestly, if we never see those two again, it would be too soon. I doubt they're stupid enough to come back to Sanctuary."

It was true that, without knowing their identities, it was a long shot to ever find them again. That troubled the detective. While Sanctuary certainly benefited from their disappearance, Maxim viewed it as a clear loss. Diego was chasing those two for a substantive purpose. If they knew anything about the man's missing sister then, just maybe, that information would also lead to his wife.

"Dwyer," said Hitchens, making sure he had the detective's attention before proceeding. "It might just be best to move on."

Maxim snickered. Moving on. That's what he had been doing for the last two years. Maybe it was finally time to stop moving, turn around, and tackle the problem head on.

He stopped Hitchens before he left. "You know, Sanctuary is a small place," said Maxim. "Maybe they didn't think they needed to run very far." The sergeant shrugged but Maxim had to complete his thought. "I really wish I could search the Seventh Sons clubhouse."

A grim expression answered Maxim's suggestion. "Son, you would lose your badge if you did that, and the MC wouldn't even let you in." The sergeant turned his back on the detective and walked to his desk.

Maxim put his feet up on the chair that Hitchens had vacated and leaned back, weighed down by his thoughts. "Yup."

ii.

The door to the office opened halfway and a man not yet thirty stood behind it. The marshal was a stoic figure with short blond hair and clean-cut features. His blue eyes and small mouth seemed hidden in the middle of his face and his big ears just accentuated his boyish appearance. Combined with the blue power suit, he exuded an aura of inexperience.

Maxim watched to see who would exit the office—there was a reason Hitchens was all worked up—but no one passed through the doorway and the marshal didn't move.

Instead, his piercing eyes bore into Maxim, and he waved his hand to beckon the detective inside. Then the marshal abruptly stepped away from the door and into the confines of his private office.

Maxim turned to see Hitchens watching him, again covering his mouth and muffling a stifled laugh. This felt like junior high all over again. The detective shrugged and got to his feet.

As he walked into the office and closed the door, the first thing Maxim noticed was that the air conditioner in here was working. It was a cramped space that was made even more claustrophobic by the hazy windows and filing cabinets encroaching on the middle of the room. The marshal sat behind his heavy desk and motioned to the two empty seats opposite him.

In the corner of the room, squeezed between a cabinet and a fake plant, was a lounge chair. Reclining comfortably was the whitest Indian woman Maxim had ever seen. She wasn't American Indian, as Maxim had assumed; that would have been normal for the area. Instead she carried an exotic charm that could only have originated overseas.

The woman had long features: her build, arms, legs, nose, everything about her was thin and stretched. Her elbows and waist created sharp edges in her casual business suit, and she wore a frilly light blue blouse under her beige jacket.

It was her face, though, that was so striking. She wore her hair back in a ponytail to show off her ears and cheeks. Her skin had a light brown tone and was softened and smooth where the light hit it. Her features stood out in the dim lighting, and her dark brown eyes and eyebrows accentuated the contrast.

Maxim nodded at the woman, but she just looked at him with an amused expression. Maybe he had been admiring her for too long.

"You know," the marshal chided, "there are reasons we do things the way we do."

The detective took a breath and sat down.

Marshal Boyd looked absurd in his leather chair. He was a short man, and the large desk seemed built for a grander presence. Maxim couldn't imagine a better caricature of a boy feigning the responsibility of a man.

"I am responsible for protecting the integrity and reputation of this entire office," he said plainly. "As a department, we need to display a judicious balance when it comes to interacting with organizations with a footprint larger than Sanctuary. That is why dealing with Federal and State agencies is my purview."

Maxim nodded, as he knew where this was going. He'd heard the same speech before and just had to patiently wait it out. A glance at the woman showed her looking intently at him. Something stirred within him, and he felt his face redden. Again this reminded him of junior high, and the detective angrily pushed the thoughts from his head and refocused on the marshal.

"The motorcycle club is a sensitive subject," said Boyd. "My policies may appear to have no rhyme or reason, but they are in place to protect us. And you. And Officer Kent."

"Sir, a man was killed within town limits." Boyd's point was only valid so far. Besides, it was dirty of the marshal to mention Kent like that.

Marshal Boyd looked perturbed by Maxim's objection but continued speaking with the reserve of a politician. "Detective, if you had properly requested to interview the club president, then I would have approved it. The key is for these determinations to flow through me so that I can keep our greater interests in mind."

There was, begrudgingly, some sense to that logic.

The marshal had only been appointed two years ago, when Maxim was just starting to make a name for himself as a detective. Between his good track record and his wife going missing, Boyd had afforded him a lot of leeway and independence. But with Maxim's increasing frustration becoming more evident through his actions, it was clear that the dynamic between the two men was changing.

"Yes, sir," was all the detective mustered. He didn't know if it was true that he would have been allowed to interview Deborah, but there was no point in making things worse. "Next time I'll come to you."

Maxim looked down at the floor, unsure of what this was all about. Boyd certainly could have made his point without this strange woman being in the room. It was obvious there was something more to this meeting and that they were just going through the motions in order to get there. Maxim was generally a patient person, but this trip was unbearable.

The marshal nodded his head in thought. He leaned back and put his hands together like he was settling in for a long discussion. "The Seventh Sons are no doubt involved in criminal activity."

He immediately had the detective's attention.

"Sanctuary is just off the Interstate, but it's still hidden in a deep pocket of the woods and mountains. It is a convenient place for truckers to diverge from their routes and accept supplemental cargo."

Maxim nodded in acquiescence. It was common for outlaw clubs to be involved in drug muling and other gang-related offenses.

"But," continued Boyd, "most of the illegal activity happens outside of our jurisdiction. Federal authorities are monitoring the situation, and we've been advised to stand down."

"So we're just supposed to shut up and stay away?" asked Maxim incredulously. It wasn't about minor collars but professional courtesy.

The marshal's phone buzzed and he pulled it out of his pocket and glanced at the screen. "It might sound derelict of us initially," he said, "but transporting contraband across state lines has broader implications. We've been asked to stay idle. However, you should feel free to follow policy and use me as a conduit to request any information you need."

Maxim hissed. "Well damn if that doesn't sound like trying to get an echo out of a black hole."

Boyd raised a single shoulder in a half-hearted shrug as he typed a text message on his phone. "Now you sound like Hitchens." Maxim waited a moment but they both remained silent.

At this point, Maxim was more frustrated than nervous about the meeting. The detective turned his gaze from one to the other before locking it onto the woman. "So which one of you is going to tell me what you're doing here?"

iii.

A full smile crossed the strange woman's lips, but it was the marshal who spoke. "Detective Dwyer, let me introduce you to the reason behind our rhyme."

The woman rose and Maxim stood up to meet her. She was taller than him and moved her lithe frame smoothly. She held her hand out in the air and the detective complied with a light shake.

"Nithya Rao," she said, withdrawing her soft fingers from his grasp.

He couldn't tell her age. She had to be a bit older than him, but she could have passed for ten years younger. And she was even more beautiful from up close.

"Ms. Rao is with the CDC," said Boyd, putting his phone aside for a moment, "and is one of the aforementioned federal authorities with whom we are coordinating."

The detective's expression must have revealed his bewilderment because the woman smiled again and said,

"You must have a lot of questions." Maxim now noticed her British accent, and it seemed to make her even more attractive. She returned to her seat and motioned for him to do the same.

"I am in charge of the Flagstaff area," she started as he sat, "and assigned to the Seventh Sons, among others. By now you are aware of the reason for such secrecy in the matter?"

Maxim couldn't believe he was about to bring the subject up in front of the marshal—but there was only one reason the Centers for Disease Control would be involved. "The wolves."

Nithya nodded. "You must know that everything I am about to confide to you must be held in the utmost of confidences. I am only requesting your assistance since it seems you are already familiar with the situation and, well, given recent events, I could use a capable officer in Sanctuary."

"What, that's it?" asked Maxim. "I find out about the wolves and interview a couple of people, and now you want to let me in?"

"Is that not enough?"

Maxim thought for a moment. It sounded like he was getting rewarded for his bad behavior. "Does this mean I get a free pass to take down the Seventh Sons?"

Marshal Boyd scoffed as if Maxim was missing the point. The detective glared at him, but the smug man just shook his head, so Maxim turned to Nithya for answers.

She looked apologetic. "Unfortunately, my agency's role

with the motorcycle club does not extend to their criminal enterprise."

"So you can't help me either?"

"On the contrary," she said. "The Centers for Disease Control and Prevention are responsible for managing werewolf outbreaks. Aside from the national interest in keeping their existence as discreet and unofficial as possible, we are also tasked with eliminating any and all threats to the populace."

Unreal. There actually was a government initiative to keep werewolves under control. It felt like something out of a movie. As Maxim watched Nithya's nonchalant behavior and business casual appearance, however, it was clear that there was an infrastructure in place to deal with the animals.

"What are you saying?" he asked. "You don't care about the contraband, so you let the DEA and ATF deal with that while you kill or capture the werewolves?"

The marshal chuckled. Nithya looked to him for a second before turning to Maxim. "We have too many liberties in this country to imprison those infected without it becoming public knowledge, or worse, creating an epidemic in the dangerous prison population. No, there is no procedure in place for a werewolf's capture."

Her emphasis on the last word was all too clear.

Maxim nodded to show he understood but too much remained unexplained. "So if none are taken alive, why aren't the monsters all dead?"

Nithya cleared her throat and fired a look of admonishment back at him. "They may be werewolves,

Detective, but they are Americans and we are government employees. We do not simply target citizens with impunity."

Maxim snickered but she ignored the contempt.

"These men and women are the victims of a disease without a cure, and we afford them every opportunity to live full and productive lives. If they choose to live peacefully within society, then there is no need to hunt them. The HIDE program is the manifestation of this implicit agreement."

"Implicit or Illicit?"

She glared at him. "Hunt If Dangerous or Exposed. Safety and secrecy are the two primary public interests. If a werewolf is attacking others or irresponsibly flaunting its abilities in public, then the CDC issues an Order To Kill for it."

"Sounds like 'Don't Ask, Don't Tell.'"

"Only with much more permanent consequences for all parties involved."

Maxim pondered the ramifications of what he was hearing. "Fair enough," he conceded. "Some discretion sounds reasonable if we're talking about sick people. So these werewolves, do they need to check in with you?"

"Sometimes," answered Nithya. "In practice, my focus is much more about keeping tabs on lycanthropic populations. I let them know that they are being watched and that they are expected to behave. HIDE is just the enforcement arm of the initiative, and it gets executed whether the wolves are aware of the program or not."

"And the Seventh Sons?"

"They know me well. They are the most organized pack in the Flagstaff area and have a lot of influence, so I remain in frequent contact with them. I expect them to set the example for the others—even the ones we don't know about. These men and women are sick but have no hope for treatment; many believe it is in their best interests to keep their condition, and their identities, a secret."

Maxim still had a hard time thinking of them as victims. "How do they get infected in the first place?"

"Lycanthropy is a communicable disease," she answered. "Rabies is a Lyssavirus that, if not promptly treated with vaccine, is believed to have a fatality rate of one hundred percent. However," said Nithya, pausing to dramatic effect, "the truth is that there are outside factors, currently unknown, that propagate the condition of lycanthropy instead."

It seemed simple enough without the science. "So if you get bitten by a werewolf and don't get treatment, odds are you'll die, but there's a very small chance that you'd become a werewolf yourself."

"Exactly." The woman crossed one leg over the other and made herself comfortable. "This is a fact that works in our favor. Rabies is easy enough to stave off with contemporary techniques, while lycanthropy remains difficult to spread."

"But what of modern medicine?" interjected Maxim. "Can't we cure lycanthropy?"

"Unfortunately not. As with rabies, once the virus

reaches the central nervous system and outward symptoms appear, the condition is permanent."

"The condition." Maxim said the words aloud as he pondered the meaning. "What exactly does being a werewolf entail?"

"Very much of what the urban legends speak of," replied Nithya. "Enhanced strength and constitution, physical transformation into a wolf when the sun and moon align, even the outward appearance of returning from death."

Maxim sat there and watched the marshal paying attention to his cell phone, casually disinterested in what Maxim thought was a fascinating conversation. "So they're pretty much strong and invincible—got it." The detective supposed there were worse diseases to contract. But then... "What about silver bullets?"

Nithya Rao smiled and softly stood up. She moved and sat in the stiff chair beside him. "May I see your left hand?"

Maxim breathed in her sweet perfume and met her open hand with his. When she looked down, he was taken in by her long eyelashes. "Silver," she said as her eyes snapped up to meet his, "as opposed to modern medicine, is an ancient remedy that has some effectiveness."

Maxim's gaze wavered under hers. He looked down and saw that Nithya was gripping the ring on his finger, his constant reminder of Lola. Maxim pulled his hand away.

The CDC agent had an impish look on her face and raised an eyebrow slightly, but then she sat up straight, retreating to a more professional posture. "Silver is bioactive. It kills bacteria and was used heavily for this purpose before the introduction of antibiotics."

"I thought you said rabies was a virus?"

"It is," returned Nithya, "but the presence or production of bacteria may interact with or be a side effect of the virus. What we know is that killing this bacteria inhibits the enhanced abilities of lycanthropes." Nithya looked to Boyd. "Marshal?"

The man opened a desk drawer and withdrew a magazine for Maxim's police-issue Glock. "Fifteen silver .40 caliber rounds." Marshal Boyd tossed the mag over and Maxim snatched it from the air.

"No shit."

The detective pushed out a bullet with his thumb. The jacket was made of copper but the slug was indeed the dull color of unpolished silver. Maxim played with the weight of the ammunition as he bounced it in his hands.

Nithya sat in silence for a moment as Maxim admired the novelty, then continued. "Tagging a werewolf with these will slowly cause it to lose any advantages it has in strength. Left with the same inherent biology as the rest of us, the werewolf would be just as susceptible to damage."

Marshal Boyd chimed in to translate. "It isn't the silver that kills the werewolf. It's the bullet. The silver just allows it to be killed." Maxim listened intently. "Silver solids in the blood are said to have the maximum impact. Make sure to target the heart."

Maxim took a deep breath as he let all of this new information sink in. Just two days ago he was being yelled at for monitoring Sycamore Lodge. Now, after questioning the Seventh Sons president, he was being introduced to a CDC agent overseeing them. The responses were disjointed and the detective couldn't make sense of it.

"So," he said, sliding the round back into the magazine, "what am I supposed to do with this?"

iv.

"Detective Dwyer," said Nithya, crossing her hands in her lap, "I am well aware of your motivations in this case."

Maxim looked cautiously at the woman. The last thing he needed was for the marshal to know he was looking for Lola again. In the absence of anything to say, he just stayed quiet and let Nithya keep talking.

"The Seventh Sons is a tightly knit group. They protect each other, stand by each other's actions. Because of this, they can be difficult to crack." Her eyes shifted to the marshal's as she spoke. "But in truth, your department is very similar."

The marshal smiled away her comparison. "We're the ones with the badges, Ms. Rao."

"Regardless," she said, turning back to Maxim, "you desire to punish the wolves for attacking an officer. You feel you must correct the embarrassment of allowing them to escape."

Those two things were true, Maxim couldn't deny that, but after his encounter with Diego, the crime became a pretense. Now his priority was the dangling thread of his missing wife. Since Lola was a motive the detective couldn't admit to, playing along with the case would get him close enough.

Nithya reached for a folder on the marshal's desk. "It may surprise you to think of me as an officer of the law, but this is my district, and I must enforce HIDE. To not hold the club accountable would be to invite further discrepancies like Officer Kent and Mr. Varela."

The image of Esteban Varela lying in the dirt flooded Maxim's mind. His death had been the catalyst of all the dark revelations that followed. He was a wolf, though, and ultimately, Maxim's interests lay with other victims.

"After the full moon," said Nithya, "you sent BOLOs out for two Seventh Sons."

Maxim nodded. "According to Deborah Holton, the club president, the other two bikers weren't members."

The CDC agent chuckled. "I am well acquainted with Ms. Holton."

Nithya leafed through the contents of the folder and handed Maxim a black and white photograph of a man lying face down in what looked to be a hotel room. "Yesterday evening, my team tracked and killed this man hiding on the Yavapai reservation." The poor image quality did not reveal many details, but the man did appear to be Native American. The local tribe was located an hour south of Flagstaff.

Maxim caught on. "You know the identities of the two escaped wolves."

"That is correct," she answered adeptly. "This is your man, Carlos Doka. We executed an Order To Kill for his part in the death of Steve Varela. In truth, it was a long time coming. He has had long ties to the criminal underworld."

"Like the Seventh Sons?"

The CDC agent paused and angled her head. "Unknown. It is likely that they were at least passingly familiar with each other just on the basis of their mutual notoriety."

She placed two printouts of IDs on the desk in front of him. The Indian man had two Arizona driver's licenses—two different names, but the same face on each card.

Maxim remembered the man lying in the clinic bed just three days before. He looked closer at the photo of the dead body and was convinced it was the same person. Except...

"His leg isn't broken."

"It very well may have been at one point," she said, "but not after he turned." When the wolves had escaped, Maxim recalled seeing their casts on the floor of the destroyed clinic room. Nithya explained further. "The wolf skin is rejuvenating for lycanthropes. They can heal most injuries during the transformation. Even back in their human form, they are as good as new. It is a vital part of their long-term health."

"So if that night hadn't been a full moon, those two would still be hurt and in custody?"

"You are looking at this the wrong way," she said with a

wry expression. "It was unlucky for them to be arrested at such a sensitive time. And as for you, without the moon phase, you would still be ignorant of the truth."

It was true. It was dumb luck that everything had worked out so perfectly. Maxim had only reacted to Diego taking action, although it was possible the man had acted on the full moon intentionally.

The detective looked at the photo of the dead man again. "So Doka was executed without being interrogated?"

"He tried to escape, and we couldn't risk him getting away again," she said defensively. "At any rate, he gave us what we needed. In the standoff, he confessed to the murder of Steve Varela and implicated the other fugitive in the attack of your police officer."

"Hmm?" Maxim couldn't make sense of that. He was under the impression that Diego had killed Varela in self-defense. Someone had to be lying. "Why would he confess just like that?" And more importantly, why would he confess at all if he didn't do it?

The woman shrugged. "Unfortunately, my information is limited."

"Does it matter?" cut in Marshal Boyd. "Varela was a werewolf and a criminal, just like the others. Off the record, I'm more concerned with the assault of an officer than the club thinning themselves out." Boyd rapped his fingers on his desk matter-of-factly. "The important thing, Detective Dwyer, is that you get to close out another case for the Sanctuary Marshal's Office."

No, he couldn't wrap things up until he found Lola. He

needed to investigate the Seventh Sons further. There was still an open thread.

Two suspects had escaped. Doka was dead but the woman was still out there. She was white and probably not in Yavapai territory. Hopefully she had escaped the reach of the CDC. "I can't close this out until we capture the blonde."

The marshal laughed as if the answer were obvious. "Who do you think the silver bullets are for?"

Nithya handed Maxim another paper. This was a rough photocopy of an old passport. The girl in the picture was much younger than the woman they had arrested.

"Nicola Makarova," stated Nithya. "We are lacking any more recent paper on her. Our guess is that she emigrated from Eastern Europe as a child and was sold as a bride or into prostitution. She is still at large and is being targeted under HIDE."

Interesting. Diego was chasing Doka and Makarova for a reason. The woman was marked for death, but if Maxim could find her first, then he could question her. If Nicola knew anything about Diego's sister, maybe that would also lead to Lola.

"I can get started right away," said the detective. He stood up, eager to get out of the cramped office and continue the investigation on his own.

He wasn't fast enough.

Marshal Boyd waved him back. "Just one minute," he called. "Sit down, sit down." Maxim looked at Nithya sitting next to his chair with a smirk on her face and complied. She was holding one last paper.

"I am confident that you are a resourceful detective," stated Nithya, "but I am afraid your skills would be superfluous in this matter. You see, I have already identified where Makarova is hiding."

The woman placed a picture of an extended wood cabin on the desk. Maxim had never seen the building before, but he immediately understood the implications of the line of Harleys parked to the side.

"This is the Seventh Sons clubhouse."

Nithya nodded.

"But Deborah said—"

"Ms. Holton is trying to survive, Detective." Nithya Rao put her finger on the picture. "This is her castle, and she is charged with protecting her pack within. You will find that all her truths serve that purpose."

Maxim sucked his teeth in disgust. Makarova was in the motorcycle club after all. The bitch had lied to him, and just when he'd thought they were getting somewhere. What else was Deborah hiding? Had she known Doka as well?

Marshal Boyd cocked his head towards the picture. "Tomorrow, under the command of Ms. Rao, you are going to raid the Seventh Sons clubhouse. I'll send Gutierrez with you as well."

Maxim sat dumbfounded. Everything he was hoping for was suddenly happening because of the CDC. Nithya Rao was turning out to be a valuable ally against the Sons. Still, it all seemed to come too easily.

The marshal assumed a stern voice. "It is imperative,

Detective, that we remain focused on the objective. HIDE gives us jurisdiction for Makarova only. Once we get her, we get out." Boyd's blue eyes were piercing, and Maxim knew he suspected deeper motives. "Understand?" The marshal was ultimately a politician whose primary concern was the public image of the department. Boyd wouldn't be a problem as long as Maxim was smart about what rocks he overturned.

The feeling was cathartic. Maxim was thrilled about going to the clubhouse. He had been so adamant about investigating this trail further that he had been entertaining the thought of sneaking there alone anyway. Now that this was an official joint operation, however, it seemed a shame if they went in undermanned.

"Shouldn't we have a larger team?" Maxim cautioned, turning to Nithya. "You said you had agents raid the reservation. What kind of support do we have?"

"This is not a tactical operation," she answered. "We are essentially serving a warrant, and I expect peaceful compliance."

The detective scoffed. "You expect Deborah, who lied about sheltering Makarova, to let us peacefully stroll in and apprehend her?"

"Apprehend," said Boyd. "Capture. There are those words again."

Nithya looked at Maxim with her large brown eyes. "Ms. Holton understands the importance of cooperating with the CDC," she assured. "If any of her pack were to harm any of ours, that would be the unconditional end of that clubhouse." A fiery certainty burned across her sharpened features that gave the detective pause.

Maxim watched the two of them as they prepared. They seethed with overconfidence. Boyd had likely never planned an operation against a threat like this before. Nithya appeared to know what she was doing and didn't lack in conviction, but did she really plan to walk into the Seventh Sons clubhouse with an escort of two officers and have things work out?

Still, Maxim was compelled to have a look inside that cabin.

Marshal Boyd chimed in. "I know you, Detective Dwyer. You're not backing out of this. Not after I've given you the perfect chance to get what you want."

Part 4 - The Den

i.

"He's still outside, watching us."

Nicola Makarova peered cautiously through the blinds at the movement in the trees. The man they had attacked was out there. He had been, for at least a day. He was no wolf, though, and silver knife or not, it would be suicide for him to try to enter the cabin. So instead he just hid, watched, and bided his time.

Nicola felt her wiry arms tremble slightly. This was maddening. If she were to fight or run, then she could flex her anxious muscles, but she didn't know how to handle this agonizing state of suspension.

Besides, she wished she could be outside again, let the sun warm her pale skin, feel the breeze throw her blonde hair across her face. She'd spent enough of her life cooped up like an animal; in her mind, freedom was always worth the risk.

"Nicola," said Melody, who made a point to roll her eyes so the other would notice, "you've been stressing me out with this all week." The younger girl had been sitting quietly on the comfortable den couches without, as usual, a care in the world. "Besides," she added, walking to the window to get a peek, "he's not that bad." The intruder outside wasn't in plain view, so she just shrugged and sat down with her iPad again.

The girl had a particular gift for getting under Nicola's skin. She treated everything like a game. Mom didn't want any of the Sons talking to Angie's brother, so of course Melody immediately had a crush on him. Only she could get away with that.

"I'm surprised you haven't thrown yourself at him yet," muttered Nicola. She looked back to see if her words had the intended effect, but Melody had already put her white earbuds in.

Nicola huffed. It had been a very bad week, but it wasn't the girl's fault. This was all on Carlos Doka. He was the one who had told them to surround Diego. He was the reason Steve had been killed. And he was the idiot who'd hurt the cop in the hospital. He used the wolfskin as an excuse, but Nicola knew better—he had always been a powder keg.

It had been a mistake to ever get involved with Doka's side business. Nicola was a skinny woman who didn't look capable of much, so when Steve asked for her help, she'd thought it was a chance to step up. A delinquent had gotten away from Doka in the woods. She had helped track him down, and Doka had pushed him over the falls to make it look like the man killed himself. She didn't know why. She didn't ask questions. Her job was to help out brothers in danger, and she had saved Steve's ass. Nicola felt like a hero that day.

Revenge killings were part of the world. You got stepped on or you got strong. There was nothing wrong with that. Over the last year, however, Nicola had begun to realize how dirty the man's dealings were. It had become clear that Doka was the one responsible for the abductions. He was the reason Diego was here asking questions, and trying to silence the man was the mistake that had finally caught up with him. Now Doka had fled to the safety of the Yavapai reservation. With Steve dead, that left Nicola to fend for herself, with Diego at her literal doorstep.

Gaston walked in and noticed Nicola's guard. "You've gotta be shitting me. How long has he been out there?" The tall man stormed to the window and trouble brewed on his face.

Melody did an encore performance of her eye roll and left the room. Gaston was one of the few people with the balls to call her out, so she tended to avoid him.

"I told him I would kick his ass the next time I saw him," said the man in a gruff voice.

"You fucking boys," said Nicola. "Too much testosterone. You think you can solve everything with muscle."

"I know you want vengeance for Steve."

She sighed. She knew Gaston had been his friend—she had been too—but was more killing the answer? Violence is what had gotten them into this mess.

"Doka started it. Where were you anyway?"

Gaston shrugged. "Diego came to me first and asked about his stupid sister. He was all up in my face, so I told him to go to hell." The big man shook his head. "He's lucky we shared some pitchers in Detroit, otherwise I would have kicked his ass just for being so demanding."

"Couldn't you just talk to him?"

"I did. I couldn't help him and he wasn't taking no for an answer. Anyway, I had some other girl all over me and had to go. Diego didn't need to start killing people."

"The man was just defending himself," she confessed. "He was just looking for Angie." It was kind of sweet, really, that the girl had a protector. Nicola could have used an older brother herself.

Gaston shook his head. Nicola knew her explanation wouldn't keep him from blaming Diego for Steve's death, but hopefully it would stop him from doing something stupid.

"Hell," he said, a lightness entering his voice, "I honestly wish I knew where she was." Nicola could tell that Gaston was wrestling with some heavy thoughts. He was a brash man, but he had a history with both siblings. "How did he even find the clubhouse?"

Nicola frowned. "I bet he followed that bitch Melody here. She's like a teenager; she thinks she's invincible and flirts with danger. And whenever she gets too deep, she calls on Mommy to protect her."

"We ain't talking ill of family, are we?" Mom walked through the large entry of the den with a snide look on her face. Speak of the devil. "What's got you all worked up, sugar?"

The woman wore her Southern charm like a disguise, but she was more shrewd than she let on. Nicola motioned outside with a nod.

The midday sun fell on the long white grass of the cabin's front yard. It was a small clearing in the middle of a dense wilderness of browning leaves and evergreen pine needles. The thick foliage in the distance cast heavy shadows, but when squinting at just the right patch of branches, it was clear that Diego de la Torre was lurking within the darkness.

Mom just grunted to confirm that she saw the man. From any other president, Nicola would have expected a course of action, a plan, but not Mom. She understood a bigger picture—she was a part of it somehow—and so she chose to do nothing.

"Why is he here, Mom?" Nicola asked coarsely. The older woman's face seemed to be made of stone. Nicola pressed her when she got no answer. "Diego should be talking to Carlos."

Mom gave her a sideways look and pursed her pink lips. She was pretending not to know how Doka was involved. But Nicola knew. Carlos was Mom's errand boy. He cleaned up the affairs that she wanted to keep the club ignorant of.

Nicola didn't hate Debbie—she was very grateful that

the woman had taken her in when she needed support to deal with her affliction—but times were fast changing. Mom had made too many compromises to stay afloat and it visibly taxed her. It made her less trustworthy. And it pissed Nicola off.

"I don't want anyone talking to the Yavapai mercenaries," Mom said sternly.

Nicola grumbled and did something she had never done before. She yelled at Mom. "Why the fuck not? What did Doka do with Angie?"

Debbie was taken aback for a moment. Even Gaston raised his eyebrows in surprise.

Nicola knew it wasn't a good idea to ask in front of Gaston—the less he knew the better—but she was the only one on the run. "Can't you see that the easiest way to get rid of him is to tell him where his sister is?"

"Nicola, dear..." said Mom, brushing her bangs aside and squinting her eyes in a look of warning. Debbie put her hands on her hips and stood tall, and suddenly Nicola regretted losing her temper.

ii.

One moment Nicola was afraid that she would face the full, twisted wrath of the woman she owed so much to, but then, just as quickly as the fire had been lit, it softened to a warm glow.

"Honey," said Mom, her voice almost cracking, "our family must persevere. We must be here for each other."

Nicola saw a hint of the maternal figure she had loved, who had saved her, but there was no denying the pressure Mom was now under. Could she ever be the same woman again?

Her thoughts were interrupted as their attention turned to the window. A white SUV turned the corner in the road, kicking up red dirt as it approached the clubhouse.

"What now?" muttered Nicola. As Debbie and Gaston followed her gaze, a sinking feeling materialized in her stomach. She recognized the government vehicle that parked at an angle from the cabin door. Even though the tinted windows were an opaque black, they all knew who the driver was.

How could they have found her?

Gaston spoke with more distaste than he reserved for Diego. "The CDC woman." There wasn't much that the man liked, but Nicola knew that the government ranked near the bottom.

They watched as the front door of the SUV opened and two perfectly white high heels stepped into the dirt. Nithya was wearing a dark business suit, but her open jacket revealed holster straps around each shoulder.

Nicola desperately turned to Debbie and wished she could take back her outburst. She was in a lot of danger now, and she felt her throat choking up. "Mom..."

Debbie, usually stoic in the face of challenge, wore a

befuddled expression. She brushed her graying hair behind her shoulders and gave Nicola a telling look. Nithya was here for her—there was no doubt about it.

"Y'all had better stay inside." Mom solemnly exited the room.

Nicola wasn't sure if hiding would be enough. As the different scenarios played out in her head, she couldn't keep from thinking suspicious thoughts. "Do you ever get the feeling that there's more going on between Mom and the CDC than she lets on?"

Gaston scoffed. "No way." His displeasure at the thought was clear.

Gaston was an idealist, fiercely loyal to the MC, but his devotion was so complete that it blinded him to anyone else's ulterior motives. The poor guy might have been the most straightforward asshole that ever lived. It made him a valuable companion when trouble went down, but he didn't have a developed understanding of how the real world worked.

Nithya stepped away from the vehicle as the back doors opened. Two police officers wearing bullet-proof vests emerged. They were two of the cops that had arrested her the other night. The Mexican boy wore a blue uniform and the other, the detective, wore a red tie under his vest and had a white hat on.

This wasn't good. Doka shouldn't have cut that cop.

"Maxim's not laying off you guys, is he?" Gaston smiled. He wanted this. He liked confrontation. Even better when it was unavoidable because then he couldn't be blamed.

The three government employees walked up to the cabin and turned their heads sharply as the front door opened. The two cops moved their hands to their holstered weapons. Nicola could feel the adrenaline starting to surge through her veins. No, she did not want to succumb to the strength just yet.

Mom stepped onto the wooden porch and into Nicola's view from the window, blocking the path to the door. She had her cowboy hat on now, and she tipped it a bit to shade her eyes from the sun.

"Ms. Rao," she said coolly, hands defiantly on her hips. "I'd appreciate some notice when you bring the police to my door."

Nithya climbed the steps and stopped a few feet from the MC president. Her tall frame, embellished by the heels, towered over the older woman. But she was the more vulnerable person here; she was no wolf.

"We have a warrant to search your premises." The CDC agent spoke with a detached authority that worried Nicola. Debbie would deny it, but the two had an amiable relationship—not so much as friends but business partners. This matter, however, appeared to divide them.

"She had nothing to do with it, Nithya. Y'all can't come in."

Maxim skirted the yard and examined the surrounding grass, peeking at the side of the cabin. The Mexican stepped back a bit and eyed the second floor windows. They were concerned about being ambushed.

Nicola turned her attention to Diego behind the tree

line. He watched intently from cover without announcing his presence.

Nithya's words drew her attention again. "She needs to answer for attacking a police officer, Ms. Holton."

What? They're gonna try to put that on her? Nicola was the one that had held Doka back that night.

The conversation escalated a bit. After some harsh words from Debbie, Nithya stepped even closer to her and shoved a finger in her face. "You know what will happen if you put a finger on me."

Nithya wasn't backing down. That was a very bad thing because her words were true. She was essentially untouchable.

Even Gaston knew his limits. "If anyone from the MC so much as scratches her," he said, "the CDC will burn this place down."

Nicola felt herself start to panic. She was in dire trouble. Maxim glanced at the window they were peeking through, and Nicola hurriedly ducked away. She pressed her back against the wall below the sill and looked up to Gaston.

"What can we do?" she rasped.

"The only thing that woman wants from all of us is blood."

Nicola couldn't accept that. She didn't hurt that cop. She didn't go against the CDC. She didn't need to die.

"Mom's gonna give me up," she said, rattled. "I'm telling you, we can't trust her!"

The big man shook his head with firm resolve. "Just stay hidden and let Mom work them."

There it was. More idealism from the big man. More belief that things would work out. Nicola was wiser, however. She was intimately familiar with the harsh machinations of the world. She knew what drove those who were in positions of power. Debbie wasn't the upstanding club leader that Gaston hoped she was. Maybe once she had been, but now Nicola was convinced that Mom was more concerned with her personal fortune than the sanctity of the MC.

Nicola poked her head up so her eyes were just visible over the window sill. Nithya and the police were still outside posturing. So far, Mom was holding her ground. Nicola glanced to see what Diego was doing in the trees, but she couldn't see him anymore. He was gone.

iii.

Screw this. Nicola needed a plan.

If the CDC woman wanted her, it was only to kill her. They had no other business to conduct. Nicola wondered about the local cops, but she was pretty sure they wouldn't help her either. Not after Doka had hurt one of them. Not if they were here backing up the CDC.

Angie's brother was the only one. He was dangerous, for sure, but he'd killed Steve in self-defense. He didn't come seeking death—he wanted information. If Nicola could find out where Diego's sister was, he would help her get out of here. It was that simple.

Angie was still alive. She had to be. Her body hadn't turned up over the falls yet. Of course, she couldn't be sure Doka had taken her, but what other explanation would suffice?

The confrontation outside continued as Nicola crawled away from the window. She wasn't going to wait to be executed. Out of view, she stood up and marched towards the back of the clubhouse. Where she was going was prohibited, but she had been the good girl long enough. The world hadn't been fair to Nicola for most of her life, and she would be damned if she was going to trust in the world to save her this time.

Nicola had stopped being a victim a long time ago. Taking action, she had learned, was the surest way to achieve an outcome. When she had been an immigrant child sold for sex, she'd tried to please her masters. She had curried favor where she could but it did her little good. She had still been a slave. And the police? Some of the men she had been forced to sleep with were cops. Nicola didn't have any delusions about her value to them.

No, no one had been there for her until she'd been bitten. It was a slow realization at first, but she had eventually learned that she was more powerful than her persecutors. It had finally been time for the world to please her. With the strength in her blood and her innocence lost, the inclination that had come to her was natural. She had torn her masters apart.

Nicola stopped at the door she wasn't supposed to open and made sure she was alone. She was thankful to the MC for taking her in and teaching her how to keep a low profile over the years, but Doka was the polar opposite of what had kept them alive for so long. Whatever they had been up to was going to bring them all down, starting right now with her.

Nicola opened the door to Mom's office and slid in gently. This felt like a betrayal but she knew: where Doka went, Mom ordered. If Angie had been taken by them, then there might be proof somewhere within.

Where would they have kept the kidnapped victims? Mom and some other members had cabins scattered throughout Sycamore, but aside from the falls, she'd never seen any strange activity in the woods. Doka visited the Yavapai reservation at times but it seemed a risky option. He was always complaining about how meddling the tribal police were. It didn't seem like a good place to start.

There was a safe on the floor, but Nicola didn't know the combination. There was also a metal filing cabinet with locked drawers. Mom kept her desk clean, so Nicola dug through the drawers, looking for anything suspicious. Pens, envelopes, small pads of paper—nothing suspicious presented itself.

There was a pistol in a bottom cubby. Nicola's fingers twitched as she pondered taking it. Did she really need the protection? The gun would just put her in more danger. If she used it against the CDC or police, she would be a dead woman. No. There had to be another way.

Her eyes scanned the room frantically. She was running out of time. Some community awards lined the walls. There were some knickknacks in a glass cabinet, little statues and such. She saw a bowl with glass beads in it, but something else inside caught her eye. She opened the glass door and ran her fingers through the beads and pulled out a small key. Then her gaze returned to the filing cabinet.

The heavy locks turned with the key. The top drawer was full of fliers and memorabilia, but the middle one looked more promising. The sections seemed to be personnel files of individuals associated with Mom. MC members were in here, too.

Nicola quickly found her name and opened the light folder. There was a death certificate from one of the men she had killed while fleeing the prostitution ring. Was this blackmail evidence against her? There was also a photocopy of her passport and copies of some of her old arrest reports, but those were public records that didn't seem important. There weren't too many papers, so she shoved them into her jeans pocket.

She flipped through the rest of the folders, looking for Nithya's name, and she was elated to find it. Inside was a scan of a recent ID for Nithya Rao. A Flagstaff address was listed. That was a start. Nicola folded the paper and added it to her collection but was frustrated at the lack of further information in the folder. No dirt on the CDC? That didn't seem like Mom at all.

Unfortunately, she couldn't find anything in here

relating to Doka.

Nicola quietly shut the drawer and opened the last one at the bottom. These were financial records: titles for motorcycles, the deed for the clubhouse under SSMC, LLC, and lots of tax forms. She was focused on looking for other files that were suspect, but nothing had the names Deborah Holton or Carlos Doka on them. Nicola shook her head. There had to be something else.

Then Nicola stumbled onto something interesting. It was a liquor license application for Sycamore Lodge. That was strange because the club didn't own the roadhouse. The listed name was a Regina Beale. Where had she heard that name before?

Nicola thought back to the incident that had first gotten her involved with Doka. She had tracked down the delinquent close to the border of Sanctuary. The roadhouse was the nearest building. At the time, she didn't think much of it.

The wolf racked her brain trying to think of a plausible theory. There was nothing special at Sycamore Lodge—she'd spent a lot of time there. There was an old farming bin out back but it only held rancid grain. It didn't make sense. Still, maybe there was something there.

In the distance, Nicola heard the muffled slam of the heavy front door of the cabin. Whoever was outside had probably come back in. Nicola had to take off. She closed the drawer and made a quick attempt to leave things as she had found them.

It was imperative that she got to Diego. Her search had

revealed no direct evidence of any wrongdoing but she had possible leads. That had to be enough to buy good faith.

The president's office was in the back of the clubhouse. It was an easy walk from there to the exit. She creaked the back door open a peek and it was all quiet, so she slipped out, wondering if she would ever be welcome inside again.

iv.

"You didn't think it would be that easy, did you?"

The crisp voice spun Nicola around, and she jumped backwards at the sight of the police detective. Maxim was standing flush with the cabin wall, holding a gun with both hands steadily pointed at her.

The strength was back. Nicola could feel it building up in her wiry frame.

"I saw you duck away from the window," he said plainly.

Nicola looked around the clearing. The CDC woman wasn't here. No one else was in sight. But she didn't want any trouble. She wasn't about to attack a police detective, and she certainly didn't want to get shot.

"I didn't cut that cop," she said, pleading. "It was Doka."

Maxim remained calm and looked at her curiously. "That's funny. He said the same thing about you before the CDC got him."

What did that mean? If the CDC had already killed Doka, then what chance did Nicola have of surviving this confrontation?

She looked to the tree line. It wasn't that far away.

"I'm packing silver rounds," said Maxim. His hardened eyes didn't miss a beat. "I wouldn't try anything."

Holding the strength back was all she could manage. She needed to remain rational here. A wild animal wouldn't make for a sympathetic victim. But she balled her hands into fists anyway, if only to fight off the instinctual pressure. Nicola took a backward step.

"Listen," said the cop, lowering the gun ever so slightly, "I just want to talk."

"Is that why the CDC is here? You know what's gonna happen to me."

It was a statement that he acknowledged with his troubled face. But his lies continued anyway.

"I can protect you if you can help me."

"Fuck you, pig," she shot back, taking another step to the trees. "You can't protect me from her."

Maxim looked around in frustration. His left hand let go of the gun as his right finger eased off the trigger. He held both palms towards her, turning the pistol to the side. "Ask yourself why I haven't called the others yet."

The overbearing sun glinted off a silver ring on his left hand. He seemed earnest, but cops, especially detectives, were trained liars. Still, even as she watched Gaston sneak around the corner of the house, he had given her pause enough to question his motives.

"I just need to know what it is you know." The detective had a tender note in his voice as he broke from his usual authoritative gruffness. "Why were you trying to keep Diego from finding his sister?"

Nicola was caught off guard. "It wasn't me," was all she said.

From immediately behind the detective, Gaston swung a fist and jarred the pistol loose. Maxim's arm buckled. He tried to snag the weapon but it flew past his fingers.

The detective recovered and forced his elbow back, catching the big man in the gut, but he barely winced. Gaston shoved the cop into the ground.

Maxim reached through the wild grass for his pistol. Nicola scrambled to find it, sprung ahead, and kicked the gun away toward the tree line. She didn't want any part of it.

Gaston gripped the detective's black vest with both hands and lifted him into the air. He righted Maxim's body and slammed him into the cabin, thrusting his robust forearm into the cop's neck.

"Don't make a sound," said Gaston. "I could have killed you."

The cop had both of his hands on Gaston's arm, easing some of the pressure on his neck. He was angry and, although overpowered, still had fight left in him. "You stupid motherfucker," he choked out. "You're going to jail for this."

Nicola put her hand up to instill reason in the big man. Gaston was a towering figure—his broad frame could've subdued the detective even without his wolf strength. He was a hothead. And he liked to fight. And he was showing unbelievable discipline right now.

"That's not how the CDC warrant operates," said the big man calmly. "You think it's a mistake that this clubhouse is outside your town? You are only here on that bitch's authority. You can't get me on this."

Maxim's shoes scratched against the wooden wall for purchase. "You can't interfere with the CDC warrant."

Gaston smiled and showed a large set of teeth. "Is that what you were doing here?" He looked back at Nicola, who didn't know what to do. "It didn't look like it."

A twig snapped and Nicola turned quickly.

"Put him down, Gaston." Diego stood some distance away, holding the detective's gun.

That was him. Nicola's heart jumped. That's who she was looking for.

"You're Angie's brother, right?" she asked. "You need to get me out of here." Nicola took another step away from the cabin but Diego was preoccupied. He was still pointing the gun at the other two.

Gaston didn't move at all, but he released what sounded like a deep, guttural growl. "You," he said, not bothering to face Diego. "What are you doing at my clubhouse?"

Maxim yanked on the big man's arm but it held strong. "What does she know, Diego?"

"I don't know," he insisted. Despite the other two still locked in a grapple, Diego slackened his pose and looked at Nicola. "Where's Angelica?"

"She's alive," she spit out. "I don't know where she is, but I can help you find her. I'm a good tracker." All Nicola needed to do was get away from the CDC and the police. She would tell Diego all about Carlos, show him the papers, and give him everything she had. Now that Doka was dead, he wouldn't care. Nicola could leave Mom out of it and hopefully not be hunted by the MC.

Maxim heaved his body against Gaston's. "Fucking let me go," he said, staring the wolf down. The big man let out a heavy hiss that sounded like steam escaping. He backed up, and Maxim slid down the wall to his knees, coughing. "You need to tell me," he said, clearing his throat, "everything you know right now if you want any chance here."

Nicola thought it couldn't hurt but it was Gaston who spoke. "We don't talk to police."

"I'm not a cop," said Diego.

Gaston was unimpressed. "You killed Steve."

"Gaston," said Nicola. "Doka told me and Steve to grab Diego after you talked to him. We kind of worked for him on the side."

"What?" he blurted out, taken aback. It wasn't the scuffle with the police detective or the gun to his back that had set Gaston on edge. It was the threat of him having to change the narrative in his head over who was at fault.

"I'm sorry. I know Steve was your friend. I should have told you." Nicola felt awful, but it had been Steve's choice. He was the one who'd gotten her involved. He was the one who'd told her to keep it a secret.

"Why would Doka attack Diego?" Gaston looked to both of them for answers. Nicola wasn't sure how to tell him. If he knew, then the CDC might just hunt him down too.

"It's about the missing people," said Maxim, returning to his feet. "Isn't it?"

Nicola saw Diego and Maxim's pleading eyes and felt bad for their pain. But it was Gaston looking at her with furrowed brows that hit her the hardest. He just stood there, at a loss.

"Yes," said Nicola, and then, "no. Not missing people. Not really." Nicola wrapped her arms around her body like she was cold. It had to be said. "The suicides."

Diego's eyes widened. "What suicides? My sister?"

"No, I don't think so. I'm guessing they have her somewhere. You have to understand that I only saw a little of it a long time ago. They didn't trust me." Nicola felt tears coming to her eyes but forced them back. "I wasn't a part of it," she asserted.

Maxim rubbed his arm and looked like he was in pain. He carefully circled around the big man, keeping a safe distance as one would with a wild animal. Then he stepped up to Diego and held his sore arm out. The biker handed the gun back to the cop.

"The Sanctuary suicides?" asked Maxim. "The ones over the falls?"

Nicola stood motionless and nodded.

The four of them in the back yard were imposing figures, each in their own way, but all allowed the silence to linger.

They each wanted something: understanding, closure, family. It was easy for Nicola to blame Doka, but she knew she had some involvement, however small, and perhaps one day what she would seek would be forgiveness. But for now, she had other priorities.

Maxim cocked his pistol to make sure it was still loaded and ready to fire. "Do you have material evidence in these cases, Makarova?"

After quietly digesting the turn of events, Gaston spoke up. "Nicola, we don't talk to the police." He stood stubborn as Maxim glared at him. "Mom won't have it."

The detective quickly turned his pistol in his hand and butted Gaston hard in the face. The wolf stepped back with a scowl but thought better about resuming violence against the cop.

Maxim puffed out his chest and held the pistol tightly. "There you go," he said. "You're learning."

Diego huffed impatiently. "Maxim, we don't have time for this. I don't give a shit about dead people—I need to find my sister."

Nicola agreed. Everything else could wait. The detective, instead of answering, just looked at the ring on his finger.

Dead people. That's where his thoughts were. Nicola moved slowly towards Diego.

"I'm taking her out of here," he said, "away from the CDC."

"I can protect her," countered the detective.

Diego shook his head. "They will kill her."

"No one is dying here today," said Gaston with unusual

restraint, "especially not Nicola." The big man positioned himself between them and Maxim, who half raised his gun. It was an act that Nicola attributed to his idealism and sense of brotherhood. It really was a shame that Gaston wasn't the MC president instead. "Diego," he said nobly, "take her."

Nicola made sure the big man blocked her from the pistol, but Diego didn't move. He just stood there, looking to the detective, waiting for his word.

Gaston urged him in a warning voice. "Diego..."

V.

Up until now they had been alone. At least as far as Nicola knew. She had been looking back and forth nervously since this began, but this time, when she looked at the cabin door, she saw it was open a crack. Inside, behind the shadow of the sun, she saw two glowing orange eyes watching them, and she knew it was over.

Debbie kicked the back door fully open with her cowboy boot and had a look of disappointment on her face. "I can't say y'all are my favorite people right now."

The others all turned as one. This was a clear complication for everybody.

Diego, furthest from the house, spoke with a sardonic edge. "You lied to me about Angelica, Mom."

The older woman stepped outside and brushed her long hair to her back. "Now honey, what I told you was a truth you didn't want to hear."

"And what about Makarova not being in the club?" cut in Maxim. "Two days ago, you swore you didn't know who she was."

"Well that," said Mom, a sly smile on her face. "I guess you caught me there." The woman laboriously looked over each one of them. Her face was cold and Nicola couldn't meet her gaze. "My agreement with the CDC had to be upheld, unfortunately. None of that matters now that you're on Ms. Rao's team."

Nicola's eyes flitted to the detective. What did that mean? It was hard to trust either Debbie or Maxim right now. All the more reason for her to go with Diego.

Mom pulled off her cowboy hat and waved it in front of her face like a fan. "My, but it is hot out here this afternoon."

"Mom," said Gaston, ignoring her theatrics, "we can get Nicola out of here right now."

Debbie raised her eyebrows and looked at Maxim in surprise. A grand smile grew on her face, and she shook her head. "Oh no. Everything's all worked out with the CDC. There's nothing to worry about. Besides," she said, pausing as she caught Nicola's eye, "you don't know anything anyway. Do you, sugar?"

Her smile, her tone—nothing was right about this. Nicola tensed her muscles.

"Deborah," said the detective, "you need to tell me what

happened to Lola right now." Maxim held his pistol tightly in his hand, but he pointed it down.

"Lola," said the woman, suddenly becoming less accommodating. She walked to Nicola and patted her on the shoulder gently. Nicola tried not to shudder at the touch as Deborah spoke. "Lola was my good friend, Maxim. We spent a lot of time together." The woman winked at Nicola and moved to Gaston, putting her arm around his shoulders. "That's more than I can say for you. You were always working, burying your head in other people's problems." Debbie walked around the big man's back and leaned on his other side. He softened his stiff posture some. "And when you finally decided to give it a rest, more than not, you would pick up the bottle."

Maxim's face hardened. Nicola saw there was truth to what Mom had said.

Debbie stepped away from Gaston and gave him a slight nod. Diego backed away from the dangerous wolf, but Mom wasn't moving toward him. Maxim was the target of her story.

"I know you have an intricate mind," she said to his face, "a detective's mind, but just because you investigate the insipid plots of the world don't mean something similar happened to Lola."

"Deborah," he warned.

"It's Debbie, hon," she said, tossing her hat onto the doorstep. "I never liked you, but your wife did. She cried the countless nights you ignored her. She never understood why your work consumed you." The others watched in rapt attention as Mom paced around the detective without masking her contempt. "Then one day—after suffering through all the drinking, after losing all the fights—one day, Lola realized that she didn't love you anymore."

A crease formed between the detective's eyebrows as he heard her words. He looked injured. The story came easily because it must have been true, and the man was about to break. But Mom didn't stop talking.

Debbie turned her back to him. "Your wife wasn't taken. She wasn't abducted." The woman returned to Gaston's side and coldly faced the troubled detective again. "Lola left you, Maxim. I should know. I helped her. She stayed at my house for a few days until she was ready to leave." Mom's voice broke a bit. Nicola thought her eyes were teary.

The cop's knees almost buckled. He wasn't looking at Mom or anyone anymore. His focus was past all of them, on a time and place far away. Slowly, the detective slid his pistol into the holster at his waist.

For a second, Mom put her face into her arms while leaning on Gaston's back, and then she wiped her eyes and continued. "Lola made her own decision, Maxim, and then she was gone."

The detective's chest heaved. He walked to the cabin and rested a hand against it, leaning over like he was ready to throw up. Nicola looked to Diego. He was uneasy.

Gaston suddenly jolted upright and let out a whimper. He dropped to the floor as Nicola saw the taser in Debbie's hands.

"Mom!" she yelled in a panic, not believing what she saw

right in front of her.

"Out here, Nithya!" Debbie called.

As Gaston convulsed in the grass, Mom rolled him over, sat on his back, wrapped her arm around his neck, and squeezed. Nicola clenched her fists and looked at the distant trees. Adrenaline flooded her body as her thin frame gained invisible strength.

"Sorry, big guy," said Mom. "This is for your own good."

Diego immediately whipped a long silver blade from his jacket sleeve, the same one he had stabbed Steve with. He feinted forward, measuring his options.

Mom noticed the knife and leaned away from it, keeping pressure on the headlock. "Detective," Mom said briskly, "I do believe that's the murder weapon you've been looking for."

Diego looked to Maxim for a moment, feet glued to the floor, but the cop didn't respond or even look. He just knelt, weeping against the wall.

Gaston had barely seen what hit him, and he was weakly clawing at his neck. His open mouth was attempting to form words, but there was nothing he could do. His head fell limp.

He would be okay, thought Nicola. He wasn't the one they were trying to kill.

Nicola planted her feet to run to Diego, but Mom launched herself from the ground and hit her square in the gut, tackling her. Nicola fell on her side and, with quick reflexes, backhanded Debbie across the face. Debbie swatted her arm away and pounded on her abdomen. Pain exploded in her gut. Nicola tried to pick up her legs to fight off the stronger wolf.

Diego advanced with his silver knife drawn, and Mom jumped off of Nicola, being extra cautious when faced with the deadly metal.

"Let's go," Diego yelled. Nicola rolled forward in a somersault and jumped to her feet as Diego retreated to the tree line. As she ran, she glanced back at Maxim with his silver bullets safely tucked away in his holstered gun. It was now or never.

Nicola wasn't as strong as most others, but she was a good tracker, and she was fast. Faster than Debbie. She bolted along the same path that Diego was taking. Power surged through her body as she pushed ahead. The long stalks of white grass bent beneath her sinewy legs.

Her stomach still hurt, but the pain didn't slow her stride. She ran hard and overtook Diego, who was only human. A sort of tunnel vision formed and all she could see was the safety of the trees and shadows getting ever closer.

A gunshot rang out. Nicola instinctively ducked her head to make herself a smaller target. She had to hope that Diego would be able to make it out alive too, but there was no time to look. Only time to go.

Nicola ran as fast as she could, but she couldn't duck the next bullet. It wasn't immediately painful but her leg just failed her. She tripped up and fell into the tall grass. As she gripped her left thigh, blood spurted out. She squeezed it tightly and pushed herself to her feet. Diego ran by her in a flash. Go. Go.

Another loud report and the tree trunk ahead of Nicola exploded, throwing pieces of bark into the air. That one had whizzed right by her. She hopped forward like a wounded rabbit. She was almost there.

Nicola didn't hear the fourth shot. All of a sudden her throat erupted in a horrible warmth and she fell to the ground.

Ahead of her, Diego de la Torre disappeared into the Sycamore forest.

Nicola put her face down in the dirt. It was difficult to move. And breathe. She coughed and blood spilled from her mouth. She summoned all the adrenaline in her body, fighting, pushing to get up, but she could only lift herself a few inches.

The sound of footsteps got closer behind her. Nicola used every ounce of her strength to roll over onto her back.

She saw the detective on his feet now in the distance, standing at attention with his hands on the back of his head in shock. His gun wasn't drawn; he wasn't the one who had fired.

Nithya Rao sped towards Nicola, holding a pistol. The CDC woman—she was here. This wasn't good. Nicola still needed to search her Flagstaff house. She still needed to tell Diego about Doka.

A strange wheezing sound that Nicola had never heard before escaped from her throat. She felt a sensation of emptiness where she was hurt. She had been shot before but this was different. Nicola's breathing became more labored as she realized why her strength was being sapped away. Her body had been ripped by silver.

Nicola had been betrayed by the woman who had once saved her. She tried to get a view of her in the distance to make one last appeal, but her eyes couldn't find their target.

"Mom..." she said, straining to get the word to sound.

Nithya slowed to a casual walk as a disgusted scowl marred her smooth face. The woman stopped next to her, standing tall and blocking out the rays of the sun. Nicola spit up a spray of blood, and Nithya's heels weren't perfectly white any more.

"I'm the one you need to worry about," said the CDC woman, leveling her pistol at Nicola's head.

There was no sound. No muzzle flash. No pain.

Part 5 - The Tail

i.

Diego wedged the door open with his boot to catch another moment of the cool breeze. Despite the clear sky and beaming sun, the temperature had dropped into the high seventies today and he meant to enjoy what he could. Fall had a pleasant spirit in Arizona, and besides, the dim recesses of Sycamore Lodge could have used some ventilation.

A table of three gruff men in sweaty clothes held his regard. The truckers were mildly focused, partaking in occasional small talk but mostly going about the business of scarfing down their greasy lunches. They carried with them a presence of questionable repute that somehow made them at home in the roadhouse. As one of them turned to look at Diego, the biker shifted his gaze to another table.

A solitary man sat heedlessly staring into nothing in particular with a mug of beer in his hand. His white panama hat sat beside his left hand as it rapped on the table. Maxim had seen better days. It was barely 2 p.m. and he was clearly drunk, with little sign of being content.

Looking to the empty bar, a familiar face smiled. Melody was working again, looking a combination of sad and bored and frustrated. She seemed relieved to see Diego. Her thin eyebrows rose and her eyes lit up. She gave him a playful wave. Diego nodded and looked around. There wasn't anyone else of consequence inside.

It had almost been a week since the raid on the clubhouse and the execution of Nicola Makarova. To Diego's disappointment, the Seventh Sons and police alike had kept low profiles in that time. The biker had been forced to resort to less direct strategies. Now, Diego finally had a solid chance to talk to Maxim, but he felt an obligation to check in with Melody first.

He removed his foot from the door, took a deep breath, and walked over to the pretty bartender as she handed him a glass of Bloody Mary mix.

"I had fun last night," she said under her breath. She brushed her magenta hair behind her ear and smiled like a school girl. Diego gave her a confident wink.

She was a fun girl, but it still felt strange to sleep with someone who had been with his sister. Same as always, Melody had continually insisted that Angelica had moved on a while ago and left no ties behind. Was Mom right that she'd used the club as a means to an end? Angelica did always want to see the world, and it was no surprise to find that their struggling neighborhood in Detroit hadn't been compelling enough.

Still, Diego had something else in common with his sister. He felt like he had hidden reasons to get close to Melody too. How could he not when the girl knew about Angelica but told him so little? So they had spent the night at her cabin and become more familiar with each other. Diego was now convinced that the bartender had no way of getting in touch with his sister anymore. Melody didn't know anything.

Diego took a sip of his drink and nodded to the bartender in thanks. "Give me a second," he said, and strolled over to Maxim's table, leaving the glass behind. He stopped in front of an empty chair and waited for the detective to look up. After a moment, it was obvious that wasn't going to happen.

Diego wiped his thin mustache with his fingers. "You're working with the CDC now?" It was a spurious question, designed to instigate more than inquire, and it served its purpose.

"Right now, I am trying to have a drink." Maxim spoke strongly but stared at the table. The man was disheveled and had the beginnings of a scraggly beard. His white shirt was unbuttoned at the collar and his jacket and tie were nowhere in sight. He held a silver wedding band in his fingers and occasionally spun it like a top on the table. Sometimes he would clap down on it with his palm before it came to a stop, but usually he would allow it to tumble out of control and make jarring, uneven noises against the wood.

Diego sighed. "This is no time to drink for days on end."

"Isn't it?" Maxim asked. He looked up finally and raised his hands in mockery. "You should've told me that days ago. Could've saved me some trouble."

"You still have a job to do."

"Loosen up," commanded Maxim. "We got them. Another case closed." The detective recited the statement with little enthusiasm. Diego knew he placed no stock in the false words.

The poor man had realized that he had driven his wife away. It had been mean of Mom to tell him what she did, but then she had meant to distract him. Though Maxim had still held his gun, he was disarmed in spirit, and he still hadn't recovered.

Diego, too, felt as if he had failed Nicola. At first, he had meant to proceed without the detective's support. Now, however, he wasn't sure how much farther he could go without him.

The biker kicked a chair back with his boot and sat down. "I don't know if she can be trusted."

The ring spun on the table and created hypnotizing shapes. Diego's inference hung heavy in the air, however, and the officer picked it up.

"Nithya?"

Diego nodded.

"What do you know of it?"

"She killed Nicola right in front of us."

Maxim blinked slowly, lazily. "It was legal. It's fucked up, but she had orders."

"I doubt it," answered Diego briskly. The biker pulled out his wallet and flipped it open in front of the man.

Maxim squinted his eyes as he strained to read in the dim light. "United States Public Health Service Commissioned Corps. That's a mouthful."

"Protecting, promoting, and advancing the health and safety of the nation."

"That too." Maxim furrowed his brow. "You in the military?"

"Not really and not anymore," answered Diego.

"You're not supposed to give that ID back when you leave?"

Diego slanted his mouth in a smirk. "I left pretty fast." Maxim just nodded so he continued. "I was a ranger with them for six years. Of course, that profession doesn't officially exist. The Commissioned Corps is a noncombatant service, but a public health need arose to teach their particular skill set."

The detective looked at him blankly but then registered understanding. "Killing wolves."

Diego winced. He never liked thinking of himself as a killer.

"We are detailed to various agencies depending on need, but in the case of the rangers, we are almost always deployed by the CDC."

Maxim took another chug of beer and looked unimpressed.

"The point is, the Commissioned Corps is the strong

arm of the CDC when hunting werewolves. They don't go after them on their own, and they definitely don't tap the local police." Diego leaned in to make sure he wasn't talking too loud. "If there was an Order To Kill issued for Nicola, the PHSCC would have been called out. Don't you find it strange that your office was asked to act outside your jurisdiction?"

"If it was illegal," Maxim countered, "why would she pull in a third party? Wouldn't that draw unnecessary suspicion?"

"Perhaps," said Diego, pondering the circumstances. "But then, you were investigating the Seventh Sons anyway. You were peeking under their rocks and poking them with sticks. What if the CDC just brought you in to placate you?"

The detective stared at him. Diego wasn't sure if he was being taken seriously or if the man was just too drunk to follow.

"Maxim, isn't it funny that everyone you arrested the night of the full moon is dead?"

Maxim took a long swig, upending the beer glass and emptying the swill down his throat. He waved to the waitress for another. "Except for you."

Yes. There was no question that Diego's actions were dangerous, but the others had been killed for what they knew. Diego, on the other hand, didn't know anything. That was his problem.

Maxim snapped his fingers and the ring popped from his hand and landed on the table in a blur, looking like a transparent globe as it spun. Diego shook his head.

The truckers beside them were exchanging heavy glances. They were silent now as the waitress stacked their plates for collection. Were they tense? That was a good sign.

"What was Nicola trying to tell us?" Diego asked suddenly, partially to himself. The answers had been so close. For everything she may have known, she left them with so little.

Maxim burped and wiped his mouth. "I've got bad news for you, Diego. Makarova wasn't a mastermind. She didn't know anything. She was a desperate woman who attacked a police officer and said anything she could to avoid getting killed."

Diego stomped his leather boot on the floor. "How could you sit here and not do anything about what she said?"

Maxim stared at the biker coldly to let it be known that he was getting annoyed with the questions.

Diego pressed the detective. "She mentioned suicides at the falls. She told Gaston that Doka was responsible for those abductions, that they weren't suicides at all, that he'd tried to kill me because I was asking after Angelica. Don't any of those count as leads?"

Maxim continued watching him with cold eyes. Then, once again, he spun the wedding band on the table.

Diego scoffed. "Look at you. You were so determined that night you arrested me. You didn't let Mom back you down before. But for what? You're all talk but no action."

Maxim hissed at him. "And you're all action but no thought. You can't just walk into a bar without a plan and flash a knife. Trust me, you might be the last of the four bikers from that night left alive, but you won't be for long if you keep this up."

A sigh escaped Diego's lips. "That's exactly why I need you, Maxim." The biker slid his seat closer to the table. "Listen, I know you're a good detective. I've asked around. There's no way you would leave something like this alone. We both know that when you're done wallowing in self-pity that you'll decide to follow up with the suicides. I am just asking for you to get there sooner rather than later."

Maxim stretched his eyes wide and let out a heavy breath. "I've already checked that out." The man grabbed his next mug from the waitress and paused until she scampered off. "There were three jumpers over the last two years. I even had the bodies exhumed. They're in the basement of the marshal's office right now: Sanctuary's private morgue." He took a sip from his glass.

"And?"

"And nothing. Cause of death is severe physical trauma on all three. I had tests run and nothing was found out of the ordinary. There's no physical evidence that supports homicide or any other suspicious circumstances."

"There needs to be something we're missing," protested Diego. "Why would the Seventh Sons be abducting people?"

The detective shrugged. "Excuse the play on words, Diego, but the bodies are a dead end."

The biker persisted. "Well, isn't the gang into drugs or something else that you can use against them?"

The detective shook his head dismissively. "Most certainly, but I can't do anything about it. That's a federal concern at this point." Maxim flicked his left hand again and the ring clattered against the table top. A wobbly ringing filled their ears.

Diego swatted down and snatched up the wedding band to silence to racket. "We need something new," Diego asserted desperately. "I don't have other leads to my sister. I'm lost, man."

The detective had a longing look on his face as pain flashed across his eyes. "Trust me," he said, "you can lose yourself in the truth just as easily."

The biker closed his eyes and leaned back. As he looked again, he focused on the wedding ring in his hand, the one Maxim often played with. It was a plain silver band, not especially shiny, with a smooth finish except for a single imperfection. There was a chip on the outside surface that cut into the edge. It was an odd shape, and the biker couldn't tell if it was intentional.

Mind your own business, bro.

His sister's words were a paradox. They were meant to push him away, but they only spurred him on more. As long as he could hear her voice, he couldn't give up.

"Let me tell you about my truth, Maxim. I've always been pretty good at fighting. It's not a surprise, really, that I ended up doing what I did professionally. But I never liked it. It always grated on me, like I was disturbing the natural order of things."

Diego swallowed. "When I was a boy, there was this older kid that picked on me once in a while. It wasn't that much and it wasn't a big deal; I just ignored it, mostly. Then one day, for no reason, he shoved Angelica into the street. I was just giving her a ride on my back. She was having so much fun. I guess this kid wanted to get her away from me so he could push me around or something but Angelica fell and hit her head and started bleeding." Diego gritted his teeth firmly. "She was only eight."

He continued. "That was it for me. I beat that older boy down with my fists so hard that I literally never saw him again. I couldn't tell you what happened to him, but as we got older, I found myself having to protect my sister again and again. I'm still doing it. And I'll always do it. It's the one time where the violence makes sense."

Diego looked at Maxim solemnly. "Believe me when I tell you that I won't let up. I'm going to keep chasing this, and in the end, I'm going to find her."

Maxim looked at the man with a softened expression. The glaze over his eyes was still there. But behind that— there was a kinship, an understanding.

"I get it," said the detective, "but I've already been traveling down that road for two years." Maxim pulled the mug of beer to his mouth and slurped up the froth. "I just hope, for your sake, that when you reach the end of your road, you can come to grips with what you find there."

The three men sitting close to them stood up and downed the remainder of their drinks. Diego turned his attention to them as they marched out the door, his eyes following them past the large patio windows, towards the side of the establishment where their trucks were parked.

"Well," said Diego, taking a superior tone. "I'm not sitting on my ass doing nothing. I've been following the truckers for a few days."

Maxim just leaned back into his chair in forced apathy. "Oh yeah? And what has that gotten you?"

Diego considered the question. It hadn't gotten him anything. The truckers always drove in, ate some food and used the restrooms, and then drove back to the Interstate. Following the gang members and truckers had been his only actionable idea, and while everything generally seemed suspicious, nothing had been cause for alarm yet.

Diego pushed away from the table in disgust and stood up. "Well, I'm going, with or without you."

"As long as you're going," said Maxim, still in a bitter mood.

Diego looked sadly at the detective. It was a pathetic thing to lose your drive, or rather, lose what was driving you. The biker wondered how he would respond if their situations were reversed, if he had found out that Angelica was beyond his help.

Diego tossed the wedding band back onto the table. It rolled sideways, but Maxim's hand caught it and immediately starting turning it in his fingers in a familiar motion.

"It means I'm coming back."

ii.

The Transwestern was the only road out of Sanctuary. It was a lonely strip of cracked asphalt that wound its way down to the civilized world nearby. It was just enough out of the way to be forgotten, swallowed by the march of time and obviated by the modern highway below.

This was what was so curious about the idea of the small town as a truck stop. Interstate 40 was the contemporary route, but it wasn't adjacent to Sycamore Lodge. The roadhouse was close enough for the truckers to find, but they would likely need a good reason for going out of their way.

Diego's interest was immediately piqued when one trucker turned west on the old 66. The other two semis continued on the only paved street and bore southeast towards the Interstate, as the other trailers he'd followed previously had done, but this one truck, this anomaly, opted to bear right, away from any sensible destination.

The laid asphalt immediately gave way to gritty red dirt. Diego stopped his Scrambler at the intersection and swiveled his gold helmet as he watched both paths. The biker was killing time, making sure to lag behind enough so as not to draw suspicion. The road was expected to be empty, so he would make it look that way.

It was easy to follow the heavy truck at a large distance because of its size and the dirt it kicked up. However, the condition of the road proved slow going. Diego caught himself getting too close a few times and had to pull back.

He needed to find a way to cool his nerves and appreciate the trek.

It was a nice ride west. The bright day and cool breeze were the perfect backdrop for a relaxing road trip. An open expanse of sand gave way to the forest, and except for the occasional trailer stationed roadside, the neglected path provided a quiet solitude that Diego yearned for. He could have gotten used to this.

After some time, the old road merged with another street, became paved, and fell in line with the Interstate to the south. They passed a small town sandwiched between the parallel highways and then the cross streets and activity disappeared again. Once more, they were among the trees, and Diego's thoughts started to wander.

The biker remembered his days in the Commissioned Corps spent as a ranger on the road. He didn't ride a motorcycle then, but he did have occasion to trail people. In fact, there was a time when he felt like most of his job consisted of tracking: finding problems, rooting them out, and helping people continue with their complicated lives.

Diego grimaced. He wasn't sure when all that had changed. More and more, instead of policing, he had been sent out to eliminate threats. He was good at it, that was for sure. He'd even done it with a clear conscience when it had been a last resort, but somehow, it had become business as usual. And being a paid killer didn't suit his soul.

Still, the biker identified with the job. He was proud of it —and it ate at him from the inside like a worm. It had happened so slowly that Diego didn't even notice until

Angelica left. That's when he had realized that he was lost. Without his family, his job, did he still have a place in this world?

Kill or be killed. No. Diego needed to find something else.

The biker may have again been on a dangerous road, just as he had been many times in his previous life, but he was decided that there wouldn't be death at the end of this one.

iii.

Up ahead, as the vegetation once more gave way to an open span of desert, the semi slowed down and turned right. There was another small town hugging the highway ahead, but this road was an offshoot well before that. It was an ashy dirt path, nowhere near the rich reds of the lands behind. It led north into the last vestiges of the forest.

Diego's bike was muffled well, but he had second thoughts as he turned up the private road. He saw a large farmhouse ahead through the trees. He couldn't just pull up to the driveway. He quickly decided to park his bike behind a wide oak some distance away. The biker pulled off his gold helmet and hiked closer to get a view of the proceedings.

The large tractor trailer came to a halt next to the old home, its light blue paint peeling in the unforgiving sun.

There was an old man with overalls out front who covered his face as the dust whisked by him. He had a white head of hair and matching beard but had the look of a hard worker. He acted as if he expected this meeting.

Was this a safe house for the motorcycle gang? Was Angelica imprisoned inside? Diego inched forward.

The trucker dismounted and greeted the old man. They talked for a moment, but Diego was too far to pick out any meaning. Then the two walked to the back of the trailer and opened the doors. The old, stout man did a cursory look around to make sure they were alone but Diego was well-hidden.

The spry trucker jumped up and disappeared into the trailer. Diego could only make out several boxes inside before the old man helped the other pull out a green plastic storage barrel. They both carried the large, fifty-five gallon drum and put it in the back of a rusty white pickup.

Maxim had confirmed that the Seventh Sons were in the drug business. Maybe the police officer had to defer to the feds, but Diego was under no such obligation. As he watched the old man secure the barrel to his truck with straps, he wondered what it was exactly that they were shipping.

The two men disappeared behind the trailer after closing it up. Diego couldn't see what was happening, but before he knew it, the big vehicle was starting up and turning around. Diego ducked down into a rosebush as the semi roared by him, likely finally headed to the Interstate.

That wasn't where Diego was going. He watched as the

man with the white beard hopped into his pickup. The biker sat and waited for him to pass and stared at the green drum in the truck bed the entire time.

That was it. Diego knew this was a breakthrough and allowed a slight grin to cross his face. When it was safe, he returned his gold helmet to his head and patiently walked back to his Scrambler.

After merging onto the highway, the old man veered onto another dirt road heading north into the forest. The back roads were remote to begin with, but this path gave way to hills and ditches and other obstacles that were not meant for his street bike. The forest grew thick with untouched growth and the dirt became loose and rocky. Eventually the trees started to thin, and then they completely disappeared as they drove into a vast expanse of dry sand.

The pickup truck wasn't as large or loud as the tractor trailer, so Diego made sure to give the old man a lot of cushion. There was nowhere to run out here anyway.

The more Diego thought about it, the more he figured that the farmhouse was just where the man lived. Besides him being an apparent hermit, there wasn't anything especially strange about the grounds. Where they were headed now was the bigger question; it was more key to the mystery at hand, Diego was sure. If there were a hidden cabin out in the desert somewhere, a place that criminal activity occurred, then it wouldn't be a leap of reason to suspect that Angelica might be there. The biker shook his head. What had she gotten herself into this time?

Eventually, the beat up truck turned off what was barely a road anymore. Diego stopped the bike and flipped up his visor. There was no civilization at all out here. No buildings, pipes, or power lines, and now, no more roads. Even if he carried his cell phone with him, it likely would've lacked a signal. They were in unmapped territory from here on out.

And he knew he was close.

iv.

After some time of plodding over rough terrain, Diego held back as he saw a body of water ahead. It appeared to be a small lake, and the old man was definitely headed towards it. Down there, in the lower land, there were numerous trees that marked an unknown oasis in the middle of nowhere.

As the truck stopped next to the water, Diego looked for a place to hide his Scrambler. He couldn't get close enough to the foliage, especially with the man disembarking. Diego killed his engine and pulled his bike into a small ditch. Unless it was directly stumbled upon, it was out of sight. He ripped off his helmet, threw it to the ground, and sprinted for the tree line.

The distance was further than it had initially looked, and the biker was nearly out of breath just from the approach. As he reached the shade he passed a decrepit sign with the words "Paradise Tank" engraved in the wood. This must have been a known watering hole for something, at some point, but the years have mitigated the usefulness of this location and society had happily marched past it.

Diego took a heavy breath and moved closer. The stout man was standing in the pickup bed, and he kicked the drum out of the back. It rolled and dropped to the sand with a thud. Then he closed his tailgate and walked to his driver's side door, doing something behind the cab.

The biker looked around. There were no cabins out here. No other vehicles either, at least not yet. The only thing he could hear on the wind were the footsteps of the man as he emerged from behind his truck.

He was wearing a fishing wader. It was a tan-colored, chest high overall held around his neck with suspenders. They connected to his waterproof boots. Then he rolled the barrel into the water.

Something wasn't right here. It looked like he was dumping the drum. He wouldn't do that if drugs were inside it. Unless...

It occurred to Diego that the man with the white beard wasn't smuggling anything at all—he was disposing of evidence.

As the stranger walked forward into the shallow water, the green barrel began to float on its side. It became easier for him to push it as he stepped deeper.

There could be some kind of chemical in the drum, something that they were disposing of illegally, but that didn't make a lot of sense. Nicola had mentioned abductions. He was looking for Angelica. She said she had still been alive at the time.

There had to be a body in the barrel.

It had to be Angelica in the barrel.

"No."

Maxim had told him he wouldn't like what he found.

There were two white caps on the top of the green drum. The old man twisted them both off and the dusky water began to spill inside. The barrel slowly started to sink as air bubbles popped along the surface. The man gave it a shove and it floated to the middle of the water tank.

Diego thought about Angelica, as a kid, hitting her head on the asphalt.

The biker abandoned the safety of the tree trunk and swiftly headed towards Paradise Tank. The grizzled man turned and began slogging through the water towards his truck. His work was done here.

No, thought Diego. Don't be Angelica. Don't be in the barrel.

As the man exited the tank, he noticed Diego de la Torre out in the open. The biker saw the barrel sinking lower and broke into a wild sprint towards it. There was nothing else to lose. The old man rushed to his truck and jumped in without taking off his wader. Diego barely noticed as he frantically started his truck and sped away.

The water almost tripped Diego as it stuck to his feet. The biker jumped forward and dove ahead, rabidly paddling his arms. The barrel was at an angle, halfway submerged, but he was almost there.

"Angelica!" he yelled, reaching ahead. He was swimming now, his feet having lost purchase with solid ground. His fingers grabbed the plastic edge of the drum as he pulled himself to it. The biker placed his head next to it to see if he could hear anything within. "Angelica!" There was no answer except for the water rushing in his ears.

He meant to paddle the drum to shore but it was sinking too quickly. He didn't have anything to pull it against. He tried to keep it above the water but it was too heavy, and as he tugged, the barrel pulled him under.

He wasn't going to be able to remove it from the water in time. His fingers scrambled around the top of the drum and yanked but it wouldn't give. Diego pulled his head above the water and saw only the tip of the barrel breaching the surface. There was a steel ring circling the plastic top. He traced around the rim with his thumb until he found a bolt holding it closed. The biker twisted at the nut with wet hands. It was tight, too tight, but he rubbed his fingers raw, and it finally turned. Diego inhaled a deep breath as he once again was pulled into the tank.

The nut spun on the bolt as he sank with it. When it fell away, Diego ripped off the top of the barrel. The water was murky, but the sun was strong, and they weren't deep enough to be engulfed in the dark. He saw an arm, and some cloth that he pulled away, then the dead face. Inside the barrel was a corpse, but it was a man. It wasn't Angelica.

Diego didn't have time to sigh in relief. Still holding his breath, he wanted to drag the barrel to shore. This was damning evidence. As his boots met the sand at the bottom, he tugged hard at the drum.

Behind it, underwater, a serene view of the secrets of Paradise Tank materialized. Through the dirty fluid, Diego could make out at least a dozen identical green barrels slumbering peacefully at the bottom.

The suicides over the falls weren't the whole story—they had only been the beginning. Down here, hidden away from the prying eyes of judicial morality, was something much larger. What had happened here was beyond his imagination, and he needed the full resources of the police to fill in the blanks. Maxim had to help him now.

For a final moment, Diego de la Torre stared in awe as he realized he was standing in an underwater graveyard. Then he coughed out air and released the drum. With an exhilarating push, the biker kicked up and shot to the surface.

Part 6 - The Dead

i.

Seventeen dumped bodies. While Maxim had been occupied with misery and drink at Sycamore Lodge, Diego had traced the disposal of a dead man in the desert and found sixteen others who shared the same watery grave.

Maxim gazed into his black coffee as if he were peering into the murky depths of Paradise Tank. The answers were muddled, but it was only a matter of time before forensics would light the path to justice. Criminals messed up and evidence didn't lie; that was the entire basis for the detective's job. Still, the confidence Maxim had in the results didn't make the waiting any easier.

A heavy breeze blew through old Flagstaff and nearly took his plastic cup's cover with it. Maxim snatched it from the patio table and clipped it into place on top of his coffee, shaking his head. For as expensive as a cup of joe was these days, he would have appreciated a solid mug. But this town sure did love its to-go cups.

Sipping the hot drink eased his complaints. The detective relaxed in the sun and glanced at the Coconino County Morgue across the street. This was the third full day after the discovery, and Maxim had made a point to check in daily. He was getting impatient for the test results, but he had been promised that today would be the day.

It felt good to be useful again, he thought, to be engaged with a purpose.

Upon the grim discovery, Diego had found a call box and rung the detective first thing. He led Maxim to the site that was unmarked on satellite imagery, then disappeared. The biker wanted to remain anonymous in the investigation so he had more leeway to make moves. At this point, Maxim couldn't begrudge him that much.

That night dredging the tank had been a long one filled with a restless hangover and many similar cups of coffee to the one he was cradling now. The following days were just as hectic in entirely different ways.

Maxim had coordinated with the county police, spoken with all the major media outlets, and done endless research. By now, he knew this case was already mostly out of his hands—he was only a local Sanctuary detective after all—but he was determined to see where the facts pointed. Since Maxim was receiving all credit for the discovery, it was easy to get people to talk to him.

A tall woman in a dark suit exited the morgue. She wore

a pink belt with a matching purse and heels and her ponytail flew like a banner in the wind. Maxim chuckled. Only Nithya Rao would think of dressing up so nicely in such a place. Her well-defined features and confident stride exuded the air of a woman who was on top of things.

Because of his frantic schedule, Maxim wasn't sure where the CDC agent had been over the last few days. This finding had been plastered all over the news so she had doubtless heard about it, but it appeared that Nithya now had an active interest in the case. He had run into her as he was leaving the morgue this morning, and she had asked to speak with him afterwards. So here he sat, waiting a longer time than her work should have taken, drinking his expensive coffee, and watching as she waved at him and then veered inside the shop to get one of her own.

Sure, he thought, he'd wait some more.

He had to admit, being on the receiving end of her smile was nice. The detective let his mind imagine more pleasant circumstances and didn't even notice when she reappeared.

"Coconino is one of the largest counties in the nation," she said with the melodic annunciation only a British national could muster, "and relatively one of the most sparsely populated. How on Earth did you manage to come across these bodies?" Nithya sat down opposite him and crossed her legs under the small mesh table.

"I'm the police," Maxim answered casually. "People come to me for help."

"Mmm hmm," she hummed, playing along. "Perhaps you are too large for the cramped confines of Sanctuary.

Not only do you break a case in the deep desert, but I must also wonder what you are doing here in Flagstaff as we speak?"

"That's funny. I was wondering the same thing about you."

Nithya squinted her brown eyes in amusement as she sipped some coffee. "Just due diligence, Detective. Mass deaths like these need to be vetted for cause. The CDC needs to rule out any outbreaks of disease."

"Or identify any, you mean."

"Of course. I spoke with the medical examiner and the lab. All the victims in question were asphyxiated, probably strangled. Postmortem toxicology found nothing unusual."

Maxim started. "They've released the results already?" Brody was useless. The medical examiner had promised the detective he would be the first to know.

"The morgue only has preliminary conclusions, but I have spoken directly with the pathologist at the lab. His results will funnel down soon enough. Regardless, it has been determined that there is no need for CDC intervention, and I will be leaving the matter to the good people of the Coconino County Sheriff's Office. You should do the same."

It sounded like the feds were making moves behind the scenes. In truth, Maxim had been doing the same, but even though his intentions were noble, he couldn't help but be leery about the news.

"Don't you know me better than that, Nithya?"

The woman smiled. "Perhaps not well enough yet." Her

sharp eyebrows softened and Maxim felt drawn to her deep brown eyes. "I do suppose adding a serial killer to your resume would get you noticed by the FBI."

Maxim wasn't buying it. "This is the organized work of multiple people. The dumping alone involved two men: the trucker to deliver the barrel and the man to sink it. And we still don't know where or when the trucker picked it up."

"Or from whom." Nithya rubbed her forehead and nodded. "I understand that the sheriff's office raided a residence?"

"I was there," said Maxim. "The old man who lived in the farmhouse had cleared out. Coconino found his pickup truck the next day in the middle of the desert. Neither provided leads. I don't think we'll be able to identify the truck company or driver either."

Nithya was listening intently but seemed distracted. She was rubbing her forehead as if she were in pain.

"Long night?" asked Maxim.

She just sighed and kept kneading her temples. "Maybe a long night is what I need." She went into her purse and pulled out a bottle of aspirin. "So you have no forensics or suspects in custody. What about the identities of the victims?"

Maxim sat up excitedly. "Now you're getting into my area of expertise." He moved his coffee cup aside as he emphatically pressed two fingers on the table. "Two of the victims were known to have passed through Sanctuary. All of them were transients. Many of them lived on various campgrounds throughout the area. Some of them were probably loners heading west or locals down on their luck. Either way, they were all easily exploitable victims. They didn't have bills to pay, appointments to meet, or families to bemoan their absence. Nobody missed them."

Nithya raised an eyebrow as she considered the facts. "Quick work." She shook out two pills from the aspirin bottle and chugged them down with some coffee. Maxim gave her a disgusted look. "What is it?" she asked.

"I've just never seen anyone take medicine with a hot drink before. It's a bit..." he trailed off, watching her amused expression.

"Savage?"

Maxim considered. "I was going to say drastic."

A light chuckle escaped her lips. "Believe me, Maxim, when you get headaches as often as I do, the definition of drastic changes."

He couldn't argue with that. They sat in silence for a moment, and Maxim caught himself smiling. It was funny, he thought. It was the small things, the items of no consequence, that endeared us to people.

"At any rate," she continued, "the clues are still lacking, but congratulations are in order. I understand why the marshal thinks highly of you."

Great.

Maxim was sure to get a commendation, possibly a promotion, if he saw this through, but that wasn't what this was about. He wouldn't be satisfied with a pat on the back. Gone were the days when jurisprudence trumped justice. Maxim looked down at the silver ring on his finger and felt that he couldn't leave the conversation at that, even if it wasn't wise to bring up his concerns with Nithya. He smiled at her and wondered what they each truly thought of the other. In the end, he decided that she deserved a chance.

"I think the motorcycle club is involved."

She looked startled. "The Seventh Sons?"

"Let me back up," said Maxim, trying to lay the foundation to his theory. "These abductions all occurred over the last two years. Sanctuary also had three suicides over the falls in the same span, along with..."

He paused for a second and the CDC agent put her hand on his and finished his sentence. "Your wife." As he looked up she reassured him. "She wasn't amongst the dead, Maxim."

He shook his head back and forth as he considered Lola's involvement. She certainly didn't fit well into his theory. "Setting her aside, initial indications are that all the dumped bodies were killed after the three suicides. I contend that both sets of crimes were part of the same abduction scheme."

She didn't look convinced. "Is there any physical evidence to support that claim? Were the suicide victims also strangled?"

He sighed. It was true that the bodies of the jumpers didn't arouse suspicion. Even after exhuming the bodies days ago, they had withstood the scrutiny of the part-time Sanctuary medical examiner. But that had been when Maxim wasn't thinking straight. His thoughts were clouded by Lola's betrayal, by his failure. He didn't see the whole picture. Now that he knew about the dumped bodies, he was taking a closer look at all the moving parts.

"They appeared to die from injuries sustained after falling a great distance," Maxim admitted.

"Were they also vagrants?"

"No," countered Maxim, "but hear me out. Isolated residents of Sanctuary go missing but are later found over the falls. The deaths are explained, but while less suspicious than homicides, the uptick in suicides can't be dismissed. Our killers have a problem. They are beginning to attract attention so they need to become more refined."

Nithya finished her coffee and listened intently.

"Sanctuary is small," he said. "Why choose victims from a pool that will be noticeable when you can pull from Greater Sycamore? Most of the forest is wild and unincorporated and governed by County. For that matter, why choose upstanding members of society when you can pick up—"

"Transients." She made a move for Maxim's cup and he waved for her to go ahead. It was his third one this morning anyway. She nodded her appreciation and took a sip and returned her hand to Maxim's. The contact felt nice. It was something he had been without for a long time.

"It's an interesting theory," she said. "Questionable supporting evidence, but compelling nonetheless. What does any of it have to do with the Seventh Sons?"

Maxim smiled coolly. "During the raid, Makarova seemed to implicate Doka in the suicides. Those men went over the falls, for sure, but what if they had been pushed?"

"The two dead wolves." Nithya shook her head slowly and incredulously. "Carlos—"

"I know. Doka wasn't one of them. Not really. But he's a wolf with strong ties to them. He was working with some of the club members, possibly under Deborah's nose. He tried to silence Diego when he went looking for his missing sister."

The woman wore a troubled expression as she pondered his words. "The other man you arrested and released?" A light went on in her head. "He was the man in black leather at the clubhouse, wasn't he?"

Maxim stopped. He hadn't meant to reveal the biker's involvement, but he had been in the arrest report. At this point, Nithya would look him up and find out the truth anyway. There was no sense turning back now. "Ex-PHSCC."

Her eyebrows rose. "You reveal your resources. Now I understand where much of your knowledge has come from."

Maxim had to bite his tongue. Diego wasn't his only resource.

Another long silence passed between them, but the detective's thoughts were less pleasant this time. If only he could get inside Nithya's head. She tapped her short fingernails playfully on his wrist. She could sense his dismay. He could tell she was trying to put his mind at ease, but he couldn't rest until he saw this through. Even though the case was in the jurisdiction of the Coconino County Sheriff's Office, even if the CDC didn't help, Maxim needed to follow this rabbit hole deeper. It just felt right.

"If I can be truthful," she proposed in a helpful manner, "I would offer that perhaps your proximity to these events is clouding your judgment. An outside observer, with the benefit of separation, might make different conclusions."

Maxim pulled his hand back from the touch of her long fingers. "And if I didn't know you better, as a third party, I might think that you were protecting the club."

Nithya Rao's large pupils revealed surprise but didn't feign offense. "Does it really appear that way?" She let a quick breath escape her lips. "Open your eyes, Maxim. I am not their favorite person after the events at the clubhouse. I am just working from empirical evidence. Show me something solid, give me something that surpasses the realm of a hunch, and my agency can help you."

Maxim watched her gulp down the rest of his coffee and felt foolish. He didn't know why; he had planned on confronting her. This had been what he wanted, but he still felt as if he'd made a mistake. He was doing too much second guessing around her and that was bad. Thoroughness was one thing; doubt was much more insidious.

"I just know," he offered, "that Deborah is lying to me. She knows something that she's not admitting."

Nithya clasped Maxim's arm once again and pulled it closer to her across the table. She had a mischievous smirk. "I suppose a detective can never be satisfied knowing only a part of the whole."

Maxim shook his head in agreement.

The thin woman leaned in so her face was right in front

of Maxim's. Her perfume intoxicated him. "I hope you don't hold it against me," she said, "but I will continue to do my best to retain some amount of mystery."

The detective almost melted as he felt his face flush and burn. Nithya was beautiful. He normally felt uncomfortable when he tried to speak to women like her, but their professional relationship made it easy. He found himself wondering what was next.

Nithya reluctantly pulled away and glanced at the time on her cell phone. "It's getting late. Buy me lunch?"

The woman wore a grin paired with heavily flirtatious eyes. She could be hard to read at times, but her intentions were deviously clear at this moment. It was still early in the day—without the test results, it was easy to submit to his desires.

"Sure," he answered. "I know a place in Sanctuary. Then you can drop me off at the marshal's office."

She gave him a puzzled look. "Your car's not in Flagstaff?"

"Don't ask."

ii.

Maxim found himself hurrying across the town square just as the air was getting crisp. The breeze had a habit of coming when it was least expected, quickly transitioning from a respite from the heat to more uninviting weather. Maxim's suit jacket would suffice for now, however. It wasn't late enough in the day or the season to concern him much.

The facade of the Sanctuary Marshal's Office looked majestic as he approached. It was an old building of brick that cast the plaza in darkening shadow. The fading light made the windows of the station glow with an eerie invitation that could only exist at dusk. To Maxim, there was something magic about moments like these; they never lasted, and perhaps that was why.

The detective peered up and his brows pressed ominously over his eyes at the sight of the shattered clinic window. The glass had been cleaned out, but they were still waiting to refit it with a new pane and steel security bars. For now, it was hastily boarded up and remained an ugly scar on the departmental building.

Barney Hitchens walked from the car lot to the front double doors, watching Maxim and shaking his head in displeasure. There was always something for the sergeant to disapprove of, and the detective was likely to hear about it presently. Hitchens gazed past him to the white SUV that had dropped him off and the woman inside. Maxim knew it was already too late to prevent the gossip.

Nithya pulled away and the sergeant walked into the station. That left only Gutierrez, the rookie, briskly walking towards him.

"My man!" he exclaimed, holding a fist in the air. "Now I see why you weren't answering your phone."

Maxim ignored the offer and pressed ahead, giving the rookie his trademark stare. "Gutierrez, for once, can you please not act like you're still in high school?"

"Not this time."

"Well, you might still technically be in high school since you never graduated," Maxim joked, "but it's time to move on."

The officer's grin disappeared. "Don't do me like that, bro. You know I've been taking business classes on the side." He hurried forward to match Maxim's pace. "I provide a valuable service to the citizens of this town."

"Whoa," said Maxim, putting his hands up. "What you do with your body on your own time is not my business."

Gutierrez forced out a mocking laugh. "We'll see who's telling jokes when you have to start taking your own phone messages and getting your own coffee. I got your back, bro. Respect that."

Maxim charged ahead. "Why were you trying to get in touch with me?"

"Oh that," said Gutierrez, stepping up to the porch and opening the door for Maxim. "Some guy from the county morgue called you. Brony or something."

Maxim stopped. "Brony? You mean Brody, the Coconino medical examiner? As opposed to a male My Little Pony fan?"

The rookie was caught off guard. "Brony, Brody—whatever, man—some white boy shit. He said he needed to talk to you."

It was about time. Nithya had gotten advance notice

hours ago.

As they walked into the office, they were greeted with a flurry of activity and a full staff. Ever since Diego's discovery, Boyd had approved overtime for the department. It wasn't that there was a whole lot for them to do, but the marshal liked to keep up appearances during the media frenzy. He was talking to Cole and some others now.

Unfortunately, Hitchens wasn't yet occupied. He found his opening.

"You know," he said, sauntering up to the two with deliberate flair, "for a detective, you sometimes strike me as awfully unaware."

The heavyset man stood blocking Maxim's desk. The detective sighed and looked to Gutierrez. "Okay, thanks, brony." The officer just shrugged and rolled his eyes. "And don't act like you don't know what My Little Pony is."

"Nah man, I'm Mexican. We don't mess with any of that stuff." Gutierrez turned and started walking back to his desk, wanting no part of the scolding on the sergeant's lips.

"What's the matter?" Maxim called back. "They don't sell those toys in the dollar store?"

The rookie just walked away, holding his middle finger up.

Hitchens looked at the two, dumbfounded. "You're in a mood today," he said. "What was that about?"

"Oh, nothing. Gutierrez just watches cartoons. But you wanted to take a shot at me too?"

The old man chuckled and sat back against Maxim's desk. "Do you really think what you're doing is wise?"

Maxim didn't know if he had time for this right now. "You're gonna have to be more specific."

"The hell I am." The sergeant cocked his head, wondering if Maxim was serious. "First you were up the MC's ass. Now who knows just how far you've crawled up with the CDC."

"Wasn't it you who told me to take a shot at her?"

"Son, that was before I knew who she worked for!" Hitchens had raised his voice but quickly glanced around the room and tried to control himself. "All I'm trying to say is that both of them are dangerous and not easily kept under the protection of this office."

Maxim hissed. "Maybe that's the real problem. No one is answering for anything anymore, whether in service of PR or to avoid being singled out. It's bullshit. Those bodies have something to tell us, and I have the feeling that neither the Seventh Sons nor the CDC want us investigating."

"Whoa, whoa," appealed the sergeant. "I didn't know the MC was involved here. I just do what I'm told and keep my head down."

Maxim saw the other officers break, and the marshal headed over to them. No doubt their conversation had caught his attention. "How are the feds involved?" he asked as abruptly as he'd arrived.

Maxim sighed. "In truth, sir, I don't know. But they've been the main obstacle in dealing directly with the club."

Hitchens spoke up. "Well don't you think they have official business here?"

"That's just it," countered Maxim as he addressed the

sergeant. "I called around. Nithya definitely is who she says she is." Marshal Boyd shook his head and puffed his chest out. "Sir, the kill orders for Makarova and Doka were legit —but they were still pending. Nithya moved ahead with the raid unsanctioned."

Boyd looked concerned. "You're saying that there's a paper trail of illicit enforcement?"

"Not any more," conceded the detective. "She jumped the gun but the orders went through. Still, doesn't that arouse suspicion?"

The marshal pressed his lips together. "We can only control our own policies, Detective." Boyd's blue eyes cut into Maxim with familiarity. "Can you honestly say that you haven't skirted procedure lately?"

"Besides," said Hitchens, "she did get the results everybody wanted. She did this office a favor, in that case."

"I'm not so sure," said Maxim. He recalled the doubts Diego conveyed to him in Sycamore Lodge. "It just feels like she wanted it handled discreetly, off the books, outside of normal CDC channels."

The sergeant let out a loud hoot. "Wouldn't that be something?" He moved his hands to his hips as he considered the implications, but the question wasn't meant to be answered.

The marshal's phone buzzed and he looked at the screen. "It's not our place to second-guess the feds, Detective." The short man took a step away from the two and paused to make a point. "These bodies are your find, and a good win for the department. That's why I'm allowing you to follow up with the case. Do not, however, go impeding the CDC or County in this matter. Do you hear me?"

Boyd didn't even wait for an answer. He flipped around and disappeared into his office, slamming the door shut.

Maxim exchanged a look with the sergeant. Hitchens just raised his hands in surrender. The heavy man pushed himself up off the desk and said, "At this point, I'm not gonna bother asking you to fall in line anymore. We both know you've gone too far for that."

Maxim looked around the office, eyeing all the personnel and wondering if he was the only one in the whole building who dared go against the establishment. Hitchens, at least, he trusted, but the man was too careful.

"Just watch your back, son," he continued, "or you might find yourself in a place without any friends. If that happens, I can't do anything for you." The man's brown eyes conveyed a dire warning. "It doesn't help to go pissing everybody off." Barney Hitchens turned to exit the office.

The detective stared grimly at the phone sitting on his desk. "I know what I'm doing."

iii.

As he eased into his seat, Maxim pulled a report out of his desk drawer. He read over it again to make sure he was familiar with the medical terminology. He was holding the test results for the three suicides he had exhumed. Originally, all screens had come back negative—nothing unusual with the bodies. However, after Diego had found the dump site by following a trucker through Sycamore Lodge, the detective had an idea to follow up on, an idea that had finally implicated the Seventh Sons.

Maxim grabbed the telephone receiver on his desk and mindlessly punched in numbers. He had done it enough over the past few days that it was already muscle memory. He nestled the phone between his ear and shoulder and kicked his feet up and waited for Brody to pick up the phone.

"Coconino M.E." he answered. The man had a scratchy voice, likely the result of too much tobacco and pot, but usually preferred to remain quiet. This gave Brody the ability to blend into the background and be unassuming even when he stuck out. He was an ideal friend to have in situations like this.

"I hear you've got news for me."

"Hey, it's good that you caught me. I was just leaving. I've been trying to reach you on your cell for hours."

Maybe Maxim had lost track of time a little. "I've been getting that. Tell me you have something."

"Okay, officially, everything came back from the lab negative. They've been really dragging their heels, though, so I suspected something was up, especially after hearing your suicides were positive."

Maxim nodded as he listened. He had given Brody a copy of the report in his hand yesterday.

"So," he continued, "since I owe you, I dug a little deeper. I have an old colleague inside." The medical examiner sounded a bit hesitant. "He made me promise not to put it in writing anywhere, but it's like you said."

"I knew it!" exclaimed Maxim, drawing the attention of other officers. He waved them off.

Brody was so excited about delivering the news that his voice cracked. "It's amazing! Every single one of the seventeen victims tested positive for rabies. On this scale, that's unprecedented! We would have never noticed unless you specifically requested the screen. This type of thing is not routinely checked without red flags."

"Is the disease what killed them?"

"Negative. Strangulation in every case. But assuming these victims were homeless and lacked access to medical care, they wouldn't have gotten a vaccination treatment. They would have been sure to die anyway."

Maxim considered the ramifications. "Maybe not..."

"Most definitely," said Brody. "Except for recent isolated cases of forced coma, the fatality rate of untreated rabies is absolute."

Maxim didn't want to press the issue. He had nearly forgotten that others were not privy to the existence of werewolves, even those in the medical community. For all he knew, Flagstaff didn't even have an epidemic.

"Listen," said Brody in a hushed voice, "I tried to keep the testing under the table." He hesitated again. "It's just hard on this type of scale. The case is too high-profile. There was nothing I could do."

Maxim's eyes narrowed. "What do you mean? What happened?"

"Well, the Centers for Disease Control happened. An agent did the rounds today. A tall woman with a British accent."

"Ms. Rao," said Maxim.

"That's her. Real pretty. She wanted to make sure the traces of the disease were scrubbed."

This was the part that Maxim wasn't happy to hear. "Scrubbed?"

"What I'm saying is, there is no documented evidence of the rabies outbreak and there isn't going to be." The man stuttered for a second and stopped himself and sighed. "You can't use it because it's not on record."

Maxim inhaled slowly. He was still in shock about Nithya's actions. "It's okay, Brody. I've been learning that things get done much more efficiently through unofficial channels anyway. Thanks." The detective hung up the phone.

Rabies. All twenty bodies. Not only did this undeniably link the suicides with the Paradise Tank victims, but it was as damning to the Seventh Sons as he could have hoped for.

Maxim's theory was proving true. The abductions had started in Sanctuary. The victims had been infected and killed and, after being missing for several weeks, were found at the bottom of the falls. They were probably thrown from the top while they were still alive. Their condition wouldn't have ever been noticed or tested for.

Doka and the club must have moved on to the transients

to counter growing attention to the cases. Less notable people went missing from a larger population set, most outside of Sanctuary, from areas without a dedicated city police force. The abductions weren't even noted because the victims were already ghosts, and there hadn't been a clamor since the bodies went undiscovered.

Until now.

Yes, the motorcycle club was involved. Maxim had no doubt in his mind. Then with the CDC cover up, he couldn't help but suspect Nithya as well. But then, he already had; he just hadn't found a solid reason to yet.

What were the feds hoping to accomplish by covering up the rabies deaths? Was it standard procedure when an outbreak has this kind of impact on society? It certainly would limit the questions if this was just attributed to gang violence. Someone would need to be blamed—but would it be the right person?

Maxim hated to admit this, but he was working against a fighter in a heavier weight class. His strikes, no matter how well placed, were not having the impact he wanted. The Sanctuary Marshal's Office needed some outside help.

The detective opened his personal laptop. He had started using it recently for the type of work that he didn't want subpoenaed. What he was doing now didn't make him proud and could easily backfire, but in a day and age where the media created many problems, maybe this was an opportunity for them to solve one.

Maxim opened his Tor client and typed up a curt email. Subject line: "CDC leak." It simply read: "Confirmed.

Seventeen Paradise Tank victims infected with rabies." He addressed it to two outlets he knew would limit the chances of this blowing back to him and stopped himself. If this didn't work out right, Maxim could find himself out of a job.

The detective rubbed his closed eyelids and took a deep breath. He could really use a hard drink right now, which meant that he would be settling for another to-go cup instead. Hey, he figured, he needed the ride anyway. He clicked send.

"Gutierrez," he called out. "Do you have some free time in a bit? I need you to drop me off at my car."

The officer was sitting at his desk looking busy, which probably meant he was watching YouTube. "No problem, sir. We can get some coffee on the way. Where are you parked?"

"The Coconino County Morgue in Flagstaff."

The rookie scrunched up his face and looked at Maxim strangely. It was odd for the detective to leave his car half an hour away like that, but Gutierrez didn't bother asking questions. Any excuse to get out of the office made him happy.

Maxim opened up a tracker program on his laptop and brought up a map of the area, focusing on the GPS coordinates of his cell phone. The little blue dot was moving east on Interstate 40. That was Nithya Rao on her way back home to Flagstaff. The detective's phone had a full charge and would provide him with a few days' worth of surveillance.

The Paradise Tank bodies had already created a media

circus. Once word got out about the rabies, pressure on the CDC and the motorcycle club would only increase. Any actors silently skirting the law in this production would start to see their elaborate covers falling away—and someone, somewhere, was bound to trip themselves up.

Part 7 - The Bite

i.

Diego stood vigilant as Maxim peered through the heavily tinted windows of the sport utility, gun in hand. The vehicle was parked and all was quiet, but it was still possible Nithya was inside. As the detective snuck around to the passenger door, his fingers etched lines in the sheen of red dirt that marred the white paint. Apparently satisfied, Maxim popped the door open and pulled his cell phone out from under the seat.

"Well, she's here," he stated with determination. "Somewhere."

Diego didn't like this. There was something he was missing.

They were standing on the edge of an old train yard, a relic from another time. The two had wound their way north on the Transwestern in pursuit of Nithya's SUV, but the location that had greeted them seemed out of place in the mountainous terrain above Sanctuary. There was a Grand Canyon transport line to the west, but the purpose of this lot, fenced off by wire and guarded by private property notices, was lost on the biker. As Diego had already come to learn with Paradise Tank, the deserts and forests of Arizona were expansive enough to keep many secrets.

Rusted hulls of train cars littered the dry grass haphazardly. Some lay on their sides and others were stacked into lines, but there was no overarching order to their placement. This was a place abandoned and it was meant to sit undisturbed, a graveyard of giant metal carcasses.

"I told you," said Maxim, scratching his cheek where the scruff had gotten too long. "Bodies uncovered, rabies exposed—we forced her into panic mode and she made a mistake."

The biker could only nod as he adjusted his new sunglasses. This was definitely a secret place. Diego had suspected there was something amiss as soon as Nithya had acted without tapping the Commissioned Corps. Now, with the ensuing media scrutiny, everybody knew.

"If she was operating independently," Diego posited, "using her government arm to pressure the Seventh Sons while also keeping her activities from the feds, then they would both be desperately looking for her, no?" Diego wondered if the woman had any friends left at all.

"No doubt. This might be a safe house where she could

lay low."

"I'm not so sure," said Diego. If Nithya simply needed a place to hide, she could have been anywhere, miles away from potential pursuers.

The sun was sweltering this afternoon. Diego unzipped his leather jacket to get some air flow and approached the train cars suspiciously. "The timing is too coincidental," he said. "It's almost the new moon."

"Don't tell me." That stopped Maxim in his tracks and the biker had to turn around.

Diego watched the man's hesitation with a smirk for a moment. "Did I ever tell you why I was at Sycamore Lodge that night that Doka and Steve and Nicola attacked me?"

"I'm a detective. I can put two and two together without needing you to tell me," answered Maxim. "You were asking after your sister."

"Yes," said Diego, "but why that night, specifically?" He walked back to the detective. "Of all the nights to voluntarily step into a den of wolves, why do it when they are close to turning?"

Maxim just stood silent, eyes searching Diego's face for the answer to the riddle.

"Wolves are big and ornery and dangerous, that much is true, but humans are far more complex and deadly. Teeth can rip you apart, but that is what makes animals much simpler. Wolves don't deal in lies or political maneuvering; they either attack you or they run. Instead of being able to hide behind their human devices, their true intentions are revealed." Diego watched the detective as he processed the information. "When wolves are close, even in their human form, you can see it in their eyes, in their mannerisms. They have no choice but to be their true selves. If you want to catch a werewolf doing something wrong, there's no better time than when they turn."

"Fair enough," said Maxim, futilely brushing dust from his black jacket. "But what if you already know that their intention is to tear you to pieces? Would you rather be fighting a large wolf?"

"Tell me, in this day and age, do teeth really concern you more than bullets?" Diego clamped down tightly on Maxim's shoulder with his hands. "A bite is more visceral, no doubt. A wild animal with frothing jaws strikes a fearful impression, but give me the pistol in your hand any day of the week."

"And if you don't have a gun?"

Diego released his grip, patted Maxim's back, and chuckled. Maxim's question was less rhetorical than it sounded and the biker suddenly wished he had more firepower. "The same holds true for them. Would you rather your foe hold a gun or growl and bare canines? Of course, neither are preferable to a nice day relaxing in the sun, as we are doing now."

"Okay," Maxim conceded. "So when the sun goes down, I should pack my silvers."

Diego was taken aback. "Is that not what you have loaded now?"

Maxim pulled a magazine from his belt and showed it off. "Nithya only supplied me with the one."

"Shit." Diego had assumed the police officer would be better armed. "Load it now, Maxim. The time is sooner than you think. Day and night are not terms that concern werewolves. What affects them is the planetary alignment of the moon with the sun. Full moons and new moons have peak alignment periods—that's when the transformation occurs."

"How long do we have?"

"Ten minutes. Twenty."

"You're kidding me." Maxim scoffed and looked at the biker incredulously. "They only turn once every two weeks, and we have the luck of being here right before it happens?"

"It's not luck," said Diego. "Wolves often display suspicious activities during these periods. They decide to hide deep in the forest. They succumb to baser instincts and become more aggressive, often making mistakes. Even more strategically, they heal immediately when they turn. If you were a wolf and you were going to do something at the risk of great bodily harm, the smartest time to strike is right before you turn. Less time to live with the pain and the injury."

Maxim nodded his head slowly and gripped the mag of silver rounds tightly in his hand. "So we followed Nithya here, now. You're saying..."

Diego didn't want to reveal his suspicions without more information—he knew Maxim was attracted to the woman—but the cat was already out of the bag. "The timing is too coincidental."

Maxim gritted his teeth and put the mag back on his belt.

"What are you doing?" asked Diego.

"Don't worry. I just don't want to waste them. I only have fifteen rounds." Maxim's face was the definition of conviction, and Diego did not doubt his next words. "I'll use them if I have to."

The two men turned as the smell of burning lumber filled the air of Sycamore. A skinny plume of dark smoke rose from within a dense bed of train cars. A fire was burning, and the two men had talked long enough.

They cautiously passed several husks of steel and saw a square formed by four storage cars. It was a loose grouping; there was plenty of space to move between them, but a large, forest green car with rivets blocked their view. Many of the cars were raised above the ground, and this one was no exception, but the base was completely boarded up and prevented them from peeking past it. Maxim motioned for Diego to take the left flank. They exchanged a last look and split off toward opposite sides of the car.

ii.

Diego slowly skirted the corner of the rail car and peeked into a makeshift courtyard. His eyes darted over the scene quickly, looking for any trouble. The surrounding trees rustled as leaves fell into the empty square of grass. There was no activity in or around the train cars. In the middle of the field was a single metal barrel with a fire in it. Diego leaned against the corner of the green car and tried to see if there was anything in the flames but it was too far to tell.

A metal grinding sound startled him, and he pulled back out of the square for a moment. Then he saw her. Nithya Rao was walking away from them. She had just exited the cab and had her back turned to them, unaware of their presence. Diego glanced to his right and saw Maxim peeking around the opposite corner. Next to him, a wooden porch stepped up towards the train car they were circling. The metal door Nithya passed through had been slid halfway open.

The biker looked back at the woman and noticed she was holding a bundle of items. He could make out what looked like a clear plastic case with vials of liquid medicine inside. Nithya placed that on the ground next to a large duffel bag and then dumped a folder of papers into the fire. She was destroying evidence.

Diego watched as Maxim inched forward slowly, both hands on his weapon. Nithya turned around and started to walk back to the doorway. She jumped and froze as soon as she saw the detective.

"Nithya, you have some explaining to do."

The lithe woman regained her composure and flashed Maxim a smile. "Detective," she said as she coolly walked towards him. "This is CDC business. If I had needed your assistance, I would have requested it."

"Not this," said Maxim, using his gun to point out the

surroundings. "This isn't official. You're on the run and your agency is looking for you. I'm authorized to take you in."

"Do you know that they broke into my house last night?" she appealed. "The Seventh Sons—they want me dead."

"And why is that?" returned the detective. "What were you doing here?"

Diego watched from around the corner as the woman struggled with indecision. She looked at the train car that she had come from, then down at the bag by her feet, then back at the detective. She put her hands out to her sides and slowly stepped closer to Maxim.

"Stop walking," he said coldly. Maxim reached into his jacket and withdrew his cell phone.

"Wait," said Nithya, putting her hand up to stop him. "Don't do that." She kept moving closer.

"Nithya," he warned, "if you keep coming at me, I will shoot you."

The detective stood holding his pistol awkwardly in his left hand as his right thumb brushed the screen of his phone. The CDC agent was very calmly closing the distance between the two. Maxim stood, somehow firm yet indecisive at the same time, as Nithya held her hand out to grab the phone.

Diego stepped out from his position on the opposite side of the car. "Stop walking," he said, repeating Maxim's order.

Nithya had not known the biker was there. She turned suddenly as he walked out and flanked her, moving further into the courtyard. Diego reached into her bag on the ground and found her pistol. Nithya gave him a hardened look. He watched her eyes closely, searching for a flash of orange or red, but it was too bright outside to tell.

"Of course," said Nithya, clapping her hands down against her thigh in surrender. "The detective's secret weapon. The Commissioned Corps ranger." She looked at the two with a newfound understanding. "You turned Maxim against me at the clubhouse."

Diego felt uncomfortable in the middle of the square. He didn't like the timing of any of this at all. He backed into the corner of the train car again.

"Why didn't you tell me you exhumed the suicides?" Nithya asked the detective.

"It was an unrelated case at the time."

She nodded with a look of defeat. "You had a local examiner find the rabies in Sanctuary, then it was only a matter of asking Coconino to use the same diligence."

"Something like that," he answered.

"I'm disappointed," said Nithya. "I didn't know how that story leaked. I thought it was some doctor who thought himself noble, but now I see that it was you."

Maxim's face showed no regret. "Did you think I would let you cover up twenty murders?"

"Look past the media story, Maxim," said Nithya, scowling. "Those men and women were taking part in a battery of rabies trials."

"They were strangled!" yelled Maxim.

"They weren't supposed to be!" she shot back. A cloud formed over the woman's face as her voice grew more somber. "I was unaware of the link to the suicide victims until you told me. Every one, each of my test subjects, were supposed to be moved to private hospice care. Past a certain point, it was known that they would succumb to the disease. The bodies, of course, needed to disappear afterwards, but the subjects were never meant to be murdered."

Diego was horrified. He felt his stomach twisting. He began to get nauseous.

"Were they ever meant to live?" asked Maxim.

Nithya's eyes wavered under his accusatory gaze. "They were willing participants," she said firmly.

Diego cut in. "And my sister? Was she one too?"

Nithya took a deep breath and blinked away her troubles. "Ask her yourself," she answered.

Diego was confused by the comment, but Nithya jerked her head towards the train car they were standing next to. The biker looked to door again and saw the girl emerge onto the wooden steps.

"It's true, what she says," she stated simply.

Diego choked up.

Angelica looked the same as she always had. She was short and dark-skinned and had long, curly black hair. She wore tight track pants with old white tennis shoes and a little tank top. She looked completely healthy just standing there, watching Diego with a smile full of joy and innocence. After a moment of his stunned silence, she giggled and jumped towards him to give her brother a hug.

"Are you—" was all Diego could muster before she wrapped her arms around and clasped him tight.

"I'm okay," she reassured him, pulling back. "Look at you, following me all the way over here! It's sweet." She kissed him on the cheek.

"I needed to make sure you knew what you were doing."

"I'm good."

Diego shook his head in disbelief. Angelica had never understood the consequences of her actions. The biker brushed past her and stepped up to the train car doorway and walked in, removing his sunglasses.

It was a large car with a wooden floor. A makeshift skylight lit the sparse quarters with a warm hue. On the far side of the room was a bed with hospital equipment, mirrored by a desk with papers and samples, which was next to the biker. The biggest defining feature of the train car, however, was the set of steel bars splitting it in two.

Diego turned away in disgust. "You kept my sister in a cage?" Nithya took a step back as he advanced.

"Mind your own business, bro!"

Diego froze as his sister uttered those familiar words.

"Nithya is helping me," she continued. "She's my friend."

Diego heaved his shoulders in frustration. "Maxim, talk some sense into her."

Angelica was not impressed. "This old man? A *policía*? I don't think so, bro."

Diego flipped his plastic sunglasses in his hand in annoyance. But the detective wasn't even listening. His gun was lowered and he was looking over his shoulder, into the distance. In a moment, Diego heard it too, and then he saw.

A light blue van, one of those large metal ones from the seventies, was hobbling up the dirt road.

Maxim was on the phone in an instant. "Marshal," he said, "you'd better get out here now. We've got Ms. Rao but we have a van incoming."

Diego looked to Nithya. "Who is that? Who's here?"

"Well," she said calmly, "it appears that my backup is arriving before yours."

Every time he bought a new pair, thought Diego, as he slipped the lenses back over his eyes.

iii.

Diego backed around the train car and gripped the pistol tightly. The marshal wouldn't be getting here in time, if at all. "Are you packing your silver?" he called out to Maxim, but there was no answer. Diego slid the magazine out from Nithya's pistol and was relieved to see that his bullets were the right type.

"Don't be alarmed, Maxim," said Nithya reassuringly. "You are not in danger. We just need to scrub this scene down and then I can smooth things over with the Center."

The van drove into the depths of the train yard and passed them, screeching to a halt behind the far car making up the square. Diego heard a few doors creaking open and some scurrying through the brush.

A man took an inhuman leap, jumping from somewhere out of sight to atop the left train car that ran towards Diego. His feet crashed down with a loud, hollow ring. A Native American man with a weathered face and a ponytail stomped ahead, holding an automatic rifle trained on the group. Something about this man was familiar.

Nithya Rao cocked her head and shaded her eyes as she looked up at the man on the train car. She had an expression of nagging doubt, like something was wrong, and in a minute it was clear what that was. Another Native American with a rifle took up the corner opposite Diego, using the right car as cover, and walking past him, right to the center of the square, was Mom.

She was wearing the same jeans and pink tank top that she had on when Diego first met her. The mirrored lenses of her sunglasses couldn't hide the amusement in her eyes, and her pink lipstick and sardonic smile didn't camouflage the gravity of the situation. This was a dangerous woman, and they were in a dangerous place.

Nithya looked up to the man standing in the sun. "You were supposed to be loyal to me, Doka."

It was him, the man who had first attacked Diego in Sycamore Lodge. At first he'd mistaken him for a gang member, but the Yavapai men were not Seventh Sons. They were mercenaries. Diego exchanged a look with Maxim, who was holding his gun lowered so as not to incite a shootout. Doka was the one Nicola had implicated in the abductions, which meant he was working with the CDC woman, but current events would indicate that he had been playing both sides.

"Should I not have called Debbie?" asked Doka with clumsy sarcasm.

Nithya practically spit on the ground. "After everything I did for you! You were supposed to be executed for attacking that officer! I kept you alive."

"You kept me alive," he repeated, "to force my hand." Doka swept the assault rifle across Diego and Angelica. "Now you have an Order To Kill to wave over my head." The aim of his weapon brushed past Maxim and rested on her. "It wasn't a good deal. For either of us."

"I can compensate you more than she can."

Mom just stood with her hands on her hips and laughed. "I highly doubt that, sweetie."

"Don't look so hurt," continued Doka. "I see you burning up evidence. You're shutting this operation down. You don't need me anymore anyway." The man's eyes on his pockmarked face twitched in an evil sneer. "I'd be surprised if you weren't already planning on killing me."

Mom was standing right next to Nithya in the center of the courtyard, next to the burning barrel. Something Doka said had piqued her curiosity, and she felt Nithya's clothes for a weapon. The CDC woman, usually stoic, was visibly shaken up, but she stood still. She knew this wasn't going to end well.

The club president squatted down and rifled through Nithya's duffel bag and fumbled with the case of injections. "I'm sorry, Ms. Rao, but we are not taking the fall for your actions." Mom dropped the case on the bag and stood up again.

"You both are more culpable than I am in this," said Nithya.

"These were your tests, dear."

"The murders were not mine!"

Mom scoffed. "You killed them, Ms. Rao, the second you injected them with rabies. Carlos strangling them was a foregone conclusion once your needle hit their skin."

"Those were the risks!" Nithya asserted. "Deep down, they were all running from something. They were desperate for this solution. Each one of them injected themselves personally. I was trying to help them."

The man on the train car let out a hearty laugh. Mom spat back. "You gave them a death sentence," she said. Diego saw the scorn in her eyes and knew this altercation had been a long time coming. "You killed every single one of them. And here you are, with one last victim remaining."

Deborah pointed at Angelica, who pulled her head back in surprise. Nithya couldn't face her and just looked to her feet while feebly protesting. "No, I came here for the moon," she pleaded. "She hasn't gotten sick yet." Her voice trailed off.

"Does it comfort you, dear," asked Mom, staring coldly at Angelica, "to know that you might yet live another week or two?"

Diego thought his heart skipped a beat. His sister had been injected? "What did you do to her?" he blurted out, not sure if he was asking Nithya or Mom.

Like the biker, Maxim had been hesitant for a confrontation given the hardware they were up against, but he finally spoke out. "What is it that all of you have been doing?"

Nithya remained a solemn statue. The fire crackled in the void of silence left by the unanswered question. It was Deborah, relishing the opportunity to gloat, who explained.

"She hasn't told you about her experiments yet?" Mom eyed the two men watching her back with rifles and casually took a step towards the detective. "The mighty hand of the CDC has been using us to get test subjects who she could inject with rabies."

"I get that," said Maxim impatiently, "but why? It's certain death without the vaccine."

"Except for my kind." Deborah's eyes flashed orange. "Ms. Rao claimed to have unlocked the mysteries of the transformation."

Diego gritted his teeth in disgust. "You mean to manufacture werewolves."

The club president shook her hair behind her shoulders and was consumed with a devilish grin. "It was a secret operation, she claimed. It was for the good of all wolves, she said." Mom turned around to face Nithya once again. "Yet here we are, with the CDC looking for you! It turns out that all these tests weren't sanctioned by the government at all. You have been coercing us the entire time, under threat of death for me and my club, and for what?"

"You agreed," Nithya yelled back. "You received benefits. Reliably reproducing the conditions for transformation was something you were interested in as well. Imagine the funding!"

"There is no money in dead bodies!" Mom threw her hands up and stormed over to the center of the courtyard, getting close to the source of her ire and locking her in her gaze. "Tell me this: how many people have you had success with?"

"It is," Nithya stammered, "it is just a matter of isolating the bacterial relationship—"

"What is the survival percentage of your project?" asked Mom with greater severity. There was something in her voice that threw Diego off.

The CDC agent could not bring herself to say it. Her defiance wavered and her eyes fluttered to the floor.

Deborah spun around and faced Maxim. Her eyebrows pushed against her creased brow as she fought against watery eyes. "Your wife wanted a new start." The woman seemed to truly feel sympathy for the detective for a moment. "Lola wanted a new life, and the club, the freedom, appealed to her. She wanted to experience things she'd never imagined before. She yearned to grasp at anything for salvation, no matter how desperate."

Angelica, in her usual straight-forward manner, cut to the heart of it. "She wanted to be a wolf."

Mom nodded. "She very much desired to be what we were when she found out. I... I fancied the idea. It was a naive dream and I didn't think it was truly possible. Then along comes this one," said Deborah as she waved at Nithya, "with a scientific theory to convert her. It was safe, she insisted, effective."

Maxim stood there as a man might when getting bad news from a doctor. Perhaps he knew his life was in danger, and he took great care to hold his gun facing the ground, but Diego needed to keep him in the moment just in case. At the clubhouse, Deborah had managed to get under the detective's skin and that fallout had lasted for days. This time, it was their lives on the line. They needed to be able to rely on each other.

"Paradise Tank had seventeen bodies in it," said Diego coldly. "Do your tears fall for those lives as well?"

Mom squinted, adversarial once more. "Ms. Rao said she was making progress. She hired the Yavapai and set this operation up. If other people had to die, so be it—I was only involved to the extent that I had to be to protect the MC."

Deborah looked down at the grass. "Protection..." she said wistfully. "Do either of you happen to know why this club is called the Seventh Sons?"

Maxim ignored the digression. "Tell me what happened to Lola," he demanded.

Deborah pursed her lips. "Nothing that can be taken back, honey." The woman reached into the small of her back and produced a small pistol.

Diego almost jumped to grab his sister but Doka was looming above him. As long as the Yavapai had the assault rifle trained on Nithya, he didn't want to attract any attention to himself. So far, at least, she was the one the gang wanted.

Nithya's voice cracked. "You can't kill me. The Center

would burn down your club."

Mom raised the pistol to the woman. "Sweet little thing, that was only a threat when we thought the CDC was directing your actions. That's why we didn't kill you a long time ago. That's why I let you execute Nicola." Deborah paused. "She was a good girl, you know."

Diego locked eyes with his sister and motioned with his head for her to get closer to him. She looked at Deborah and took a subtle step away.

Nithya continued pleading. "They know about the rabies now. They'll already be looking for wolf's blood. I'm still the only one who can protect you."

"You kill Nicola to cover your behind and then all of a sudden get the charitable itch to protect us?"

"That's an appropriate description for your actions as well."

Doka shot an uncomfortable glance at Mom but she laughed it off. "They'll be knocking on my door soon enough, with or without you," said Mom gruffly. She turned and stared into the fire. Diego grabbed Angelica's hand and pulled her to the train car. Whatever happened to Nithya had likely been brought upon herself, but he wouldn't have Angelica paying for the other woman's crimes. This, everything he did, was about keeping her safe.

"You didn't burn it all, did you?" asked Mom, looking into the flames. "You see, Ms. Rao, it's too tempting for you to turn invisible and leave all blame for the rabies on us. We'll be sending your injection schedules and evidence to the CDC. They'll see that the disease came from medical procedures, not wolf bites. They'll blame you for this, and with any luck, they'll leave my club alone."

"It's too late for that. They know about you."

Deborah's cheeks puffed into a smile. There was no doubt that she enjoyed the game they were playing. "They know of the Seventh Sons, yes, but they don't know that we've been illegally kidnapping victims so you could go against directive and spread the affliction. They don't even know that this train yard exists. Your lies have caught up to you, Ms. Rao. If we killed you here and now, there would be nothing tangible that linked us to this."

"But," stammered Nithya lightly, "the police..."

Deborah's smile slowly vanished and she took a long breath. She lowered her weapon and turned her head halfway to Maxim, as if she couldn't fully face her decision, or if she hadn't made one yet.

"Maxim," she said, "I'm sorry you had to be here to see this. This all could have been tidied up without your intimate knowledge."

The detective's visage was stone. "Where is my wife?" He continued to struggle with the obvious, even when it was right in front of him.

"Lola was different from the others. She deserved better. She was my friend." Mom's grip on the pistol tightened as she thrust it out toward her enemy. "Putting Ms. Rao down will be doing everybody here a favor. She has hurt people that we all loved." Deborah was going to shoot.

"Don't absolve yourself of all the blame!" Maxim blurted out. It was an instinctual reaction, Diego knew. He was trying to save the woman's life any way he could, no matter how feeble.

The biker felt for the detective. This surely wasn't how he'd imagined things ending, but it was an end. It achieved what they wanted. This was a case where being a police officer would not help the situation.

Maxim continued. "For two years, you stole people, not to help them, but for profit."

Diego needed to stop this. "Maxim, this isn't helping," he cautioned.

"For two years, you let her kill people."

"Shut up," warned Diego.

A darkened crease formed on Deborah's brow. "What else could I do?" she spit back.

"I'm a cop!" he yelled. "You could have told me about it."

Deborah exploded into defiant laughter. Even the stoic Doka let down his guard and released a bellowing chuckle. He lowered his weapon and squatted down on his perch on the train car and watched with amusement.

Mom recovered from her hysterics. "Open your eyes, Maxim. You don't think the CDC controls the offices of the mayor and the marshal?"

The marshal. If he was in with Mom, then the backup that Maxim was expecting might not have been on the way. If the three of them were without support out here, truly alone, then what chance did they have of making it out alive?

"Why do you think none of the other cops, the sensible

cops, come anywhere near us?" Mom banged her gun against the steel drum in the middle of the courtyard and took a moment to contain her rage. "A rule which, I might remind you, you used to wisely obey."

"Listen to me," urged Diego, stepping forward. "Deborah, you know what drove us to ignore your warnings. You know why we are here now. For us, this has never been about you."

"You expect me to believe that?"

"I do. From the beginning, I've said all I cared about was Angelica." The biker exchanged a heartfelt look with the girl. "I just wanted my sister. I know you were being forced to keep a secret. I understand why you couldn't help me before. We can put that behind us."

Mom pursed her pink lips as if she were considering his words, although Diego was unconvinced that she wasn't acting. "And what about the detective?" she asked.

Diego looked to the man who had been standing firm with indignation. Since the night they had first met, after Diego had mentioned unexplained disappearances, the detective had shown a newfound spirit ignited within him. Was it possible now, after everything that had occurred, for the fire to be quenched?

"We can come to an agreement," Maxim afforded.

Mom seemed to scoff under her breath, and she paced around the barrel and Nithya. "Maxim," she said, talking to the air more than him, "the uncompromising detective, about to allow me to go free?" There was something in her eyes that was telling.

Diego backed up. "Don't do this, Mom. We can go. We can just go."

Doka chuckled. "Go?" he boomed. "You've had plenty of chances to go." The callous man regained his feet.

"I'm afraid any cooperation from Maxim on this matter is impossible." Mom shot Diego a scornful look. "I ain't your mom, and I hate to break it to you, but I sent your sister to Nithya under the precise assumption that she would end up in the tank." Deborah's dialog became more bellicose, and the sun again glinted orange off her eyes. "This slut," she said, pointing at Angelica, "fucked her way into my club, attaching herself to Gaston as if that was a free pass. Then, when the idiot finally wised up and realized that she didn't love him, she turned her charm onto Melody."

A smug look flashed across Angelica's face. She put her hands on her hips and stood with one leg shot out to the side. It was just as if she were having an argument with a high school friend. Somehow the presence of armed men didn't sway her, and it almost appeared as if she were looking for a fight.

"Can you imagine?" asked Mom in disdain. "One of my own. A lesbian! Falling in love with this short thing? A cute smile and a full behind, and Melody was putty in her arms. Disgusting!"

The biker saw Maxim's stern expression and realized the reason for it. The detective was unyielding to some extent, that was sure, but there was more here. Because of his wife, he'd had a relationship with Deborah. He knew her, maybe better than anyone here, even Doka. Maxim had probably known that they were dead men the moment she had stepped between the train cars and revealed herself.

Now, with the revelation that Mom was planning to have Angelica killed all along, their fate was all but sealed. Conversation wasn't getting them out of this, and the marshal wasn't coming.

Diego shied the high sun away with his arm. Doka stepped to the side and eclipsed the blinding light. His silhouette on top of the train car outlined a menacing figure. The rifle he held fired faster and had more bullets than the pistol in Diego's hand. Sure, he had silver and they didn't, but when did a copperhead ever lack efficacy against human flesh? The three of them weren't surviving a shootout.

The sun caught his eyes again. Doka was shifting back and forth. The man was getting antsy. Something was making him restless. Mom, too, continued to pace in the courtyard.

Aggressiveness, agitation, malcontent—those were all signs that Diego had been trained for years to look for. How long did they have?

Like a man treading water with the final life of his muscles, Diego had to stall for time. It seemed futile to bargain for only a moment more of life, but Maxim had stayed Deborah's gun and the CDC woman was still alive. She might still end up dead, but other possibilities existed. That's all that mattered.

And so Diego, too, began the dance.

Deborah tilted her head to the sides as she stretched her neck muscles. Once again she raised the gun, only this time, it was pointed at Angelica.

"You're focusing on the wrong person," said the biker. Diego readied his hand in case he needed to fire.

Mom fluttered her eyelids dismissively. "Oh, I'm quite sure I want her dead."

Diego took a step towards Doka's train car to diminish his firing angle. "Not death. I'm speaking of acceptance."

Deborah wasn't comfortable. She was annoyed that she didn't know what he was talking about. "What?" she asked unceremoniously.

"My sister has always had dangerous tastes—that's why she landed on the doorstep of your clubhouse—but no one is forcing you to accept her. The Seventh Sons don't need to vote her in. As president, you could guarantee that. Accepting Angelica was never your real concern."

Diego looked to the Yavapai in the opposite corner. The man had a bead on Maxim, who was further out into the courtyard than Diego was. The detective was closer to Mom, and Doka had a clearer line of sight to him too. The biker shot Maxim a glare to give him a heads-up that it was almost time. He could only hope the man understood the message.

Diego saw Mom watching him with a suspicious eye. "You asked the question," he said. "A long time ago, dedicated mothers and fathers, who would never otherwise have dreamt of hurting their children, hiked out into the unmapped woods and placed their babies in the grass. Boys would be abandoned simply for being a seventh son. These children were communally considered unlucky and were feared to be—"

"Werewolves," finished Deborah, putting her gun at her hip and stepping closer to the biker. There was something curious about the way she studied him. "Are you a fan of historical mythology, Diego?"

He raised an eyebrow and cocked his head. "It was never my best subject, but the Commissioned Corps maintained an active interest in such matters."

Doka grumbled and Deborah's orange eyes lit up. "So you're an assassin?"

"I didn't like the killing. I quit."

"I see," said Mom with a scornful look. "So you're a killer who's studied your prey. It doesn't surprise me that you know the origins of our name."

"I also know of the lesson."

A spiteful grin consumed the president's face as she turned to share a laugh with Doka. But she nodded and agreed to humor the biker. "And what lesson, pray tell, is that?"

Diego spoke earnestly. "Werewolves, seventh sons, were spurned by their loved ones and left out to die. They were and still are considered outcasts, but you and I know it doesn't need to be this way. My sister may rub you the wrong way, but the person that you really care about, the one who you must truly learn to accept, is Melody."

Mom's head pulled back in disgust and Diego continued. "The girl is being treated as an outcast by you, and all this posturing and complaining is ignoring the root of your ire."

Mom stared at the biker with wild eyes, perhaps

struggling with a truth she must have already known. The woman was not accustomed to looking inward, Diego thought, and after her actions over the past two years, it would have been difficult to like what she saw. People usually didn't react wisely when their perceptions of themselves became disjointed.

"A killer with a conscience," said Mom dryly, as if to write him off. She waved her pistol at his sister. "A slut with ambition. And," she said, giving Maxim a look of hatred, "a fool with a cause. All of you have proven to be dangerous."

Maxim grunted in frustration. "You blame everybody but yourself!" Deborah raised her gun at the sudden outburst. "You turned Lola against me. I had my part, but you cultivated our split. You convinced Lola to turn. She had no dreams of becoming a wolf without you. She didn't even know who Nithya was; you were the one who Lola trusted. Silencing the people who remind you of your problems doesn't do anything to actually fix them."

Aside from wood crackling in the fire, the train square was silent for what seemed like an eternity. Deborah stood defiant yet wounded, with watery eyes. Nithya was much worse, already broken. She stood in the sun yet her mind was in shadow, and she couldn't bear to look at anyone. Maxim was heaving, nearer to the two of them, carelessly putting himself at risk. The Yavapai in the distance was flexing his shoulders, and Doka continued shifting from his right leg to his left. And Angelica, without a care for the hardware or resentment they faced, puffed her chest out as if her confidence were weapon enough.

All was serene for that moment until Diego heard Doka's rifle cock above his head. The biker didn't know if he was checking his weapon or if he had reloaded it, but Diego took a step closer to the base of the platform to break the foul man's line of sight.

Mom gathered her thoughts enough to speak. "I intend to live, and I do apologize, but leaving you alive would lower those odds." Deborah looked to the sky even though the new moon wouldn't have been visible. "You know what time nears, assassin. Perhaps, had you remained in service, you would have been equipped with silver, but you and I both know that little gun of yours is useless now."

Diego pulled the sunglasses from his face, sighed, and threw them to the dirt. Then he brought the weapon up a measure and made a show of examining it.

"It's not my gun," he said plainly.

Deborah cocked her head slightly. She jerked it to the side and looked at Nithya's bag, which was on the ground beside her. With a quickness Diego hadn't seen from her before, Mom spun around. "That's a CDC weapon!" she yelled to the others. She sprung away from Diego, running past the burning barrel, away from the two men. "They've got silver bullets! Kill them!"

iv.

Everything happened at once.

As Deborah ran deeper into the courtyard, she pointed her pistol backwards and fired at the group. She was more concerned with not getting shot than hitting anything, however.

Maxim, whether trying to suppress her or put her down, immediately raised his gun and fired a burst at her. She grunted as a round penetrated her shoulder. The panicked woman stopped shooting and pressed to the edge of the opposite train car to exit the shootout. She was, however, the least of their concerns.

The Yavapai behind the right rail car waited for Mom to clear his line of fire before sending a barrage of automatic rounds Maxim's way. The detective ran back and jumped onto the steps and into the half-open door of the train car they were standing next to. A quick succession of bullets panged against the thick steel of the wall, sending them ricocheting into the dirt and sky.

Nithya Rao immediately dropped to the floor. She feebly covered her head for protection, scrambling to pick up her duffel bag and case of medicine.

Diego's main concern was defense, not attack. He needed to get his sister out of the middle of this war zone. He thrust his arm straight up into the air and fired some silver shots at the looming figure of Doka as he pressed his body against the train car the Native American was standing on. Diego held his free hand toward Angelica, trying to pull her behind cover. She looked at him, her eyes shaking, for the first time understanding their predicament, and extended her arm to his.

As she stood there in the sun, her frantic motion was reduced to a single moment where she appeared stationary. Her pose was mired in beauty and desperation as she reached out to her brother. The beam of light that fell across her face was cut out as a figure blocked the rays of the sun. Then the shots rang out.

A quick series of bullets from above cut through Angelica's side, running up her thigh to her ribs. She hopped a step towards Diego before her body shut down, and she crumpled to the ground.

"No!" yelled Diego, trying to jump up the side of the car and angling his pistol over the edge. He fired a few harried shots that almost certainly missed their mark. Flush with the surface of the steel, he could neither see Doka, nor was he exposed to his fire. Diego stared at his sister as she struggled to lift her head from the grass. She wouldn't make it long and he needed to kill Doka before he could attend to her. He needed to draw the man away.

"Hold on," Diego whispered.

The biker heard some loud steps on top of the car and looked up. Doka peeked over the edge. They both shot at the other, but Diego jumped away and retreated out of the square, taking cover behind the green train car that Maxim was inside. That wouldn't be far enough.

He heard a solid crash as Doka jumped from one rail car to the other. An empty clip dropped on the floor next to him as the man above reloaded. Diego ran as fast as he could away from the courtyard.

Automatic rifle fire opened up and trailed in the dirt behind the biker. As he reached an old rusted husk suspended on blocks, Diego slid into the gravel and slipped underneath the steel barrier to the other side. Gunfire rang out loudly against the metal—it jarred his senses but did not penetrate through to him.

Diego picked himself up and stood with his back to the structure, against the supporting cinder blocks, breathing hard.

He had succeeded in drawing Doka away from the square. Now what?

V.

Maxim hunched over his knees with his back to the wall. His second mag was empty. It had taken a lot of fire to suppress the Yavapai with the assault rifle.

The detective patted at his chest and stomach under his jacket. Was he hit? Why hadn't he worn his vest today?

He looked down. No blood. He had probably just landed on a rib when he dove to the floor.

The detective quickly peeked his head around the

doorway. The Indian was waiting in the same spot behind cover. He was leaning against the back side of the right train car, exposing only his head and right arm as the rifle rested on a metal railing.

Maxim barely pulled back as bullets whizzed past his head and into a cabinet on the far wall. The Yavapai had a bead on his position. Maxim couldn't continue peeking out from the same spot.

The detective reached for his belt and pulled out his remaining magazine. Fifteen silver rounds. If this was the last of his ammunition, he would need to be more accurate. The smooth metal of the cartridge slid into his Glock with a satisfying click.

His only chance was the draw the man out. Maxim stood up and wondered how he would manage to escape the train car without getting hit. He needed to see into the courtyard first, to see what was out there. The open door was near the back of the train car, but he was standing on the left side of it. All he could see was the right train car that the Yavapai was behind.

Maxim took a nervous breath and crossed the doorway to reach the back of the car. More shots butchered the cabinet but he was left untouched. Although Maxim didn't have a nook to tuck away in and was exposed to whatever was outside the door, the Yavapai's angle of fire had been cut off. He would need to step out into the courtyard to fire upon Maxim, and that's the spot he trained his gun on.

In the meantime, Maxim could monitor the scene to the left of the doorway now, into the square. He saw Nithya crouching against the far train car, holding her bag, in the opposite corner he was in. She was petrified.

He also saw Angelica's legs in the corner of his view. She was lying on the ground motionless, probably hit. Maxim would have needed to poke his head out to see more, and he couldn't afford to do that just yet.

Where was Deborah? She had escaped to the far side somewhere. Surely she was close by, waiting to strike...

The Yavapai stepped into Maxim's sight with his weapon raised. Maxim popped off five shots and at least two of them met the man before his opponent had managed to pull the trigger. The Indian buckled and carelessly fired the rifle towards the detective, before pulling back to his previous position. The man was hurt. Now Maxim could see what that silver was worth.

Suddenly, Nithya screamed. Still in her heels, she ran clumsily, trying to get away from something. A wolf with brown and white markings trotted into view. The animal wasn't especially small or large, but it had a ferocity that was unmatched by normal wildlife.

The beast leaped and landed on her. Nithya was tackled onto her chest as the animal bit down into the top of her shoulder, inches from her neck. The wolf shook her head violently back and forth, twisting Nithya like a rag doll.

Maxim discharged his weapon. The wolf moved away, biting down with her teeth, dragging Nithya beneath her. It took three more shots before the wolf released her prey and bounded away.

She slipped behind another train car—hiding like the

rest of them. He thought it odd but he could've sworn that the wolf, running away, had no tail. No matter. Maxim didn't have time for such trivialities. He knew that the animal was just around corner, waiting.

Nithya ripped her business jacket off. The top half of her white shirt was soaked in blood. As she awkwardly tried to sit up, she held the jacket against her wound to stop the bleeding.

The detective picked up movement in the corner of his eye and looked to Angelica again. She wasn't there. It was quick, but it looked like she had been dragged away.

Shit.

The detective returned his attention to Nithya. The woman was giving herself a shot from a small syringe. The plastic case she had collected was sitting open next to her. What was she doing?

Then Maxim saw the brown and white wolf reemerge from behind the distant rail car. He squared his pistol, taking careful aim, and released a round.

The wolf's jaw clamped down on Nithya's hand and jerked her backwards.

Suddenly, bullets whizzed by Maxim's head. The detective ducked and saw the Yavapai back in the open. Maxim ran to the left and fired two more shots to back the Indian off.

Now, Nithya and Angelica were both missing.

The detective huddled next to the doorway again and listened as Doka and Diego fired at each other in the distance. Yet his two foes remained silent.

What was going on out there?

Where was the marshal?

And what could he do with only three bullets?

vi.

Diego knew Doka was back there. He could have been right around the corner. Ideally, he would have waited longer and let the man reveal himself by making a sound, but Angelica didn't have that kind of time.

The biker spun around the corner of the metal husk and brandished his pistol. Nothing. Diego pulled back around.

Some automatic weapons fire emerged in the distance. It was followed by a shot from Maxim. Good—he was still alive.

Diego ducked down and peeked under the train car, between the cinder blocks. He didn't see any movement, so he hopped lightly to the other corner.

Suddenly, right next to him, Doka emerged at the end of the barrier. At point blank, Diego pulled his hand up and fired a shot. It penetrated the Yavapai's shoulder and the man screamed in pain.

Instead of firing again, Diego saw Doka's rifle rotating towards him. He pressed both hands against it to hold it off.

Doka discharged multiple rounds right next to the biker's face.

Everything went quiet for a moment as the two became locked, pushing their metal together. Diego's ears rang loudly as his hearing returned, and he almost seemed to lose his balance under the force of the stronger man.

Diego's pistol was pressed against the rifle—he couldn't pull it away or he'd be dead—but he tried to aim it at Doka as much as he could. He pulled the trigger and fired two shots.

Doka bent away to the side to avoid the attack and tried to do the same. The automatic rifle clicked as it spent its remaining ammo.

The two men look at each other as they quickly processed the new development.

The biker pushed himself off the Indian and backed up a step, homing his pistol on the man's torso. A good central hit should weaken the man and suppress the wolf.

The Yavapai swung the empty rifle down in a graceful motion and slammed it against Diego's gun as it discharged. The biker's hand erupted in pain, and he couldn't hold on to his weapon. It fell to the dirt at his feet. Diego dropped down to recover it. As his fingers brushed against the metal, the butt of Doka's rifle swung upwards and met him square in the face.

The sound of Diego landing on his back was muffled. Something in his head spun and he struggled to remember where he was. His mind was whirling.

Through his blurry vision, he could see Doka standing

tall before him. Diego blinked back the blood that trickled past his eyes and could barely make out the Yavapai throwing his rifle to the floor and stepping over him.

The gun. It was in his hand. Diego had managed to pick it up before getting knocked back. He lifted his heavy arm and fired. Again, and again.

Then he was empty.

Diego de la Torre lay quietly on the ground. Nothing was happening. He wiped his face with his hand and his head stopped spinning. He was sprawled in the dirt, next to the metal barrier, alone.

Then Doka, with a victorious smile on his pockmarked face, slowly came around the corner again. He was holding his left arm where it was bleeding above the elbow. Diego had hit him twice but didn't inflict any fatal wounds.

In the distance, Maxim's weapon rang out and they both heard a stifling yell. The lumbering man turned his head to the sound.

"Doka!" yelled the other Native American in a gurgled voice.

Doka's eyebrows scrunched over his eyes.

"Doka!"

A single pistol shot echoed in the air, and the man didn't scream anymore.

Dried leaves fell past Doka's hardened face and settled on the ground. The man burned with determination and focused on the biker. And then Doka's head spasmed.

Diego sat up on his elbows. His right hand hurt, more than his head did. It looked like it was swelling. He wiggled his fingers as pain seared up his arm.

The man in front of him fell to the dirt, catching himself with his hands. Doka let out a gruff bellow from deep in his gut.

It was time. Diego crawled backwards through the dirt. He was stuck by the occasional rock but he ignored it. He needed to get distance while he had the chance.

The biker peeked under the rusted train car. He didn't see Maxim anywhere. They were alone.

The transformation was almost instantaneous. A dark brown wolf with a wide chest lumbered before him, staring ahead with cold gray eyes. A deep growl rumbled as Doka bared his teeth. This was it.

The animal covered all the ground in between them in a single pounce and was on top of the biker in a flash. The weight of the beast almost knocked the air from his lungs. Diego felt the teeth scrape his left arm as he frantically protected his face.

But Doka whimpered and jumped up over his head, off of him.

Diego spun around in the dirt, rolling onto his stomach and picking himself up on his injured forearm. Grains of dirt scraped into his open wound, but the biker trained his eyes on his target.

In the distance ahead, the large brown wolf scampered away, limping, favoring his left front leg. In his left side, Diego's long silver knife was lodged in the animal's rib cage. He had missed the heart, but with all that silver, that had to be a kill shot.

Doka ran ahead until his escape was covered by the other train cars. Diego put his head down and thought he heard scurrying.

vii.

"Are you okay?" Maxim kneeled down and clasped Diego's arm. "We've got to get out of here."

The detective pulled Diego to his feet. The biker felt dizzy as the blood rushed from his head. His mind swam again for a moment. "No, we need to find Angelica."

Maxim wrapped his arm around his shoulders as he forced him ahead. "She's not here anymore. She's gone."

"No. We need to check."

"It's too dangerous. The wolves are out there and I spent all my ammo."

Maxim pulled Diego back to his unmarked sedan, ignoring the biker's protests, but something wasn't right. Diego saw movement behind the dirty car windows. He wiped more blood from his eyes.

When they approached, a brown and white wolf revealed itself from behind the car. It jumped up on top of it, standing and growling menacingly. Its large eyes burned bright orange.

Diego immediately knew who he was looking at. "Mom."

The biker instinctively reached for his wrist but

remembered that his knife wasn't there anymore. It was somewhere lost in the woods, likely resting in the corpse of a man.

The three of them stared at one another in a standoff until another wolf's scratchy howl interrupted them. Mom pricked her ears up and faced the source of the challenge. At the tree line on the side of the road, they all saw a heavy wolf with a dark gray coat.

Deborah growled at it. The other wolf returned the sentiment with raised hackles. Mom's sharp teeth snapped ahead as a threat.

The dark wolf broke into a gallop toward Maxim's car. Mom braced herself against the larger animal. They collided in a blistering crash and the momentum pushed them into the grass. Deborah rolled away and scrambled to her feet in a blink.

The two wolves bit at each other with a fierce intensity. They locked down on each other's necks and pulled and tore. Rarely had Diego heard such horrible growling and gurgling, and he knew the two animals were not merely asserting dominance. They were hungry for blood.

The beasts tumbled some more but eventually broke away and resumed growling and gnashing. Deborah moved to flank her opponent, and Diego noticed she had a slight limp. As the two continued to circle each other, they saw the big gray wolf breathing heavily. He turned and revealed a vicious gash across his face that cut across a bloody eye. He was badly wounded.

Mom slowly advanced on the other wolf and it backed

away, but then she suddenly stopped and looked behind her. The two animals sniffed at the air in confusion.

Diego looked back and saw a different wolf with a light brown coat sprinting towards them. It was smaller than the others, but it still squared up against Mom aggressively.

Deborah was outnumbered.

The brown and white wolf turned her head back and forth between her enemies and suddenly spun around and ran off. The other animals did not give chase.

The two men relaxed as they stood together, exchanging relieved glances. The big gray wolf was shaking its head and trying to swipe at its closed eye with its paw. He was a mighty specimen with a guttural bark, but he was in pain.

The sound of blaring sirens slowly got louder and the injured wolf lumbered away. Maxim leaned Diego against his car and walked toward the road.

Diego just stared at the little brown wolf, standing motionless and looking at him curiously. It couldn't be, could it?

Several vehicles kicked up dirt as they skidded around a bend, flashing red and blue lights. Two cars were speeding towards them with a Fire Rescue truck in tow. It looked like Maxim's backup did answer his call, after all.

Diego turned to the last remaining wolf again. Maybe it was the beating he'd taken, but it seemed as if he had to fight away a tear. The animal cocked its head.

"Go," he said, softly. "Get out of here."

The wolf raised its expressive eyebrows and darted into the forest.

Part 8 - The Hunt

i.

The door to Maxim's green sedan closed with a clunk. He hated this car. It was faded and old and wasn't nearly as flashy as the Expeditions issued to the sheriff's office, but Sanctuary had a smaller department with significantly less resources. As the detective strolled past the two shiny white trucks, he waved to the Coconino County deputies inside.

It was an overcast day, the beginning of fall, and just one day after the shootout at the train yard. Nithya and Angelica were both missing, Doka was presumed dead, and Deborah had propelled herself to public enemy number one.

Nithya needed to answer for her crimes, and the CDC was looking for her, but Maxim had the sense that her involvement was being marginalized. A federal conspiracy, after all, wasn't a favorable headline. Especially not when an outlaw biker gang could have been running the show.

Maxim Dwyer crunched over dried leaves as he made his way to the doorstep of the club in question. County reported the Seventh Sons to be holed up in their clubhouse, trying to sit out the fallout.

Good, the detective thought, that made things easier for everybody. Not that he expected Deborah to be waiting for him inside. That would have made things too easy.

The front door rumbled as Maxim pounded it with his fist. It opened quickly, as if he were expected, and he was greeted by the spiky-haired brute who just might have been able to help him.

"Gaston."

The towering man rested his muscled arm on the top of the door and scoffed. He had a tight-fitting black shirt on and a bracelet and belt studded with spikes. He also had spikes in each earlobe and a slew of rings running up his left ear. "Have you come for round two?"

Maxim smiled dryly. "I thought it was Deborah who took your title belt."

The man ran his tongue under his lips in disgust and grunted. "If that's what you want," he said simply, "she's not here."

The detective nodded knowingly and raised his upturned palm, pointing inside. "May I?"

Gaston turned and walked inside, leaving the door open. Maxim entered the wolves' hallowed ground and followed the big man into the next room over. Gaston sat down on a leather couch and raised his feet to the coffee table.

The adjoining room was connected by a large archway where two bikers had been shooting pool. They had noted his interruption, however, and were looking on intently. A bearded man with a red jacket was standing upright, holding a pool cue across his outstretched shoulders like a cross. The other one, a younger boy, was sitting against the table with his arms folded over his chest. Maxim remained standing.

"How's Coconino treating you?" he asked.

"They've got no warrant," said Gaston, stretching his right arm over the back of the sofa, "but we've shown them around a couple times. Ever since your office put the APB out on Mom and Doka, they've been watching this house."

Maxim glanced at the white trucks stationed outside through the window. "Which means you don't know where either of them are?"

"Don't know and don't wanna know. I hope it stays that way."

"A club needs a president," said Maxim nonchalantly.

"They've got one."

The detective turned around and noticed Gaston holding his chin up proudly. He was talking about himself. The kid with the black hair was laughing and the bearded man was nodding his support.

The detective narrowed his eyes. "Deborah's out?"

"She's old news," he answered. "The MC needs protecting, and I can do that better than she ever could. I got all my guys inside here, laying low, staying out of trouble. We don't want any part of these headlines."

Now it was Maxim's turn to chuckle. "You've got to be

kidding me if you think you can still walk away from this."

"The Seventh Sons didn't have anything to do with those abductions. The Yavapai mercenaries were the heartless bastards who did this."

"Led by Deborah."

"An outcast."

Maxim paced towards the new president. "Varela and Makarova knew."

"Only partly," Gaston said. "They helped Doka with a thing or two—Nicola said as much—but they can't be punished any more than they already have been." The big man dropped his boots back to the floor and leaned forward. "It's water under the bridge, Maxim. I know this thing can tear the club apart, so I'm willing to leave it alone if you are. It wasn't Diego who killed Steve or you who helped kill Nicola. This was that CDC bitch and Mom and the Yavapai. If we keep them out, then you shouldn't have any business with us."

The detective just looked at the three men solemnly. "Doka might be dead."

"Humph. I've heard that before."

"Nithya too."

"Now that wouldn't surprise me," said the big man. "It takes balls and brains to get the best of Mom, and Nithya didn't have either."

There was more chuckling from the pool table. Gaston lifted himself up and walked over to a small refrigerator in the back of that room. He grabbed two bottles of beer and returned, holding one out to the detective.

"I'll be straight with you," said Gaston. "The deaths, attacking the police, that shit should never have happened. As the new boss, I won't let any of that slide."

"Mmm hmm," intoned Maxim, eyeing the beer carefully. "So no more muling contraband through the truckers?"

Gaston's face remained blank. "Let's have that conversation another day."

Maxim ignored the point and waved his hand at the offer of beer. "I'd better not. There's a lot to get done."

The man shrugged and placed the extra bottle on the coffee table. As he resumed his seat, his face softened. "Mom, Doka, the CDC bitch—you've told me what happened to everyone except for Angie."

A crease formed on Maxim's hard brow as he took a moment. "She's a wolf, I think."

"No shit?" asked Gaston. "I bet she'll be pushing for membership then." The man became thoughtful all of a sudden. "Between us, I don't know if I want women in this club. They don't respect guy code."

Maxim nodded absently at the remark. Gaston still had Melody left to deal with, at least. But thinking of Angie as the little brown wolf brought to mind other concerns.

"Speaking of which," said Maxim, looking over the three men, "who's the large, dark gray wolf that was out there with us?"

Gaston exchanged looks with his men but shook his head. "It wasn't any of us."

"Come on, guys. I'm not going to arrest you for fighting Deborah."

Gaston appeared nonplussed. "What wolf?" Maxim made a living reading people and the big man's ignorance was convincing. "You don't think we're the only ones in Sanctuary, do you? Trust me, if I had a go at Mom, she wouldn't have gotten away."

Interesting, thought Maxim. He had assumed it was Gaston who had helped him, although he hadn't been able to figure out why. It made sense now, knowing that he took over the club, but why would he deny it?

Maxim gritted his teeth as he tried to go through all the angles. "Well, maybe you can help the marshal's office in another way then."

The president sighed. Working with police officers must have been new to him. "What do you need?"

"Where does Deborah live, for one?"

"You're looking at it," he answered.

That was strange. "This lot is registered to the club."

The big man nodded. "She doesn't keep anything under her real name, something to do with trouble in Alabama." Gaston scratched at his tall hair. "She almost always slept here, but you can bet she has a place to hide. Most of us do. It's in our nature to disappear for days or weeks at a time."

"That's not overly helpful," said Maxim. "We're going to need to track her down and arrest her somehow."

"We?" he asked incredulously. "Have you seen the police staking me out? We have too many eyes on us. Think of the publicity our actions will stir up."

"Not good enough." Maxim walked to the back of a recliner and put both hands down on it to lean towards the man seated opposite. "You can't stand on the sidelines for this one, Gaston. The Seventh Sons are involved, like it or not. You want to protect them? You need to work at it."

Gaston clenched his jaw several times. "We can't make any moves until the police outside get reassigned. If you do that for us, then we'll have room to work."

The detective shook his head emphatically. "I have no pull with County, and I'm not going to put my job on the line for somebody I don't know if I can trust."

The big man shrugged. "That sounds like a 'you' problem."

Maxim rocked the recliner away from his hands and chuckled. He looked to the ceiling as he scratched the back of his head. "You misunderstand me, Gaston. The years of this club doing whatever they please in Sanctuary are done. You need to think about this long term. The fact that I don't trust you is a big problem for you, and I intend to make it a worse one if I need to. You want to convince me that you had nothing to do with the abductions, that the club is innocent in all this? Then you need to prove that to me. You need to do something to claw your way out of this." Maxim stared at Gaston's darkened face. "It's time to make a choice."

Gaston rested his elbows on his legs as his hands met his forehead. This was hard for him, but there was something he was holding back. He'd lived by a code that prohibited talking to police, but he also knew that he needed to protect his club above his own life. What happened when those two ideals contradicted each other?

Maxim pressed him. "Gaston, it's time to put your money where your mouth is."

The man pulled his head back up. "What about Deborah's money?"

The detective fired off an inquisitive look. The president snapped his fingers and directed the boy to bring something to him. When he returned, the kid placed a metal briefcase on the table in front of Gaston. Maxim walked around the recliner to take a look inside.

The big man kept his strong hand firmly on the top of the case, holding it shut. "When she allowed Nicola to be killed to protect her secrets," he said solemnly, "she turned her back on all of us."

Maxim waited with sympathetic patience.

Gaston clicked the latch and unfolded the case. Stacks of bills, mostly hundreds, took up the majority of the space. "This is her 'go' money. There's some cash in there, and also some passports and credit cards and other things she might need in case of an emergency."

"Like right now." Maxim tried to quickly ballpark the cash amount, but he had never been involved in anything like this before. Sanctuary was a small town with small problems. At least, it had been. "She hasn't come around for this yet?"

"Not with the police sitting outside, but she will, eventually, as she gets more desperate." Gaston stood up and walked to the window. "I'd rather not have that play out on my doorstep right in front of law enforcement."

"How much is this?"

The biker president smiled as he turned back to the detective. "I can't say. It's uncounted. I wouldn't be able to give anyone an accurate number, assuming they asked."

Maxim returned a sly smirk. "Just in case any were to go missing."

Gaston raised his hands in ignorance. "I wouldn't know."

The detective rifled through the money again. It was real. Regardless of what Deborah intended to do next, she would almost definitely want to recover it. She was on the run, probably wounded, and not welcome back at her clubhouse, her home. She may have killed a federal agent and attempted and failed to kill a police officer, not to mention the civilians. She'd even been implicated by the media as the mastermind behind the Paradise Tank abductions. Whether that was ultimately true or not didn't change the fact that she was Arizona's most wanted, and she would either get caught, get killed, or get out.

As Maxim flipped through various identification documents with aliases, he was surprised to see Melody on a passport. He held it up to Gaston. "Where does she fit into all this?"

"Melody," he asked, confused by the question. "She's her mom."

Maxim waved the passport in his hand. He thought of Gaston's comment about not allowing women in the club. He recalled Deborah's dispute with Angelica and the personal nature of it. "Mom, as in club president or—"

"Why do you think Melody acts like she doesn't need to bother with anything? She's a princess, and she's in for a rude awakening next time she sees me." Gaston ground the sole of his boot back and forth into the floor. "Debbie is her birth mother. I thought you knew that."

Maxim threw the passport back into the case and slammed it closed. "I thought you said the entire club was in here."

Gaston shrugged weakly. "Like mother, like daughter. Half the time she's off doing her own thing. Melody likes to play. She probably has a new boy or girl. Anyway, she's almost never around club business."

"And her house?"

"She stays here too, unless she's spending the night with one of her toys."

Diego.

Maxim stomped towards the door with the briefcase. He was determined to get this over with quickly. No mistakes.

"Contact me if you see her." Maxim stepped outside with haste. "And Gaston," he said, turning for only a quick moment, "I may be calling on you for some help. I trust you'll find a way to shake County and come through."

Maxim hurried back to his car. How could he have been so stupid?

ii.

"It was just a bite," said Diego. "What's the worst that could happen?"

Maxim looked down at the man. He wasn't sure if the biker understood the irony of what he had said, but more likely than not, he knew what he was doing when it came to these matters.

The two men were in the same clinic over the marshal's office where they had first had a chance to speak freely. This was a nicer room, however, meant for the general populace. Diego was not handcuffed and the room lacked the security measures of the other. Not that the security had been a strong point two weeks ago when the werewolves broke out, but that was being corrected. As they spoke, drilling and hammering created a racket in the background as construction workers replaced the broken window.

"I'm already inoculated," continued the ex-CDC operative. "You could say this was a common job hazard. As long as I'm pumped with antibiotics to keep from getting any infections, I can get out of here soon enough."

Maxim nodded away the man's insistence to be released. "You're lucky it was your shoulder and not your neck."

Diego shifted in the bed and grimaced. "I could say the same thing for him. I cut him pretty deep. If I had gotten his heart, you would have found him by now."

The detective scratched his scraggly neck. "I don't get it. Both Deborah and Doka are ghosts. No one's reported seeing or hearing from either of them. Considering the added resources from Coconino, it's troubling that they haven't turned up."

"Wolves have learned to run their entire lives." Something caused Diego to halt the line of conversation. His thoughts had turned to another topic, and Maxim saw the worry in his countenance.

"They're not looking for Angelica, are they?" he asked. "I don't want her in the middle of this."

"Don't you worry about her," assured Maxim. "My office is leaving the two of you out of the detailed reports. Even the motorcycle club is doing everything they can to skirt interest. Blame is landing solely on Deborah and Doka. Even Nithya is being investigated as a possible victim."

"But where's Angelica?" Diego didn't care about the investigation as a whole. He kept hammering at the point about his sister, and Maxim didn't blame him. He had been so close at the train yard.

"It must be rough. You almost saved her and lost her on the same day." The detective fumbled with the words he had meant to be comforting. "If she's a wolf, then she should be healthy and able to defend herself."

"I've gone over that myself," said the biker. "She was gunned down right before my eyes. I'd thought she was dead—probably the only reason she's isn't is because of the evil we've uncovered in Sycamore. But if that's the case, if she is safe and out of trouble, why wouldn't she come to the station?"

Maxim sighed and looked around the serene room as if an answer would come to him. All he could muster was,

"Sometimes the ones we love don't always do the things we want them to."

The two men said nothing as Maxim's sentiment echoed through their thoughts. The words were not profound but they were profoundly true, and even though acceptance of the dictum conceded a loss of power, Maxim felt that it allowed him to somehow be greater than what he had been before.

Lost in thoughts of salvation, Maxim didn't notice Barney Hitchens enter the room.

"Sorry that I didn't keep up with her out there," said the gruff man.

They both turned at his announcement. The man was in his fifties, set in his ways, liked to complain, and rarely apologized. He was wearing his blues and standing with his arms crossed, leaning against the door frame. Running through his wiry black and graying hair was a black strap holding an eye patch over his left eye. Maxim almost laughed for a second until he realized what the face reminded him of.

Diego also recognized the man. "The gray wolf."

Maxim's jaw dropped and he took an instinctive step in retreat. Hitchens? A werewolf?

"Son," said the man in a surly voice, "don't look at me like that. I'm the same man you knew. Mostly." The sergeant peeked down the hallway and then approached the bed to speak more discreetly. "Not all wolves are bad. For instance," he said, looking to Diego, "your sister is one now."

Maxim was still amazed at the man's secret. "That's why you were never around the station on new and full moons. You always had a day off, like yesterday, or just disappeared."

Hitchens nodded and showed his big teeth. "I guessed it would be hard to hide it from you any longer. Do you realize I need to wait two weeks for this to heal up? I'm telling everybody I had cataracts surgery."

The man laughed it off, but Maxim was still in shock and wasn't ready for humor. He wasn't quite sure that he liked the ramifications of this development.

"Who else knows about this?" he demanded.

"Nobody," said the sergeant. "And I'd like to keep it that way."

"Not even the marshal?"

"Especially not the marshal! He is close to the mayor and the feds, including the CDC. You think I want to be on their radar? You see what Nithya did with her knowledge of the club. She extorted them into doing her illegal business. That is not happening to me, you can count on that."

Maxim swallowed. The thought of Nithya being the mastermind left a sour taste in his mouth. He didn't want to believe it, but he couldn't deny what Hitchens said. Still, the man's statement didn't absolve him of any involvement. "What did you know of Nithya and the Seventh Sons?"

Hitchens shook his head vigorously. "Whoa, don't put that on me," he reassured. "I'm not one of them. The people in this here building are my team. I've never seen the CDC in the station before and had no way of knowing what the MC was up to. We're told to stay out of their affairs—as acting sergeant, I enforce that. That's my job."

"It's not much of a job," said Diego, visibly upset about the policy.

The sergeant flashed the man an indignant look. "This didn't happen overnight," he said. "It was a long, slow burn that got us here. But, I tell you, that match is nearly out. The marshal is lucky that none of this shit is landing in Sanctuary, but he'd be downright negligent if he didn't start keeping a closer eye on things from now on."

Maxim wanted to trust his friend, but it was his nature to ask questions. "If you had the day off yesterday," he asked, "how did you know where we were?"

"I followed you," said Hitchens smugly. In response to Maxim's suspicion, the sergeant's face was overtaken by a grim expression. "Maxim, I could see that you're were trying to get yourself killed over this whole Lola business. We both know that there is death at the end of that road. I just want to make sure it's not you who's dead."

The older man glanced around for something sturdy to place his weight on and settled for the nightstand next to Diego's bed. "What I need to know from you is if your sister's going to be a problem out there."

Maxim thought Diego would've acted offended if he weren't so banged up. "She's fine," said the biker. "She hasn't made the best decisions in her life but she isn't violent."

Hitchens nodded in satisfaction. "That's good. The last thing we need is a bunch of new wolves flooding into this already waterlogged town. Not now."

"Angelica's the only one," said Maxim. "It appears that all the others before her succumbed to the rabies."

"Does that mean the woman finally found a successful formula?" asked Hitchens.

Maxim shrugged softly but it was Diego who answered. "I don't know," he admitted. "Twenty people died in service to those experiments. Did the injections have any beneficial effects at all, or was Angelica just lucky?"

Maxim pondered the question. "There wasn't any significant evidence left behind in the train car after what Nithya burned and what went missing." He was talking about the case of medicine that he had seen Nithya use on herself. The woman's duffel bag had been wrapped around her shoulder and was dragged off with her.

Hitchens shook his head and released a long hiss from his lips. "So what, all that, for nothing?"

The three men's thoughts were clouded with the cold reality. Evil didn't always make sense, thought Maxim. In his line of work, he'd had to get used to it.

"Don't worry," said the detective, "she'll be put to justice. I'm more worried about Deborah Holton. She's the one most dangerous to us."

"And she's likely already in Mexico," said Diego.

Hitchens laughed heartily. "That woman don't know a lick of Spanish."

Maxim waved their comments off. "She's still here and the Seventh Sons have turned their backs on her. The clubhouse is locked down. Interestingly," said Maxim, turning his attention to Diego, "I found out that the only other club member missing is Melody. I can't get in touch with her, and she's not working at Sycamore Lodge."

"And you think she's hiding Deborah?" asked Hitchens. "It seems risky for her to be an accessory to that kind of heat."

"Not if she was Deborah's daughter."

Diego nearly jumped as he heard the news, but Maxim could tell that he understood. It made sense in retrospect. Maxim found himself in the roadhouse a lot but had a habit of staying away from women. Diego didn't find himself with a similar liability. He was closer to Melody in the few weeks he had been in town than the detective ever had been.

"I'm sorry," said Maxim, "but I already searched your hotel room on the way here. I would have called, but we both know you don't carry your phone on you and I couldn't take the chance of missing her just in case she was there."

The sergeant leaned forward. "And?"

Maxim just shook his head.

"I know," said Diego, putting his hand to his forehead. "I know where she has a small cabin that she uses when she wants... privacy."

Maxim Dwyer stretched his lips into a larger smile than he had managed since he had known the biker.

Hitchens suddenly jumped up from his lazy post. "I'm backing you up with Cole and Gutierrez this time, and I won't take no for an answer." The heavyset man stormed to the door and stopped in his tracks with a surprising agility as the marshal entered.

"Where do you think you're going?" asked Boyd in his brisk, condescending manner. He shoved his way past the sergeant and approached Maxim. Even though he looked like a man who hadn't slept in days, his crisp blue eyes were sharper than ever. "If we have a lead in this case then we must notify County."

The two officers looked at each other cautiously; their plan seemed to be in jeopardy.

"They don't know about the wolves," pressured Hitchens. "It's a risk."

Marshal Boyd put his hand up to silence the man and raised his head to the ceiling with impatience. "I cannot—"

"He has a point," assured Maxim. "Marshal, if Coconino gets involved, then the CDC gets involved. They created this mess and will likely burn everything in their path to disassociate themselves with it. You and I both know that this town is built on secrets." Maxim locked eyes with a man who likely had very different motivations than he did. He just had to hope that he tugged at the right one. "How much of Sanctuary will be left standing?"

Boyd gritted his teeth and mulled over the thought.

"He's right, sir," added Hitchens. "We can handle it."

The marshal met Maxim's stare and fumed for a moment. He quickly shook his head and then spun around and walked to the door. The detective looked to Hitchens in a moment of panic, but Boyd suddenly froze.

"We'll need deniability," he said.

The sergeant tried to stutter out some words, but Maxim

was already on top of it. "We're not even after Holton, sir. This is a routine follow-up with Melody."

The blond man gave a curt nod. "Good enough." As he prepared to leave them to it, he turned halfway. "And Maxim," he said, abandoning his diplomatic reserve, "get your answers and come back in one piece."

iii.

Maxim braced himself against the passenger door of the squad car as Gutierrez hit a dip in the road at full speed. The suspension seemed to buckle on the landing, but the tires held their traction and the rookie pressed on.

It was difficult to see. Red sand filled the air where Hitchens and Cole weaved ahead, sirens blaring. Their cruiser skidded to a halt on the gravel in front of Deborah's safe house. Gutierrez pulled up beside them and the four officers jumped out of their seats with their weapons ready.

As Maxim was getting into position on the small porch, Cole was the first to the door. The brawny man kicked it down on his first try. The detective wondered if the man was a werewolf like his friend and realized that life would be much more complicated with his newfound revelation.

As the two veterans stormed inside, the detective signaled Gutierrez to go around the back. Maxim paused a moment to decide what to do with himself but his decision was made for him as the officers surrounded Melody as she sat on the couch, sobbing. She put up no resistance as the pistols were trained on her.

"Keep going," said Maxim, stepping out of the crisp air. Even though the afternoon hours still lingered, temperatures had been dropping earlier in the day, and it wouldn't be long before it was coat and scarf weather. Hitchens and Cole continued clearing the premises and Maxim surveyed the scene.

The kitchen, dining room, and living room were all combined in a quaint open area, and it was all in a shambles. A shelf was knocked down, a lightweight breakfast table was snapped in half, and various objects had been thrown about the room. A sliding glass door connecting the kitchen to the backyard had been shattered and a small amount of blood was spattered on the glass and anything else that was remotely sharp.

As for Melody, she was wiping her eyes as she curled up in a corner of the sofa. It was clear that she had been crying for some time because her eyes almost matched the deep red of her hair. Even worse, however, was the fact that she was bruised up and held an ice pack to her head.

Maxim gave the girl a sympathetic glance and holstered his Glock. "You okay?"

She sniffed and simply shook her head.

Maxim approached her and took a better look. She had some blood on her, but her wounds appeared superficial. The blood in this cabin didn't come from her.

"Melody, what happened here?"

Her tears slowed but the damage had been done—black lines of mascara ran down her moon-colored cheeks. It was an element of flair that seemed to fit her Gothic image except for the fact that it was genuine. Her presentation was stripped down, less deliberate. What remained was very honest.

Maxim took in a deep breath and moved a wicker footrest to the girl. He gently sat down and showed Melody his true concern. "Diego's in the clinic, by the way. He's okay. I thought you might want to know."

"I saw what she did," she said lightly, "on the news." Melody brushed her eyes again to fight back any remaining urge to cry. "I didn't know."

The detective nodded understandingly. From what he could tell, the girl lived a life of blissful ignorance, in some ways probably more innocent than any of the other club members.

"Was she here?" he asked softly.

She nodded. "After the rabies hit the news, she told me to hunker down in the cabin. She said things might get worse before they got better. I didn't know what she was gonna do! I never questioned her."

"It's okay," said the detective. "Just tell me when you last saw her."

"She came here, earlier today." The girl pulled her knees up to her chin and covered her bare feet with her hands. The red paint on her fingers matched her toes, but the spatters of dried blood were a darker shade altogether. "I was just here waiting, like she asked, and she showed up, dragging that CDC woman with her."

"Nithya's alive?"

Another nod. "She was hurt real bad. I didn't know how, at first, but I'm pretty sure Mom bit her. She looked awful. Real pale."

The three other officers returned to the room. Hitchens looked frustrated. "The house is clear. There's no one else here."

Gutierrez raised his eyebrows as he saw the sliding door. "Bro, what happened here?" The detective looked back to Melody.

"She's a different person!" exclaimed Melody. "She came in here, demanding that we leave Sycamore. She wanted us to run away, but I told her I didn't want to leave the club. I didn't want to leave Angie." Melody crossed her arms on her knees and buried her face in them. "That's when Mom flipped out. She said I was abandoning her when she needed me. She never liked me hanging around Angie and accused me of being depraved, so I slapped her."

Gutierrez was more impressed with the story than with the damage. "A catfight over another girl? That's hot." Cole gave the rookie a smack on the back of the head.

Hitchens stepped closer to the girl and waved at the destruction in the house. "You two did all this?"

"No," she answered, lifting her head. "I mean, we did get rough, but out of nowhere, Angie burst in and jumped on her. I don't know how she got here. She fought Mom off a little. She was trying to defend me and help Nithya, I think, but you know Mom. She doesn't back off. She's too strong." Suddenly, she burst into tears again, failing to fight off her sadness any longer. "Everyone was bleeding. Everything changed!"

"What happened?" asked Maxim more urgently. "Where did they go?"

The girl covered her face with her hands. "I don't know," she said. "I hit my head. I woke up a few hours ago. Alone."

Maxim pushed himself up and kicked over his wicker seat. This was worse than he thought. Deborah had been trying to run, but now revenge might have been her priority. He couldn't let that happen, even if it meant doing something he didn't like.

"Melody," he said, taking some steps back and motioning to the officers, "I need you to work with us, okay? We're going to need to take you down to the marshal's office."

Hitchens nodded to his friend and Cole whipped out a set of handcuffs and stood the girl up. Melody complied with wet eyes, hands behind her back, apathetic to the world. "She's not my mom anymore. She doesn't love me."

The poor girl. Maybe it would do her some good to be under watch.

"I don't get it," said Gutierrez. "Why would a fugitive drag two people around with them? She can't get far. What's her end game?"

The rookie was quickly realizing what Maxim feared. Nithya may have been deluded, but she wasn't as dangerous as the ex-president. Doka was just a mercenary, not a fanatic. Deborah, on the other hand, was spiteful and had plenty of people that needed a lashing.

Maybe Gutierrez had a point, though. Maybe Deborah would stay close out of necessity. Unfortunately, in the dense brush of Sycamore, everything was close and impossibly far away at the same time.

"Where can she go, Melody?" asked the detective.

The girl just stood quietly, forlorn, and shrugged in helplessness.

Maxim put his hand on her cheek and lifted her head to his. "Did she say or do anything suspicious?"

"She said she was gonna kill them both."

"Anything else?"

Melody blinked several times as if she was reliving the bad memory but her thoughts found purchase on something worth remembering. "When she first got here, before we started arguing, I was cleaning the CDC woman up in the kitchen and Mom was doing something out back somewhere. When she came inside, I could tell she was crying before anything ever happened between us." Maxim nodded gently as he wiped Melody's eyes and pulled his hand back. "We always did wear our hearts on our sleeves, me and her. She tries to be colder, but it's not her nature."

Maxim watched as the officers walked her outside and loaded her into the squad car. "Keep an eye on her and go over everything inside that might lead us to Deborah." As for the detective, he walked into the kitchen and through the portal of broken glass.

Sycamore. This cabin was smack in the middle of it, just

as it seemed everything was. This lot had no real fences or landlines; it was just a small clearing surrounded by an army of trees. Fortunately, the backyard was smaller than most.

The detective strolled past a flower garden lining the outside wall. Colorful purple blossoms with red tips and other unfamiliar flora looked generally well-kept. While the non-potted plant life did grow in wild patches, Maxim's overall impression was that this had been managed by someone with a green thumb. That was something he had never known about or suspected of Deborah.

He turned and looked at the house and surroundings. It would have been easy for Angelica to sneak up on the property through the thick vegetation. With her newfound strength, Diego's little sister was probably confused and desperate. Could Melody have been correct about the woman's motivations?

Being a wolf was, in all likelihood, something that Angelica did sign up for, whatever Diego would let himself believe. After the train yard, there was no love lost between her and Deborah, but maybe the girl did see Nithya as a friend and truly wanted to rescue her. Perhaps, in her own strange way, Nithya actually did think she was helping her victims.

The detective spun in a slow revolution to take in a panorama of the grounds. A tangled hose lay parched and cracked in the sun. Some long grass had overgrown a little-used brick oven. The sound of wind chimes picked up in a new chill breeze as the sun, fighting its last of the day, shone down and reflected a glimmer of light from deeper in the woods.

It caught the detective's eye.

Maxim approached, stepping into a clumped patch of leaves and ducking under bare branches. He noticed some ivy draping around a piece of stone and saw an object resting on top of it. It shimmered in the spotty sunlight that managed to pierce through the evergreen canopy.

Maxim Dwyer stepped up to the slab and picked up a silver wedding band and the piece of paper it sat on. The ring was smaller and thinner than the one on his finger but it held the same brushed sheen. Like his, there was a small imperfection etched out of the face. Maxim removed his band and lined it up next to the other. Both half heart symbols merged flawlessly into one.

Maxim's heart skipped a beat and he unwrapped the paper slowly and deliberately. It simply said, handwritten in blue ink, "You were right, Maxim. It was my fault."

The detective brushed away the strands of ivy as a pit formed in the center of his stomach. The rock was an unmarked headstone, but Maxim knew for certain who was buried underneath.

Part 9 – The End

i.

Sycamore Lodge was not its usual self tonight.

The weather was crisper than it had been all year, the first cold snap of the season, but there were no lights on inside the roadhouse, no lively fires on the polished stones of the patio. The line of parked cars and Harleys was absent, in its place only dirt and the occasional car belonging to the most dedicated of all-day drinkers.

It was an odd night. Even the moon was strangely absent from the vast, star-filled sky.

What the hell, thought Maxim. He wasn't here for company or celebration. He had just found out that his wife, Lola, was dead. He had already suspected as much, but after two years of being without her presence, it felt like a great release to be able to know with certainty. No, the detective did not need company on this night, but he was not here to drown either. He just wanted a single drink, a final toast to the life of his love.

There was nothing else to be done for now. His gambit of tracking Melody down had seemed promising, but they'd missed the action by hours. Now, the CDC was packing into the Sanctuary Marshal's Office and combing through the new information. It was only a matter of time before they came to the same conclusion as Maxim: there were no leads to Deborah remaining.

As the detective bounced up the patio steps and approached the door to the building, the eerie stillness overcame him. A slow night would have been desirable, but what he was witnessing was the quietness of death. The red wooden blinds had all been pulled down to cover the windows. Even the glass door was barred with a screen, and Maxim was deflated to find that it was locked.

That was strange. It wasn't especially late. Today wasn't a holiday. Even if it were, that would have proven a boon to business. Maxim tried to peek in past the screen, but it was too dark inside to see anything of note.

The detective turned to go and held his face in thought. Of all the nights for him to be barred from his drink, why tonight? As Maxim strategized his next course of action, he was interrupted by the ringing of his phone.

"I'm off work, Gutierrez," he answered.

"Sir," started the rookie excitedly, "I hope you don't mind, but I was looking at the land deeds. Remember you mentioned that Holton doesn't keep any property in her name? Well, the cabin we raided is registered to a Regina Beale."

"Huh." Where had Maxim heard that before?

"It's a DBA set up, a corporate shell name. I figured Holton might have used the company for other purchases. I was right. Guess what local business was recently purchased by Regina Beale?"

The detective turned his head and stared at the roadhouse behind him. "Sycamore Lodge."

"What—? How'd you know? Did you already find this?"

"No," said Maxim. "Just a feeling I suddenly got." Maxim scratched his beard as he pondered his next move. "Are you at the marshal's office? Put Diego on."

Gutierrez was chagrined. "Well, sir, you see... Diego skipped out of the clinic."

Maxim raised his hand to his forehead. "What? Where did he go?"

"He said we could get in touch with him at the clubhouse."

"Shit." The last thing the police needed was another brawl between the bikers. What's worse, Diego's distaste for technology meant he wouldn't be carrying his cell phone. "Okay, just get him in your sight."

"Sure thing, boss," said Gutierrez. "What are you up to?"

"Having a drink. I'll get back to you if I need you. And good work, rookie. Looks like I can't give you shit for those community college business classes anymore." Maxim disconnected the call.

The detective stood in the cold night. His skin was alive but it wasn't because of the weather. He knew Deborah had to be inside Sycamore Lodge. Moments passed. He paced in the roadside dirt and stared at the shuttered bar and pulled his suit jacket tighter around his body for warmth. He was in this situation now and was determined to make the best of it.

Maxim drew his gun and marched straight for the door. He used his mass and momentum, as Cole had done hours earlier, and put his foot to the lock, careful to avoid the glass. The frame buckled under his solid kick and the door flung open and crashed into a wooden panel within.

Maxim pressed his shoulder flush with the outside doorframe and peeked both ways. As he had anticipated, it was dark inside, too much to make out anything past the first table. He took a minute to see if anything transpired but was met with silence. All signs pointed to him being alone, but the detective didn't buy it. He could feel the black warning him away. In a place like Sycamore Lodge, the quiet was more damning than the chaos.

Maxim stood with his Glock at eye level, elbows tucked against his stomach.

"Deborah?" he called out.

Everything, still, was quiet, but the detective waited.

There was an instant where he heard a breath, and then the ex-president of the Seventh Sons finally spoke. "Good work, Maxim." The southern tang on her words didn't mask her displeasure.

Her voice came from the back corner of the room, near

the hallway to the kitchen. She was centered in the building there, with an encompassing view of the entrances and the option to run in multiple directions. Going around the back seemed just as risky.

Deborah didn't say anything else as the detective mulled over his options. No matter what he did, he thought, nothing would change the fact that she was a wolf and he didn't have silver.

Maxim Dwyer sighed as his grip loosened on the pistol next to his face. He looked at the wedding band on his finger and knew his outlook had changed. There had already been so much fighting, so much death. Maybe the solution was to skirt that path entirely.

The detective brushed his jacket back to place his weapon in his holster but paused as he noticed the bushy plant next to him. Maxim cocked his head in thought and then dropped his Glock into the base of the planter.

Maxim slowly moved out of his cover. He swallowed hard and stepped inside the darkness, ready to confront whatever he found within.

Suddenly the bar was filled with an evil red light. The sconces along the walls, ornamented with deer antlers, buzzed to life as Deborah hit a switch. The main overhead lights that would have allowed patrons to see what they were eating remained off, but she'd achieved what she wanted. There was an ominous glow in the room that allowed him to see her and the others whom she had taken hostage.

Three men, older Sanctuary residents, were sitting on the floor in a line against the right wall. They had probably been drinking here when Deborah had taken over. Helen, a motherly bartender who Maxim recognized, was also present, sitting next to a young cook. He was new. They all had plastic ties around their ankles and their hands were behind their backs, similarly bound.

The devious woman who'd orchestrated this affair was standing over Nithya, who was the only one sitting in a chair. Deborah had rested a gun casually on the woman's right shoulder and patted her on the head with her free hand as if she were a wounded pet. It was hard to determine Nithya's condition in this light, but it was clear that she was stricken with a subdued apathy, an unsettling detachment that caused her to carry her head in a dizzying sway.

Maxim examined the setting and wondered if Doka was here. There was a stage area, a step down and further to the side, with the stone floor where Varela had been stabbed. That was the event that had set all of this into motion, and Maxim thought it fitting that they might find a conclusion in the same place. Upon inspection, the stage area, as well as the bar and the kitchen hallway, were empty.

Maxim cleared his throat.

"How'd you know I was here?" asked Deborah, pursing her pink lips as she waited.

"Regina Beale," said the detective.

"Ah," she said plainly. "A creation of my own, a throwback to Edward Fitzgerald Beale."

That's where Maxim had heard the Beale name before. Deborah loved to talk about how the man was commissioned to forge the passage west. Sycamore Lodge was originally built as an outpost for that work.

"Interesting man, really," said Deborah, her eyes glazing over as if they saw another time. "You could say that he started our tradition in the West. Have you ever heard of the Camel Corps?"

Maxim did not respond, carefully scanning the surroundings while affixing his attention on her. He didn't see any other threats. The Yavapai weren't a worry—they were dead. It was just him and the old woman, but she was danger enough.

The fallen president made a smacking sound with her lips, disappointed that the detective wasn't encouraging her to tell one of her stories, but she continued anyway. "For people of our affliction, camels provided a host of advantages over horses. They don't spook around wolves, for one, but they aren't as fast and don't fight like horses either. They live on less food and water. Out here, with supplies at a minimum, nothing is worse than having to feed your food."

Maxim knew the woman took a strange pride in carrying old traditions forward. She wasn't from here, having relocated from Alabama many years before, but she seemed to find solace by immersing herself in fresh histories. The detective clenched his jaw and let the woman say what she needed.

"Do you know that it's illegal to hunt camels out here?" She chuckled to herself and patted Nithya on the shoulder. "Not that you can find one anymore, but the animals became synonymous with werewolf activity. Edward Beale was a distinguished man who had special dreams, but his efforts out here didn't last long. He had to flee back east. But his empire, his legacy, still remains in us. Of course, I'm not his kin—I'm a noble daughter of the South—but our blood shares enough in common now. We have become a kind of family."

The detective peered at the woman, trying to get a feel for her state of mind. "Family is why I'm here," he said.

"Of course," she answered. "You know, it's natural to want to protect your kin. They provide you with a reach that, perhaps, drives you to expand it. That's why I may be guilty of being... overzealous with Ms. Rao's volunteers."

"It's past time for me to protect my family."

The woman looked directly into his eyes for the first time, sizing him up. It was as if the sudden realization of what was happening had finally hit her and she was forced to address what had to be done.

"It was plain stupid of you to come in here," she said. "You know that your authority don't mean squat to me now."

"I'm here for a trade," said Maxim, without emotion. His eyes swept the room. "Where's Angelica?"

"Safe," said the woman curtly. "I had to lock her up due to her recent developments."

Maxim nodded and walked over to the bar with soft steps. Deborah drew her pistol to him, but the detective merely raised his hands to show he meant no harm and continued on his way. "I found her grave and your note."

Deborah's mouth pinched into a frown. "I knew Melody

would call the police after that little scuffle. She never had the heart to fight."

Maxim opened up a low refrigerator and grabbed a bottle. "She didn't tell me. Diego knew about the place."

"Oh that," said Mom, blinking back her anger. "You could say she had too much heart where that was concerned."

Deborah kept her pistol in the air and approached Maxim as he twisted the cap off of the bottle he'd procured. "Give me your gun," she ordered.

Maxim silently shrugged.

Deborah patted at his jacket and found his empty holster. She furrowed her brow and felt his arms and ankles. The detective just waited until she was satisfied.

"I told you. I didn't come for a fight." Maxim pulled a stemmed glass from overhead. "God, I fucking hate white wine," he said as he poured himself some. "She loved the stuff."

As the man took a sip, his dead wife's friend lowered her weapon. She fetched and poured her own glass.

"The last time I saw her, we split a bottle. Years before that, at our wedding, we drank it from the same glass. It was always special to her, so I shared the wine and the moments and never complained." A heavy sigh escaped from the bowels of his being. "Now, I can taste it for the last time and say goodbye."

Deborah watched in silence as the detective finished his words and then she held her glass high in the air. Maxim regarded the gesture dryly but then did the same before sipping from his glass. He took enough time to appreciate the moment, to draw it to a respectable conclusion, but he knew the impending business wouldn't allow him the serenity that he had hoped for.

"Lola's dead," said Maxim, picking himself up from his perch on the bar and walking back to confront her other killer. Deborah moved to protectively hover over Nithya once more. "We all had a part in that. But I loved her, even if I didn't show it, and I understand the bond of family. All of us here, we can still get out of this. You could see your family again."

The red light created jagged lines on Deborah's weathered face, and she shook her head with predetermined resolve. "Melody disowned me. She'll never look at me the same again after she found out what I did." The woman balled her free hand into a fist and pressed her lips tightly together as if she were about to blow, but then she let the feeling escape her hard heart. "I've made missteps. In retrospect, I had a funny way of protecting the MC. I don't expect you to understand, but she should. I did it for her. The cabin, this bar, Regina Beale, it was all set up for her legacy. No, Maxim, you and I do have something in common. It's that we were both big disappointments to our families. Unlike you, I've decided not to drag mine down. The best thing I can do for Melody is to leave Sycamore."

Maxim took a step closer. "Maybe you're right. Maybe we are both fuckups. Maybe neither of us deserve redemption, but Angelica is Diego's family. We can both choose not to destroy that. We can both choose not to spread our misery to others."

The woman's head fell as she looked at Nithya, nearly broken, close to death. Deborah's teased hair fell over her eyes.

"I don't care about the price," said Maxim. "Not anymore. I came in here to save her life." The detective took another gentle step forward as he appealed to whatever was left of the woman's empathy. "Let her go and I'll stay."

Deborah brushed her long hair behind her ears and gave the detective an uncompromising glare. "You may just have to stay anyway." The woman raised her gun to him again.

"Don't do anything drastic, Deborah. You know we have Melody in custody."

She nodded. "Then it's in your best interest to leave her alone and help me get out of town for good. Sanctuary will do better without the likes of me."

"I'm fine with that, but only if we play nice. Let these hostages go. Let me arrest Nithya so she can serve time in prison. And let's get Angelica out of this mess as if she had never been involved."

Deborah scoffed. "Do those complete your terms?" she asked mockingly. "Why is it that you fight so hard to protect Ms. Rao's life?"

The detective couldn't explain it. He wanted to believe that Nithya hadn't acted out of malice. "Look at her," he answered. "She's dying."

Maxim studied the faces of the other hostages. They were deathly afraid, whimpering in the corner, staring at the floor boards. Sanctuary was meant to be a place where people could escape their troubles, not this. If he had to deal with the devil to free them, so be it. The fate of his soul was a good sacrifice for theirs.

"Okay," said Deborah, "we can work together. You need to release Melody and let her be free to do as she chooses, whether she stays or goes."

Maxim nodded.

"You will also let me go. And I give you my word that you will never see me again."

"I have no pull with County or the CDC."

She eyed him carefully. After a moment of deliberation, she smacked her lips again, as one might chide a child or pet. "Maxim, you want to bet it all, and you haven't even put your chips on the table yet."

He was confused by her meaning. "How's that?"

"A little birdie told me that you have all of my money. I don't need sway with the CDC or Coconino deputies, but I do need that. That's a sticking point for me."

Maxim smiled. Gaston must have told her over the phone in an effort to keep her away from the club. It was a smart move. "So you heard?" he asked coyly. "The president is dead. Long live the president."

"Honey," said Deborah, unfazed, "titles are overrated. It's power that makes a person."

ii.

The next hour that Maxim waited with the hostages was agonizing. He had never spent that much time in Sycamore Lodge without a drink in his hand. It's not that the temptation wasn't there, but this was far too important. Maxim had to remain sharp.

Deborah had allowed him to make a call to set up the exchange. Then she had confiscated his phone and left him sitting at a table by the front. He had taken to watching the hostages, wondering about their lives, trying to make eye contact and soothe them with a confident countenance. Nithya was the only one who wouldn't look. Whether weakness or shame kept her head down, he didn't know, but he desperately wanted to hear her voice again.

It was only when those feelings became unbearable and he was afraid his resolve would fail the hostages that the hum of a motorcycle rolled closer. With permission, Maxim twisted open a set of blinds as Deborah approached the window. Between the red slats, a lone figure in black leathers and a gold helmet stood straddling a Triumph Scrambler. He kept to the edge of the road and appeared as unthreatening as possible.

Deborah peeked through the blinds and looked up the street.

"I told him to come alone," assured Maxim.

She nodded in her domineering manner. "That better be the case. Remember, if I see anyone else, or if the assassin tries to come inside, I start killing hostages." She brushed him away with the gun in her hand. "Run along now."

Maxim walked to the door and heard one of the men whimper. The detective put his hand up and encouraged them not to lose hope. He looked to each of them and knew it was his duty to protect them. The only problem was that he didn't know how yet.

For that matter, he didn't even know where Angelica was. Deborah was keeping that from him as her last trick. Maxim watched her brazenly eyeing him, standing by the window, arms crossed, waiting for him to get to it. The detective slipped outside.

It was freezing in the open air. The combination of vacant heat and constant breeze was peculiar and unsettling. In the alcove by the patio door, where Deborah could not see what the detective was doing, Maxim recovered his Glock from the planter and holstered it out of sight. Then he pulled his suit jacket tightly around his body and stepped into her view.

Maxim kicked up gravel as he stepped impatiently towards the bike. He knew Deborah was watching them closely from behind. He needed to make sure this went smoothly. He saw the metal briefcase waiting in the biker's arms and reached his hand out for it.

"Hello boss," said Gutierrez from under the helmet.

The detective almost jumped at the unexpected development. "Where's Diego?"

"He's in Gaston's pickup truck, down the road."

Maxim couldn't hold back a smile. Diego had finally thought of a plan before jumping into a fight.

"Okay, well we have six hostages inside. One of them is Nithya. I don't know where Angelica is, so I'll need to trade her for the case. When she comes out, get her on the bike and get her out of here. She needs to be safe. Deborah needs to see you leave. After that, if she doesn't release the other hostages, Hitchens and Cole need to come in strong while I keep her from killing anybody. Don't focus on me, worry about saving the hostages. That's our job."

The detective couldn't see the rookie's face under the tinted visor but he could imagine the troubled expression. "What's the matter?"

"That's the thing," said Gutierrez. "The CDC took Melody to County for questioning."

"Don't worry about the girl."

"Hitchens and Cole are in Flagstaff with them."

Maxim blinked before it settled in. He had been counting on their strength.

"I don't know what happened. The CDC is getting pissy. They wanna talk to you too."

Maxim sighed. It was useless to worry about that meeting right now. "Let's see how tonight goes first."

Behind him, a loud rapping on the window rang out. Maxim turned and saw a dark shadow watching them. He nodded and faced the rookie again.

Maxim extended his arm and took possession of the case. "Did the feds ask about the club?"

The gold helmet shook back and forth. "Nah. Melody laid this at her mom's feet. I think they're still interested in the Yavapai, but so far, they're limiting themselves to simply watching the Seventh Sons."

"Good."

"Why are you protecting them, sir? A bunch of monsters tear through our station, almost kill Kent, and you are lying for them."

Maxim looked back at the roadhouse and imagined the people inside, what they've done, what they had yet to do. "I don't know, Gutierrez. Everyone has a right to be good, I guess."

"Until they do something bad," countered the officer.

The detective turned his head to the rookie again and gave him a single slight nod. "Until then. And that's when it becomes our job to stop them."

The rookie didn't say anything and watched as Maxim turned and started back toward Sycamore Lodge. "Stay here," said the detective. "Don't get off the bike."

Maxim's steps were more deliberate on his walk back. He gripped the case firmly and stared at the window where Deborah's figure and the horizontal blinds formed a perfect black silhouette against the red glow of the lodge. As he approached, she moved backwards and her form blurred and lost its clarity.

Maxim stopped at the stone steps.

"Deborah," he called out. "Send Angelica outside." He heard the woman stomping around within.

"Not until you give me that case."

Maxim stood up straight and summoned his most authoritative voice. "If I go in there, you have the money, Angelica, me—everything you want. I would be defenseless.

You still have other hostages. Let Angelica ride away with Diego so we can deal alone. Then I'll give you the case."

The woman didn't even consider the offer. "You need to come inside and let me make sure that case has my money in it."

The detective's head fell. He had never known Deborah to be reasonable. Was he wasting his time appealing to her now? "At least let some of the hostages out."

"Can't do it," she replied plainly.

Maxim closed his eyes and gritted his teeth. If she was being this uncooperative now, she would only get worse once she had the briefcase. He needed to handle this in a different manner.

His eyes bounced around the property. The detective ran his hand across the wiry hair on his cheek and frowned. If Angelica wasn't inside the bar, where else could she be?

Maxim turned on his heels and walked away from the patio, skirting the roadhouse around the left side. He heard Deborah yell for him to get inside, but he marched on, out of view from her or Gutierrez.

There was a rolling warehouse door on the edge of the building. Maxim saw that it hadn't been bolted down for the night, bent down to grab the handle, and heaved it up. It stuck at the height of his shoulders and he lowered himself to peek in. He saw several emptied kegs of beer, a dumpster, and broken down cardboard boxes. It was a small space, and he could tell at a glance that no hostages were in there.

Maxim continued around and found himself in the back of Sycamore Lodge. It was all dirt besides the occasional patch of brown grass. During the day, truckers would park their trailers on the far side from him. There was a small stoop by a rickety back door with a glass window. Cigarettes spotted the ground where patrons often lurked in between drinks.

Deeper in the clearing, to Maxim's left, was an old grain storage bin. It was a large tower of corrugated metal that had been left idle for at least a generation. The detective recalled Deborah's stories of how Sycamore Lodge used to be an outpost for moving food and supplies west for the surveying of Beale Wagon Road. Maybe there had been an attempt at farming here at some point as well.

Maxim approached the structure to investigate. It looked decrepit but not especially suspicious, and he was about to circle the bin when he heard the creaky bar door pushed open. Deborah was standing in the back, fuming.

"Maxim Dwyer," she yelled, "what in the Sam Hill do you think you're doing?"

That was a good question, one without a clear answer. It certainly didn't appear as if anyone was out here, but when Maxim saw Deborah drawn to the back door, he decided to improvise in another direction. If he couldn't get the hostages away from her, well...

"You want the case? Come out and get it."

They were about fifty yards from each other. That was a safe distance to have a standoff. He was in a clearing and could pull his weapon before she ever had a chance. Sure, they both had guns, but Maxim was willing to bet that he was the better shot.

She scowled at him from the safety of the lodge, staring him down until she suddenly withdrew inside. Maxim squinted his eyes as he watched, and waited, for her to reappear, and she did, only she was pushing Nithya outside onto the porch while she remained by the door.

So Deborah wouldn't relinquish her position so easily. She stood like a vigilant sentry and it was Nithya who made her way into the open yard. The wounded woman's movement was labored and slow and Maxim had plenty of time to reflect on his thoughts of her before she arrived. Still, somehow, when she stood before him, he was at a loss for words.

Nithya Rao looked terrible. The space between her shoulder and neck featured torn flesh that had been given little attention. She was hunched over so that Maxim appeared the taller of the two, and gone was her confident air. She was a broken woman, yet in some ways, she was prettier in her sickened state, less prim, of course, but more authentic. There was an honesty about her eyes that pervaded his impression. Perhaps, he thought, it was the peace of resignation.

For the first time in days, she returned his gaze and looked straight into him. "I'm not a monster," she said firmly.

Her voice nearly broke him. "Nithya..."

"I've committed crimes. I've abused my position. Believe me, I understand my role in the deaths of those people, but I was being deceived by the bikers as well."

Pity forced Maxim to feign a weak smile. "You kept them

in a cage."

She remained resolute. "They weren't coerced. They gave themselves the first injection. Once they were subjected to the program, they could not be free to leave it. Allowing their departure would have been a greater ill to society."

"So they were strangled by a madman to benefit society?"

Nithya trembled at the thought. "Once the rabies showed outward symptoms, once it was clear that the patients were to die, they were supposed to be moved to a secret hospice. Deborah assured me that they were allowed to die peacefully, privately."

"Dumped in an abandoned water tank."

"They had to be disposed of secretly. The number of deaths and the presence of rabies would have brought us down."

"It did bring you down."

"I kept telling myself that I was helping more than hurting."

Maxim raised his voice. "How was Lola helped by you starting all of this?"

The woman shuddered slightly under his question but answered with the calm detachment of a scientist. "Your wife wanted a change, Maxim. Deborah didn't want to turn her friend because of the dangers, so she brought her to me. Lola personally conveyed to me her thoughts of flinging herself from the falls to end it all. She wanted to kill herself, Maxim. She was dead without me. I knew it was illegal, but I saw an opportunity for the both of us."

Nithya paused for a heavy moment, perhaps realizing the irony of her words. "When Lola got sick, we did our best for her. We kept her at Deborah's cabin and treated her, but she was overtaken. Lola had met her desired fate after all.

"We had a quiet burial for her. Deborah was devastated, as was I, but I thought I was on to something. I asked about other volunteers. Deborah latched onto the process, no more as a helpful hand to a friend but instead as a business decision. We started by using the basement of Sycamore Lodge. Deborah had just purchased the property, and it served its purpose until I found better, more neutral ground. Deborah negotiated special consideration from the CDC for the Seventh Sons and was well paid. She continued to push for more. More trials. More people."

At this point, Maxim was numb to the news. "And what of your reasons?"

Nithya sighed and clasped her elbows for warmth. "I have a brain tumor, Detective. I have been healthy all of my life, yet here I am, not even forty, and I do not know how many years I have left. The mass pushes against my skull, causes incessant headaches, and will one day rob me of my reason. Then I will die, alone, probably in a mental ward, without dignity."

Maxim looked to the woman softly. It seemed she was still able to stir sympathy in him, whatever her transgressions. It was no matter. She would answer for her part, one way or another.

"Lycanthropy," he said, working out the same premise

she had staked her livelihood on. "You wanted to be able to heal like them."

She gave a weak nod. "Werewolf physiology stands up surprisingly well to degenerative diseases. Late onset deterioration tied to aging is nearly nonexistent. Imagine not needing to watch your cholesterol in your later years. Imagine not having the crippling burden of caring for a parent. The old get to keep their graces."

Maxim thought over her words with a furrowed brow. "So you never desired to become a wolf?"

Nithya laughed as her face was wrought with irony. "It's tragic," she said, looking up to the stars as if their worlds held answers other than this one. "I've been sick, in pain, dying, and all I've wanted was to live. Not an abnormal life, not selfishly long, just long enough to be able to look back on my time and be proud of the differences I've made. Yet the bulk of my test subjects had purely temporary problems and wished to snuff themselves out with little thought. I've failed them. And I've failed myself."

"What about Angelica?" Maxim asked.

She smiled weakly. "Perhaps my lone accomplishment. Or perhaps she was predisposed to lycanthropy without my help. But I am happy that she can move on. I am sorry that was not the fortune of your wife."

The detective listened in silence. Imagining what could have been was as fruitless as lying to oneself about the past. There had been no mystery cure for his relationship with Lola, no more than Nithya could control the tumor in her brain.

"Hey!" called out Deborah impatiently. Maxim had almost forgotten the hostile terms that encompassed this dialog and looked to Deborah, who was still standing outside on the stoop. "Get on with it."

Maxim nodded and returned his attention to Nithya. "You haven't saved Angelica yet until she is free from that woman. Where is she?"

"Holton has her locked in the basement." The woman held out her hands to receive the briefcase.

Maxim studied the backside of Sycamore Lodge. He hadn't realized the old building had a basement before Nithya's story. There was no entrance against the outside wall, so it was likely that the lone access point was within. His eyes moved to the wolf standing by the back door. Deborah was getting increasingly agitated by their delay. Maxim would need to create some space between her and her captives.

"Last chance, Deborah," he yelled, holding the reinforced briefcase high above his head. "Send the girl out and I'll give you your money. I promise."

The breeze grew more intense, and it whipped Deborah's hair wildly about her head. She stared mercilessly at Maxim as he made his demands, then smiled a cruel smile and simply said, "You can't take charge of this one, Maxim."

The two stood defiantly opposed to each other, neither giving an inch. The detective waved the case in the air as a taunt.

"It seems that you want more blood on your hands," said the woman. "I think I'll start by cutting Helen's throat."

Deborah stepped into the door to retreat inside.

"No!" screamed Maxim, advancing forward. He couldn't let that happen. He unlatched the briefcase and upended it with both hands. The contents spilled into the dirt. Stacks of bound bills and passports fell to his feet as he shook the case empty. Deborah paused in the threshold of the bar and shot him a look of despair. The detective threw the case to the ground and picked up a wad of cash.

"What is it that you want more?" he asked, insistent. As a hard wind blew, the detective ripped the tie that held the cash in a bundle. "Misery—or riches?" He ruffled the bills loose from his hands and they were picked up by the angry air, exploding into a mass of individual actors haphazardly fluttering to freedom.

Deborah could stand it no longer. She sprung from her perch as if propelled by a rifle.

She closed the distance between them more quickly than Maxim had anticipated, charging straight for the source of her ire. He'd barely drawn the Glock and she was upon him. He fired some reflexive shots. The wolf sidestepped and ducked under the near misses.

By the time the detective was pulling the trigger a third time, he was tackled by the savage woman. She dragged him to the ground next to the grain bin.

On his back, Maxim brought the butt of his pistol down on Deborah's head. It was a solid blow but it barely phased her. She overpowered his hand and banged it into the ground until he dropped the weapon.

Deborah rained down vicious punches to his chest and

face. Maxim instinctively drew his arms up to protect himself before he felt the pain that would have buckled his body had he been standing. He tried to kick her off, but she was too strong; in a moment he was helplessly pinned.

From behind her, a metal briefcase swung around and knocked Deborah in the head. The unexpected strike swept her to the floor, but the agile woman rolled to her feet and faced her attacker. Nithya Rao stood above the woman, wildly swinging her awkward weapon.

Deborah easily lunged between the blows and swatted the case to the ground. Then she did the same to Nithya, putting her fists together and slamming them into the woman's chest. Nithya sailed backwards ten feet and collapsed in the dirt.

Maxim struggled to get up as Deborah turned her attention back to him. To complicate matters further, they heard an engine revving loudly. The detective, still on the floor, bent around and saw a metallic gray late-model pickup truck skidding past the lodge and bearing down on them both.

Gaston, thought Maxim as he saw the big man at the wheel. That meant that Diego couldn't be far behind.

The next events happened in a heartbeat, but some combination of heightened awareness and adrenaline allowed Maxim to take in every detail.

The detective saw Deborah reach into the small of her back.

He frantically rolled toward his weapon and scooped it out of the dirt.

Maxim heard shots ring out and kept his head down, but as he turned to his opponent, he saw that she was firing on Gaston's truck.

The windshield shattered into a spider web of fragments, somehow held together except for the distinct holes that the bullets had traveled through in front of the driver's seat. Some of the rounds must have hit their mark because Maxim swore that he saw a streak of crimson paint the broken glass.

Deborah, meanwhile, was attempting to flee from the path of the impending vehicle. She ran toward it at an angle as she fired, trying to sidestep it. Maxim raised his weapon and shot at her as he pressed his back into the abandoned farm structure. He couldn't tell if his aim was true.

Suddenly, Gaston turned the truck sharply to the left. Deborah was almost nimble enough to avoid the maneuver, but the broad steel bumper of the pickup caught her hip and slammed her to the ground. Her weapon flew from her hand and she was pulled under the careening vehicle. Deborah was dragged through the dirt until the tire bounced over her body.

In that moment, Maxim realized the truck was about to barrel into him.

The detective leaped from the ground to his left. The pickup, massive at this immediate proximity, smashed into the large grain bin just a foot from his right arm. The impact was catastrophic, pushing shards of glass and slivers of metal forward. Gaston's truck, which had seemed to have been moving impossibly fast to stop, was instantly motionless and half-embedded in a corrugated metal wall.

Maxim had only half a moment to breathe as he steadied his feet and gripped his pistol tightly, eyes searching the ground where Deborah should have been. The reprieve was not long enough to get to safety.

A colossal sound, like that of a stampede of buffalo charging his direction, assaulted his ears. Maxim's feet were swept forward suddenly by an unyielding wave of rotten grain spilling out from the fractured bin behind him. The detective fell on his backside and fought to get up out of the sliding wheat, but it was acting as if it were quicksand. As he struggled, the deluge continued to pour over his body and head, burying him under its increasing weight.

The detective tried to take a panicked breath and sucked in the harsh grain. He coughed it up and the rancid stench almost caused him to pass out. Maxim moved to cover his mouth so he had space to breathe as the load over him got heavier, and he was afraid he would be crushed.

Hold on to the gun, he thought. Hold on to the gun.

iii.

Diego ducked underneath the half-open door to the Sycamore Lodge storeroom. He had seen Maxim slide it open moments before. The detective was now drawing attention to the back of the lot. This was the biker's best chance to sneak in and find Angelica.

The room was full of garbage and kegs. Up a couple of stone steps, double doors provided side access to the bar. Diego peeked through the small panes of glass in the metal doors and saw a hallway. A small closet was open on his right and the entire length of the left wall was shared with the kitchen, which had two entrances. At the end, the passage intersected with another hallway that eased travel between the main lodge area and the back of the building.

The biker jumped as he saw Nithya taking this same path, crossing past him in the other hall, followed closely behind by her captor. Deborah was pushing her toward the back. Perhaps this sideshow would allow the biker to move unnoticed within.

After waiting a short time to make sure Deborah wasn't coming back, Diego slipped the door open and quietly entered through the threshold. One by one, Diego took each agonizing step with supreme caution. The doorways to the kitchen had swinging doors with windows. Looking inside revealed nothing but ovens, flattops, and other appliances stained with grease. As he reached the end of the passage, the biker took a breath and peeked around to the back.

The rear door was closed. Diego could see Deborah through its large window, standing with her arms crossed looking on at some development outside. The hall down in the opposite direction looked clear. With silent haste, the biker walked backwards, watching the dangerous woman the whole way until he found himself in the familiar confines of Sycamore Lodge.

The bar looked empty but the biker heard startled gasps. A clump of people were tied up in the corner that he had just walked away from. He didn't know any of them. More importantly, Angelica was nowhere to be seen. Was she not here at all? Is that why Maxim didn't make the trade and left Gutierrez stranded outside?

"Where are the others?" he asked impatiently.

One of the truckers said, "She took the woman out back."

Diego wasn't here for Nithya. "Anyone else?"

The group just shrugged. An older woman gave the only other information. "We haven't seen anyone else besides Detective Dwyer."

Diego's heart sunk. According to Melody, Mom would have been the last one to see Angelica. If she wasn't here...

He shook the thought from his mind and stomped to the front door, peeked past the shade, and swung it open. The biker waved in the rookie sitting on his Scrambler.

Diego rushed to the bar and looked for something sharp. He snatched up a pair of scissors and joined Gutierrez as he came inside. As they walked to the hostages, Diego put his arm across the officer's chest to stop him. They needed to cross the view of the hallway to get to the corner. Diego poked his head over and still saw Deborah outside, looking away. The biker nodded and they quickly moved past.

"We're gonna get you out of here," said Gutierrez to the others as he saw Diego cutting through the plastic ties around their legs. The rookie looked down at his black leather clothes. "I'm a police officer." The man pulled a utility knife from his pocket and followed Diego's lead.

"Where else could Deborah be hiding somebody?" asked Diego in a rushed voice.

The older woman answered again. "Uh, kitchen, storeroom, basement, bathrooms—"

Diego cut the woman's hands free. "Where's the basement?"

She pointed around the corner to the area where the stage was—where Diego had stabbed Steve. The red sconces that lit the bar and hallway were absent in the dance area, and although the eerie light carried well where it was not obstructed, much of the side room was left bathed in shadow.

The group froze as they all heard the creak of the back door. Diego put his finger to his lips to tell the others to be silent. They could hear Maxim yelling in the distance and the biker gripped the scissors tightly. Then the door slammed shut and they heard gunshots. That was Gaston's cue.

Diego jumped into the hallway and saw no one there. He helped up the older woman and looked to Gutierrez. "Get them all out of here." Then the biker jumped to the stone floor and headed to the darkness in the back. He pressed himself past a heavy door and then found another. After undoing the deadbolt, it revealed a stone staircase down.

Light emanated from the depths, and as Diego carefully made his way down the steep steps, he saw a single bulb hanging from a chain. It illuminated cramped quarters, not very useful for more than storage because of their size, but even lacking for that due to the difficult entrance.

Lining the wall were several green plastic drums, the same type that had recently made their way to the bottom of Paradise Tank. The biker realized that the bar was in between the train yard and the farmhouse. This dusky cellar was likely where the victims had met their ends before being packed and shipped off like cargo.

Lying in the corner, peacefully asleep in a weathered cot, was his sister.

"Angelica!" cried Diego. "Wake up. Are you okay?" He shook her shoulders to rouse her and clipped the ties around her hands and feet. The girl opened her eyes and smiled weakly. Her face was bloody and bruised but she was in one piece. As Diego helped her sit, he realized that she lacked strength and must have been drugged. "It's okay, it's okay," he said, drawing her arm around him and standing up.

The first few paces were difficult, and the biker thought he would have trouble at the stairs, but Angelica contributed more of her power to the effort as she shook the numbness away. Very quickly the two were through the shadow and back under the tendrils of the red lights.

The bar was empty, its door flung open to the cold wind inside. Diego flipped up a single blind with the tip of his scissors and saw Gutierrez in the road, leading the five rescued men and women towards the town on foot.

"Go join them, Angelica," said Diego firmly. He noticed his sister's confused expression. "I'll be along in a minute."

Angelica shook her head. "I'm staying with you."

"That would be a first," said a sardonic voice from behind them. They started at the sound and saw Mom standing in the back hallway, holding the metal case that she had suffered for. She limped ahead and clutched her right hip with her arm, which was bleeding from a bullet wound. On her left, the entire side of her face was obscured by a mix of dirt and blood. She didn't look well as she stood there, but somehow, managing supreme composure, she still summoned the audacity to be dangerous.

"Where's Maxim?" asked an exasperated Diego.

The woman gave a careless shrug. "That man was in such a rush to join his wife."

The biker took a step forward as his hand tightened on the scissors.

Deborah smirked. "You planning on cutting my nails?" The woman moved into the center of the room and looked at Angelica standing to the side, forlorn, avoiding eye contact. "Diego de la Torre. You walked into this bar two weeks ago with a focused desire—to rescue your baby sister. It must pain you to know that she is now part of my family as well, sharing blood with those you have mindlessly slaughtered. Still," said Deborah, approaching the man, "she is alive and you have accomplished your objective. Don't tell me that you require something else?"

The biker heaved his shoulders as he listened to the smug words. He had tried to leave on civil terms in the train yard before. She had ordered them shot down. Now Maxim was dead because of her, and maybe Gaston and Nithya as well, and who knows how many others.

Diego stood firm, blocking her path to the door.

Deborah took a final step to bring herself immediately in front of the biker. She cocked her head and the light caught her ravaged visage. The true horrors of her heart had finally breached the surface of her skin, even if the wounds only lasted until the next time she healed. Ignoring the pain she must have been in, she stared him down and held up the briefcase. "A deal is a deal: the money for your sister."

The biker ground his jaw down in frustration. He looked to Angelica, young and hurt. Diego knew he couldn't overpower a werewolf, even a wounded one, and he knew any action on his part would pull his sister into harm. The man swallowed his pride and took a step to the side, clearing access for Deborah to exit.

The wolf smiled triumphantly as her eyes flashed orange. She strutted as she walked past him.

Angelica, having already been beaten and still drugged, kept back. As Diego watched her standing there weakly, covered in blood, he knew that she was a wolf and that she would heal as well. She was strong inside, no matter the feelings that welled up within him when he saw her in that condition. It dawned on him that the sweet, innocent projection he had of his sister was a relic of the past. It didn't do either of them good anymore.

A horrible feeling burned within Diego that caused him to feel that he was committing a great wrong. It was the same creeping sensation that the biker had nearly drowned in when he'd hunted werewolves, and it had caused him to ultimately quit. Only this time, Diego was much more receptive to the realization.

"It wasn't my deal," stated the biker, and he swiftly swung his arm around, burying the blades of the scissors in the back of Deborah's neck. The woman turned halfway around and locked her evil eyes on him once again. "Maxim was my friend," he said.

Deborah was not prepared to go down so easily.

She slammed the metal case against Diego's chest. It knocked the wind from him and he crashed into a neighboring table. As he fell to the floor, he thought he heard his sister scream, but he was gasping for breath and could not recover.

Angelica leaped at Deborah fiercely and threw a barrage of punches. Deborah fell and dropped the case, but she kicked out and caught Angelica, who was already partly dizzy, in the head.

The biker pulled himself up on the table and looked for the scissors. He didn't know where they'd gone and didn't see any other weapons nearby.

Both women regained their feet and continued battering each other. Deborah's leg was failing her—she could not move and roll away from strikes as she once could—but she was by far the stronger of the two. She reverted to absorbing Angelica's blows and, when the moment was right, caught her with a haymaker square in the stomach. Diego's sister flew over a table and landed on another.

Diego was unarmed, but he suddenly noticed that the scissors still protruded from the back of the wolf's neck. In a final effort, he ran to the woman and reached for the blade. Deborah Holton turned and caught his neck with her wounded arm.

Diego's boots left the wood floor. The wolf lifted him and squeezed, and he felt the airway in his throat constrict. He tried kicking the woman but she was too powerful. He could only watch helplessly as his sister lay on the floor, groaning.

A gunshot rang out. Then another. And another. The death grip around Diego's neck loosened. As the biker took in a deep breath, he heard two more shots and watched the luster depart from Deborah's bright eyes. They both crumpled to the floor.

Diego caught himself on his hands and lifted his head. Standing in the hallway, coming from the back door, and with a jacket littered with grains of wheat, was a man holding a spent Glock.

iv.

Maxim Dwyer stood with his offhand pressed against the wall, allowing it to support his weight and managing to feel battered yet unbeaten all at once. He had been dreading this moment. It meant losing another link to his dead wife, however depraved.

No matter. He had seen Deborah's vile nature. It was

true what she had said: Sanctuary was better without her in it.

The detective caught Diego's eyes and they shared the exhausted sentiments of their struggle.

The biker jumped to his feet to help his sister up. She brushed away the aid and forced herself up using a wooden chair for support. She was a strong-willed one, that much was clear.

They heard someone's hurried steps rushing over the patio and looked to the entrance as Gutierrez rushed in. "Everyone okay?" he asked.

"Call it in," said Maxim calmly, "but leave the others out of it."

The rookie nodded with firm obedience. "And the fed?" he asked, referring to Nithya.

"Just get the paramedics here. This is finally our jurisdiction. The marshal's office will handle this scene for as long as we can." Gutierrez returned outdoors to use the radio.

Diego watched Deborah's body on the floor with apprehension. Maxim looked closely and thought he could see the faintest of movements in her broken frame.

"She said you were dead," started the biker, keeping his eyes on the woman.

Maxim cringed as he recalled the sensation of being buried alive. "I was dying," he answered calmly. "Bracing against an irreconcilable weight. But I was dug from the ground."

Diego looked at him strangely. The grain bin would be

explained when he saw it. For now, the biker turned his attention to other concerns. "What happened to Gaston?"

The detective shook his head weakly. "Shot up pretty bad. He was barely moving." At those words, Angelica went to the backyard.

"Don't worry," said the biker, returning his eyes to the woman on the floor. "These wolves don't die so easily. Neither do you, apparently."

Maxim thought about the man's words as they both heard raspy breathing getting heavier. Deborah was definitely still among them. The detective immediately reloaded his weapon and bent down over her, rolling Deborah so that she was on her back.

"Idiot," spoke the wolf with a spirit that made them both jump. She had coughed up blood, a doubtless sign of a punctured lung, yet she had the strength and alacrity to grab Maxim by the neck.

The detective put a hand on each of hers, one tugging on her grip and the other, holding his gun, vying to keep her other arm at bay. She pulled his head down and bared her teeth. Diego leapt forward and buried his knee into her shoulder to keep Deborah pinned to the wood floor.

The bloodied wolf was not able to overpower the two men on top of her but did not yield. She was intractable, even against the threat of oblivion. The three locked themselves in a tight embrace and pressed with all their might.

"We're not going to die, Maxim," she said, laughing up spittle.

The detective twisted out of the woman's choke and suddenly found his weapon free. He put the Glock 22 to Deborah's heart at point blank and pulled the trigger several times.

"Fuck!" he yelled. "Can't you see you're beaten?"

Her body slackened and both men eased their grips. They rested next to her, their chests heaving as their drained bodies recovered. Gutierrez ran to the door but stopped short as he saw they were not in danger. He turned and left them alone again, perhaps allowing them to do what needed to be done.

"She's not lying, Maxim," said Diego. "You didn't shoot her with silver. She's powerful. She may recover."

Maxim contorted his brow. "Don't you have another knife or something?"

Diego shook his head. "I'm afraid silver daggers are fairly expensive. Until we find Doka's corpse, my weapon is lost in the trees of Sycamore."

They sat in silent frustration for a moment. Maxim needed to end this, and not only for Lola. The detective found himself, as he often did, mindlessly rubbing the ring he still wore on his finger. If he was to truly move on then he needed to stop living with that old promise. With bittersweet release, Maxim Dwyer pulled his wedding band off his finger for the very last time.

He looked down at Deborah and knew that this would be the end for her as well. Maxim set his jaw and plunged the ring into the cavity in her chest, pushing deep until the silver rested inside the woman's heart. He glanced at Diego, the expert in these matters, who nodded his satisfaction. Deborah Holton would not return.

The sound of sirens jarred him from his stupor. There were still loose ends to tie up. Maxim sprung to his feet, holstered his gun, and left Gutierrez to greet the responders. The two men exited from the back door.

Gaston's pickup truck had lost its shiny luster. What hadn't been consumed by the grain bin sat mostly buried by its contents. The passenger door was open. The man was now sitting against the back wheel with Angelica tending to him.

While Gaston looked critically wounded, Maxim was not so worried, especially after the eye-opening events inside. The detective gave the big man a nod of thanks that the wolf returned. Although a cold exchange, there would forever be an understanding between the two.

Nithya stood behind the truck, fearful of the coming police. She laboriously moved deeper into the forest.

"Hold it," called out Maxim, once again drawing his weapon. He strode closer to the woman that he couldn't help caring for. But he knew he had a duty. Even if it was sad, it was just. "You can't simply leave, Nithya."

She looked at him with heartfelt eyes as he raised his gun. "I could have left you buried, Maxim." When she saw that the detective's pistol remained steady, she added, "I never lied to you about my feelings."

Maxim's hand wavered. Part of him felt that she had told him everything he needed to hear. His heart had been closed for two tortuous years, maybe even longer than that, and he was now faced with arresting the only woman who'd been able to reawaken his emotions. Still, Maxim held the gun raised.

Nithya smiled. There was a moment of happiness in her eyes, as if she had seen in him a flash of his quality that she adored, and turned to continue walking away. "You'll have to shoot me then."

The detective sighed, swallowed, and put his pistol away. "I don't need a gun to restrain you, Nithya." He stepped forward with a heavy heart—but stopped short with surprise when Angelica moved in between them.

"She helped me," said the young girl. It was dark out, but for a moment Maxim saw a flash of yellow across her brown eyes. She intended to help Nithya leave.

"You were lucky," proclaimed Maxim. "You could have died just like the others." He looked back to appeal to Diego, but the biker kneeled silently next to Gaston.

The short girl lifted her head proudly and brushed her curly locks behind her shoulders as she stood in his way. "It's what I wanted."

"You may have lived but many others died. What she did was wrong."

Angelica was obstinate. "They can't tell you the truth because they're dead. I'm the only one left alive that you can ask, and I'm telling you that what she did wasn't wrong."

Nithya again turned to Maxim. "There is a tumor in my head, Detective. I had hoped to have the time to discover what I needed in order to survive, but the pain is greater every day. What's more, I've been bitten by Deborah, savagely. I am likely to succumb to the rabies for all my efforts."

"No," said Angelica. "You can treat yourself like you did me."

Nithya shook her head. "One out of twenty-one lived. That accounts for less than five percent of all subjects. Those numbers are similar to the control." Nithya was overcome with a tragic smile. "Two years of effort, and all of my work has been in vain. Now, in two months..."

"No," repeated Angelica. "You did help me!"

Nithya watched the girl sadly before addressing the detective. "Is it really so hard to let me die with my freedom?" she asked. "Allow me this, Maxim. My last moment of happiness."

She turned to walk away.

Angelica had tears in her eyes but Maxim still stood earnestly. Could he really just let the woman escape? What justice had fate orchestrated for her?

"Let it go," urged Diego with calm sobriety. Maxim's gaze fell upon his friend, who was now standing next to him. "There's been enough fighting."

Something stirred inside of Maxim. For most of his life he had never broken the rules that were set before him, but recent events had presented him with many opportunities to reconsider. Was he truly sure that sticking to such extremes was the right thing to do?

Maxim discovered that he did nothing as Nithya Rao disappeared behind the grain bin.

"You need to get out of here too," he said to Diego and

his sister. "If your names are in the report, the CDC will follow up with you. You don't want to be on their radar." He looked to Gaston, who was bloody but breathing in a controlled manner. The wolf needed medical attention and wouldn't be going anywhere.

Angelica smiled at him. "You're all right, old man." The girl considered for a moment. "For a *policía*." She then tugged at her brother's shirt but found him holding his ground.

"The hostages have seen me," said Diego. "I've been in the marshal's office twice. They already know about me. Besides, Gutierrez has my bike and is wearing my clothes."

His sister let out a laugh but she waited, thinking he was only joking. "Come on, bro," she insisted.

The biker firmly shook his head. "You need to get out of here, Angelica. You'll be fine now."

Maxim could see the resolve in the man's brown eyes, and his sister did too. The girl sprung away without taking further issue, and the men heard the bustle of the officials impending behind them.

Over the course of the night, the paramedics attended to Gaston and loaded him into the truck. Deborah was pronounced dead at the scene and taken away by the medical examiner. The gray pickup truck was extracted from the grain bin and towed. Hordes of investigators swarmed the scene like ants and the feds got involved. And then, finally, Sycamore Lodge was allowed to rest.

As the morning stirred, the sun one again commanded its place in the sky.

Epilogue

The black Scrambler roared in the middle of a greater thunder, a throng of bikers returning from the Flagstaff hospital where Gaston was recovering. The new president was respected among the remaining MC members for managing to keep the CDC from shutting them down.

As they halted at the first stoplight in Sanctuary, Diego glanced to his flank and saw Melody on her hog, sharing a smile with him. She winked and he returned the gesture even though it was sure to have gone unnoticed behind his helmet.

The light switched to green and invited them to resume their pleasant ride. Up ahead, a large camper was parked awkwardly on the side of the road and a shiny silver TT was positioned behind it. As they got closer, Diego saw Maxim standing in the grass, wearing his white hat, circling the abandoned vehicle.

The biker signaled to the rest of the group and broke

away. As they disappeared around the bend ahead, Diego slowed to a stop next to the detective and removed his helmet.

Maxim rubbed his smooth chin. "You're riding with the Seventh Sons now?"

Diego shrugged. "We're just coming from visiting Gaston."

"Is he demanding beer yet?"

"He's okay, aside from the annoyance of having to wait out the entire moon cycle."

The detective chuckled. "Yeah, well, that works out in his favor. He'll be released to the Sanctuary clinic before the two weeks are up, and we can give him leave before he turns. If he stays out of sight for a month or so after that, nobody will notice anything strange the next time they see him."

Diego was impressed. The town was finally living up to its title, providing a haven for a persecuted people. His gaze fell on Melody, who was parked some distance ahead, waiting for him.

Maxim caught the gesture. "Are you sure this one isn't going to get you into any trouble?"

"Can't be any worse than my sister."

The detective raised his eyebrows in agreement but stayed silent.

"By the way," asked Diego, "are you coming to Sycamore Lodge tonight to send her off? She wants to thank you again for everything you've done."

"So she's set on leaving, huh?"

The thought would've troubled Diego a few days ago, but he had found a way to accept it. He was surprised at the liberation he felt. "Sycamore was just a speed bump for her. She wants to find her own place in this world. As her older brother, I need to encourage that."

"And Nithya?"

The biker shrugged. "She's gone. They're not traveling together. Angelica might be back here someday, though. She knows where to find me, at least; I found an apartment in Sanctuary. I think I might stick around for a while."

Maxim drew his head back in surprise. "So this little party is going to be a regular treat." He was talking about the MC.

"Sanctuary is married to the Seventh Sons. With Gaston down and the deaths of the others, the club is at half its normal size. They don't object to hanging out with a like mind."

"Your motorcycle doesn't make you like them."

Diego nodded. "I can never be a wolf because of my vaccinations, but through all of this, I think the MC has recognized the importance of friends over circumstantial ties. They trust me enough."

"They run drugs."

"I've heard," said the biker. "I don't want any part of that. It's not action or money that I'm after. Speaking of which," said Diego, pointing behind him, "I see you got a new ride."

Maxim smiled as he admired what he could see of his sports car on the other side of the camper.

"Yeah, well, I think it's time that I opened up to some new experiences myself."

The biker chuckled as he examined the aggressive lines of the small roadster. "The silver's a nice touch."

The police officer thought intensely for a moment. "A new promise to myself."

That's when Diego noticed that the man had no rings on. He could have recovered the keepsake if he had wanted, but would there have been a point?

Diego placed his gold helmet on his head again, leaving the visor open to talk. He motioned to the old camper Maxim had been studying. "Anything going on over here?"

"Just the usual," said the detective dismissively. "Sanctuary is a lot more boring than you'd probably expect."

"Need any help?"

Maxim scrunched his eyes. "Nah. I can handle it."

Diego patted his friend on the shoulder and readied his bike to go. "Brotherhood and the open road, Maxim, that's why I'm here."

The police officer crossed his arms and shot Diego a suspicious look. The biker shut the black visor and pulled away from the inquisitive stare.

"Besides," he called back, grinning, "you really do have some beautiful forests out here."

-Finn

Read Next:
The Blood of Brothers
Sycamore Moon Book Two

Continue the Sycamore Moon series
where Domino Finn books are sold.

DominoFinn.com

Be notified when new Domino Finn
stories are released, right to your inbox.
Sign up at the website and never miss another book.

Connect

If you're reading this, it means you demand more from your urban fantasy. Dark forest monsters are good for a scare, but they're nothing without a layered cast of characters and realistic plot drivers. *Sycamore Moon* is my stab at a cut above the rest: driving mystery, true friends banding against impossible odds, and themes that hopefully make you put the book down and ponder, if even for only a minute.

My writing process demands quality control at every step of development. I hope you agree *Sycamore Moon* is the premium product I strive to make it. Unfortunately, doubling down on originality and quality in an on-demand world has drawbacks. It's simply not possible for me to get you a brand-new novel every month or two. The process takes time.

That's where you come in. Together we can build a better book.
All you need to do is connect.

- Join the Outlaw Underground, our private Facebook group. (www.facebook.com/groups/dominofinnfans/)

- Leave an all-too-important review where you bought the book. Each one helps more than you know.

- Recommend this book to your friends. Link it on social media.

- Join my reader group newsletter, get a free story, and hear from me only when I have new releases or important news. You'll never miss another launch sale again. (dominofinn.com/newsletter/)

Simple, right? Five minutes of your time makes a world of difference to me, Maxim, and Diego. Thank you for your heartfelt support. I'll keep writing as long as you keep reading.

- Domino Finn

Preview:

The Blood of Brothers
Sycamore Moon Book Two

A 6 a.m. phone call was never a good thing. Whether a family member in trouble, a friend who needed a favor, or a telemarketing recording from another time zone, it didn't matter—the call was a recipe for immediate anxiety. An overbearing ring that demanded attention, right at that moment. It was a jarring, imbalanced way to wake up, creating an edgy tension that wouldn't dissolve until the day ended with a beer in hand.

In short, early phone calls were unwelcome.

As the sole homicide detective in Sanctuary, Arizona, Maxim Dwyer knew these calls heralded an entirely different kind of pain. To a lot of people. And he was the lucky one.

The darkness of the morning was foreboding. In the peak of the summer, the bedroom should've been bright by now. Some days it was a struggle just for the sun to come up. But it always did, in the end. As did Maxim.

Sanctuary was a small town. The police force was nine men

strong, including the marshal, and Maxim was the only assigned detective. That meant he handled all sorts of calls: robberies, violent crimes, and cases that required tact. The uniforms managed the day-to-day stuff: domestic violence, drunk and disorderlies at the biker roadhouse, accidents, theft, and vandalism. Most of the work this season involved keeping ornery groups of campers in line. But the officers on duty were trained to handle light investigative work if needed. For Maxim to be summoned this early, there was only one explanation.

No time to shower or shave. No brushing or flossing. A slap of cold water to the face was an amazing stimulant when it needed to be. And breakfast was overrated.

Maxim threw on an old suit and headed to the crime scene. An unnatural fog hung in the air, blocking out the sky. On the way, his sleep-filled eyes squinted as the sun gained ground in the sky. It pierced the glaze of weather and seemed to burn it away. By the time he pulled his silver Audi TT into Sanctuary High, daytime was official.

The detective idled past the large building of gray and brown brick. Wide paths of concrete and asphalt with newly painted lines covered the lot all the way into the parking area in the back. It was summer break, so the only two cars present were the brand-new cruisers driven by Hitchens and Cole, the department's oldest veterans. The cars were pretty slick for Caprices, making it look like the Sanctuary Marshal's Office had better resources than it did.

Maxim parked his coupe between the squad cars and

scratched his prickly chin. He gazed across the large green field before him. Surrounded by a chain-link fence, it shared the school's back grounds with the parking lot. The asphalt section didn't need an outer fence, however. The curb was enough.

Besides the current police presence, nothing appeared amiss. An empty school, an off-season, and a whole lot of quiet. Immediately, Maxim decided the serenity of the location played a part in the crime.

He exited his car and spied the police tape across the field, where the metal fence kept out a thick cluster of trees. The forests in the greater Sycamore area were dense. The tree line had only been cut back as much as the school needed, and even that encroachment seemed unwelcome. Sanctuary was a beautiful town precisely because it hovered on the edge of civilization. Its inhabitants appreciated being reminded of the wild. As the detective watched Hitchens and Cole work outside the fence, he realized nature had inched a little too close to society once again.

Maxim strode through the open gate and made his way across the field. The lawn was freshly cut and still wet with dew. The expanse was mostly wild grass, natural in this climate and easy to maintain. The football field, along the street beside the school building, was laid with sod and more meticulously cared for. Closer, there was a cement court for basketball and other activities. The larger area here, where it was more natural, was mostly used for pick-up games of soccer and other general activities, like running.

Large swaths of grass were cut, but other sections grew long and appeared ignored. Maxim noticed the ride-on mower on his side of the fence, right next to the scene, and immediately ran the events through his head. The groundskeeper was mowing the lawn as he probably did once a week, judging by the grass length. He had only managed to do about a third of the field before he made the grisly discovery and called the police. As Maxim approached the officers standing on the other side of the fence, he noticed a Mexican man in his late forties hunched next to them. He wondered why he hadn't seen his car in the parking lot, and made a mental note to check on that.

As Maxim reached the fence, the other two officers shared a smile.

"How's it going, rock star?" asked Cole through the chain-link. The tallest of the three, and the most built, he was an imposing figure, but his demeanor alternated between bouts of sobriety and jest in a way that was unexpected. He wore black nitrile gloves and held a small camera—standard investigative procedure for crime scenes.

"I told you not to call me that," said Maxim tiredly. Ever since he'd closed out a federal case the year before, things had been different. To the media, he had captured a serial killer. To the Centers for Disease Control, he had saved their reputation. It was a huge win for the marshal's office and for the detective, but the unwanted attention made his job more difficult. And that was without the added torment of his fellow officers.

"Sorry, just trying to make you feel good after we rousted

you from your beauty sleep."

Maxim clenched his jaw. Hitchens and Cole weren't like most veterans who punched in and out of work watching the clock. They were in prime physical condition. Even Hitchens, who didn't look it because of the extra weight. They liked action and they liked the midnight shift. Maxim knew they were as reliable as any on the force, and they knew the same of him. The banter was just how they passed the time. "I work nights when I need to."

"Yeah?" asked Cole. "I'll remember that next time a drunken camper stabs his buddy with a s'mores stake."

Maxim grimaced. It was Cole's favorite story. Only two weeks old, he repeated it loudly and often. Two best friends had gotten into an argument. One had stabbed the other straight through his forearm with the metal wire. The hot end of the pole had gone in and out cleanly, but the melted marshmallow and chocolate burned his skin pretty badly. Cole had handled the call without involving Maxim.

"If I hear that goddamned story one more time..." grumbled Hitchens. He had less patience in this early hour than the others. Unlike Cole, he hadn't been on shift, but as acting sergeant, Hitchens had been awakened alongside Maxim. He appeared especially irritable today. "I don't wanna hear about s'mores or rock stars. I don't wanna hear about how the media attention got extra funds for the department and that's the reason we have our new cruisers. I don't wanna hear that the CDC gave us a wide berth as thanks. And I especially don't want to hear anymore goddamned Spanish today."

Maxim and Cole shared a look of warning. Within the span of seconds, Barney Hitchens had simultaneously predicted and headed off the direction of their banter. They knew not to press him.

Allowing the rant to simmer, Maxim again looked to the groundskeeper. The man sat in the grass on the other side of the fence. "He doesn't speak a word of English, does he?"

Hitchens scowled and turned his back to them. Cole shook his head. "Negative."

"And none of us can translate." Maxim chuckled to himself. Arizona was a good place to know Spanish. He'd been meaning to learn. But who had the free time? "I assume you have Gutierrez en route?"

Hitchens turned around. "I called his ass three times. Imparted to him a sense of urgency." Then he stormed off again. Maxim smiled. Poor guy. As the rookie, Gutierrez would be feeling the brunt of the sergeant's ire today.

The detective could see part of the body from where he was standing, as the groundskeeper first did, but he preferred to walk through the crime scene systematically, examining the stage before he watched the play. "Any vague translation of the 911 call?"

"Didn't call it in," answered Cole. "Doesn't have a phone. He flagged me down in the street as I happened to be driving by."

"Any sign of anyone else? Any other vehicles?"

"Negative. Just him. I've seen him cutting the grass here before. He works alone in the summer."

"So what do you know?"

"Well, it's pretty clear the man was working and stumbled on the vic. He ran around with a wild look in his eyes for a while until he calmed down. I think he's worn out from the shock. What do you think? Can you use your famed 'stubborn grit' to understand Spanish?"

Maxim flashed a fake smile. The veterans liked to quote media reports to comedic effect. Maxim was just happy none of them had picked up the line comparing him to a pit bull. It was just part of the extra shit he had to deal with for being on TV. Apparently, the joke still wasn't old nine months later. "I'll wait for the translator. And you shouldn't believe everything you hear, Cole. All I am is an observer of life. I know what people do and why they do it."

Cole nodded, only half listening. "Yeah, well, not this time."

Something in the man's voice, a sense of surrender, said he didn't even want to make jokes about this. Maxim peeked past the tall man again. He could already tell this was a morbid scene. Refocusing on the officer, he decided to cut to the chase. "What about the vic?"

Cole stepped away from the chain-link toward Hitchens. "Well, I think you'd better come to the other side and take a look."

Maxim considered the high fence that separated them, then checked down its length to the left and right. "Where the fuck is the gate?"

Cole chuckled. "Tell me something. If you're such a great observer of life, then how'd you manage to wind up on the wrong side of the fence?"

Maxim's face turned red as his eyes traced the path to the street, past the school. There was probably a gate there but it might be locked. Better to go around the back way, where the cars were, and circle the outside fence from the parking lot, through the wild ground. "Well, why the fuck didn't you drive your cruisers around?"

"The groundskeeper jumped into my car and I drove in before I knew where to look."

"What about Hitchens?"

Cole shrugged. "I guess he just parked where I parked."

Maxim cursed and considered climbing the obstacle but figured that would only give the officers a better story. He turned and made his way back to his car.

"For the record," called out Cole, "the sergeant didn't fall for it."

Maxim Dwyer smiled, careful not to let the others see. It was a funny joke. He would need to repay the favor.

When the detective got back to his car, he considered driving it over the curb and into the hilly grass, but only for a moment. Sports cars weren't built for that abuse. Looking at the shiny new police cruisers, Maxim realized that Hitchens had the same thought. Maxim hiked up and around, carefully examining the ground for any clues that might have been left by the events earlier in the morning. He reached the others without seeing anything amiss.

There were two lines of crime scene tape, each tied to the fence on one end and a tree on the other. Cole hadn't bothered closing off the border in the trees. The officer held the tape up as Maxim ducked underneath.

"I didn't touch a single thing," said Cole. "You might not want to either until the doc shows up."

"You have the ME on the way? I thought Medina was on vacation?"

"Nope. ME-dina just came back yesterday. You believe that luck?"

Maxim whistled. He'd assumed they would tap the morgue in Flagstaff. That would have been slow going because County had a larger caseload. Sanctuary didn't have a backlog of autopsies to deal with. Having the doc back meant they could expedite things locally.

Maxim approached Hitchens, who silently contemplated the body. Maxim stepped in line with him and caught the whiff of a butcher's shop. "Hell of a way to go," said the sergeant.

A large sycamore towered above its neighbors. Its stout trunk split into two main branches. Hanging on the heaviest outcropping, upside down, was a mutilated man. There was no skin on the body.

Maxim grabbed a pair of black nitrile gloves from a cardboard box and snapped them up to his wrists. "I don't suppose anyone checked vital signs."

"Oh shit," said Cole. "Did I forget that?"

A thick rope tied to the overhanging branch held up both legs by the ankles, which were bound together. The victim's hands hung loose, barely brushing the ground, leaving his head at waist height. Empty, dark eyes stared from a meaty skull. Bone was visible in some places, but most of the surface area was exposed muscle and fat. The naked man had been strung up and skinned like a deer.

The grass on this side of the fence was unkempt. Deeper beneath the canopy, the shade prevented too much from growing, but the growth along the tree line fared better. It was thick enough to prohibit footprints.

"How close did either of you get?"

"This is it," answered Hitchens. "Cole figured there might be all kinds of evidence that fell around here."

Maxim nodded and stepped forward carefully. He circled the body, giving it a wide berth. As he passed the tree trunk, he carefully examined it. Even though there was plenty of sunlight, he took out a flashlight and ran the beam up and down the bark. Not finding anything, the detective finished his circuit around the body.

"Well, he wasn't killed and skinned here," he said.

Hitchens shook his head slowly. "Not enough blood."

"Not enough is right. The vic was drained dry. Time of death is gonna need to wait for the lab, I think. Lividity and body temp are gonna be thrown off by the drainage. Probably rigor, too."

Hitchens let out a heavy sigh that seemed to empty his wide frame. "Have you ever seen anything like this?"

Maxim shook his head. "It's cold blooded. Calculated. Meant to incite emotion."

"Or vomit," said Cole.

Maxim ignored the remark and carefully inched closer to the body. He noticed a blackened section of muscle over the rib cage. The flashlight revealed some yellow-white puss. He would need to wait for the ME to figure that one out. Moving down the body, it was clear that the flesh of the left arm was torn. The bones in the forearm were more exposed, and the thumb was missing entirely.

"These look like animal bites," said the detective.

Maxim knew the three of them were thinking the same thing. Sanctuary wasn't like other American towns. This one had a large population of wolves, present company included.

The older men scoffed. "New moon's not for another two days," said Hitchens. "Besides, you don't think the Seventh Sons would be this stupid, do you?"

Maxim didn't answer. The Seventh Sons were an outlaw club affiliated with criminal activities. They were brash, tough guys who frequented town and had a clubhouse in the woods. They were werewolves, but they weren't stupid, and they knew it was in their best interests to keep a low profile.

As far as the moon was concerned, not a month went by when Maxim wasn't aware of it. Not in Sycamore. Not anymore. The wolves came out every fourteen days. As

Hitchens had said, it was too early, and there was no way this body was twelve days old.

"I don't know," said the detective, finally. "This looks ceremonial. Supernatural, maybe. I don't take the motorcycle club that way. But we will need to rule them out. Let's assume the time of death was early this morning until the ME tells us otherwise."

A double chime interrupted Maxim's next thought. Hitchens checked his phone and read a message. "It's Gutierrez... I don't believe this."

The rookie was the best option to translate and it appeared he would be late. "What's he say?"

Hitchens grunted. "Verbatim: 'Shit my pants. Going to Starbucks.'"

Cole let out a bellow. Maxim rolled his eyes. He was past joke-telling time and was getting impatient. The longer it took the rookie and the medical examiner to show up, the later he would be up tonight. The longer before he could settle down with a beer. He stomped over to Hitchens and grabbed the phone from him.

Maxim was stunned to see that Hitchens had not lied about the contents of the message.

"What the fuck?" Maxim exclaimed, tossing the phone back to the sergeant. "What sense does that kid make? Those two sentences don't go together. You can say, 'I shit my pants. Going home.' Or you can say, 'I want coffee. Going to Starbucks.'" Hitchens and Cole started giggling like kids, and

Maxim slipped into a smile in the middle of his rant. "What you cannot fucking say is, 'Shit my pants. Going to Starbucks.' That's a non sequitur."

The officers laughed some more, and Maxim imagined Gutierrez walking into the Starbucks bathroom with a load in his pants and couldn't hold back anymore. He joined them. It felt good to release some tension, and they would surely call on this laughter in the future just as often as Cole brought up the s'mores story. The rookie wouldn't live this one down.

"Fuck it," said Maxim, wiping his eyes with the sleeve of his jacket. "Tell him to meet you at the station. You mind taking our wit down there until I meet you?"

Hitchens strutted away. "Was waiting for you to ask. I don't want to smell this meat market anymore. You all have a good one."

"Wait," said Cole. "Tell him to pick me up a vanilla Frappuccino."

Hitchens and Maxim both stopped what they were doing and turned to the officer.

"What?" Cole asked. "It's getting hot out."

Hitchens shook his head and continued on his way. "You better hope that boy washes his hands."

Maxim turned to the body and felt his smile leave him. Hitchens was right. This vic was a piece of meat. Chewed on as an animal might do, but drained and skinned as only a person could. Of course he had to consider the werewolves. But until he had an ID, ruling anybody out would be difficult.

Maxim kneeled next to the body. He turned the flashlight on again and searched for clues in the grass. Some blood was below the body, of course, so it hadn't been left out to drain for days. The smell was still fresh. This morning was still looking good for time of death.

"Did you get pictures of this blood down here?"

Cole carefully inched closer. "I was afraid of disturbing the evidence." The officer leaned over and took a few shots. Then he turned the digital display to face the detective and scrolled through his pictures. "I got all angles of the body, wide shots with the tree, the rope, the knots, the trunk."

Maxim nodded. "Get close-ups of the wounds. The tearing in the arm and shoulder. The missing thumb. The puss on the torso." As he spoke, the body spun slightly on the rope, and a flash of the skull caught Maxim's eye. He shined his flashlight at the right side of the suspended head and saw a small indentation between the ear and the temple. "And get a picture of this gunshot wound too."

It was difficult to detect on the massacred body, but there was a tiny hole. A single, long strand of black hair stuck out, glued to the head by matted blood. Maxim leaned around the body to check the other side. The skull had no other anomalies.

"Probably a small round that bounced around in the brain and never came out. I bet it's still stuck in there. Hopefully the slug's in good enough shape for ballistics." Cole silently nodded as he snapped several pictures.

Maxim stood up and shined the flashlight along the rope. It

was rough hemp, possibly littered with fibers or DNA, but nothing visible to the naked eye. Maxim allowed his gaze to travel up to the tree and just stared, as if the new perspective would help him. He thought of the common crime scene adage: never forget to look up. Evidence could end up anywhere. It almost made the detective laugh. This was one crime scene where nobody would need to be reminded to check the tree. Almost dizzy, Maxim shook his head and backed away.

The detective peered up and down the corridor between the high school fence and the tree line. To his right, through the football field, was the street. The left was the back of the grounds, where he had come from. Somebody could have skirted the property from either direction to get here. Then Maxim considered the trees. He looked straight into the forested lot and saw how quickly everything turned to piles of leaves and brush. Maxim hated outdoor crime scenes. There was too much to rule out. Some early guesses at this stage, if incorrect, could tank the investigation.

Maxim moved towards the football field, seeing what this path offered in the way of criminal harbor. The field was set off from the school building but directly adjacent. There was no entrance to it from this outside lot. However, a gate at the corner led into the basketball court. Maxim noticed a rusted chain and lock holding it closed. A quick inspection left him confident that it hadn't been opened in a long time.

Maxim turned away from the school, walking along the football field now, parallel to the front street. This was no stadium; it was an open-air arena with bleachers. While it didn't provide full cover from the street, the combination of size and seating afforded a large amount of privacy. Maxim walked the entire length, searching the grass for anything out of the ordinary. At the far corner he made his way to the street. Dirt sat flush with the asphalt, impressed with tire tracks.

Immediately, Maxim imagined the crime as it occurred. The vic was strung up at another location. Skinned. Drained. Shot in the head either before or after. Then he was brought here in a vehicle, likely a truck or van of some sort. The killer pulled to the side of the road, unseen in the early morning hours, and lugged the body along the fence in relative privacy. He strung the dead man up and disappeared, waiting for its inevitable discovery.

But why here? Why Sanctuary High?

Maxim shook his head as he made his way back to Cole. He would tell the officer to rope off the area by the street and take pictures of the tracks. It wouldn't likely lead to anything, but it was worth a shot. Along the way, every twenty feet or so, the detective kneeled, turned on his flashlight, and shone it across the grass. He could barely see the light he cast against the daylight, but he was confident in the technique.

When he was almost back to the body, he made one last sweep with his flashlight and saw a glint reflected back his way. Maxim cocked his head and tried to make out the object in the tall grass. He pushed up against his tired knees and advanced on it, smiling when he stood over a skinning knife. It had a small, stubby blade that was shorter than the handle. Three colors of wood were glued together to decorate the length, but the bottom half of the handle was a carved deer antler. The blade was covered in blood.

"Cole. You'd better get a picture of this."

This wasn't the murder weapon, Maxim guessed, but it was damning all the same. The detective knew the biker it belonged to.

Also Try:
Black Magic Outlaw

Did you know Maxim and Diego aren't the only ones standing up to the supernatural?

Did you know they're part of a wider shared universe of everyday heroes?

Did you know that sometimes the good guys use a little magic too?

If you're into bullets, black magic, and an extra helping of action, check out Cisco Suarez, a too-cocky-for-his-own-good necromancer in a tank top.

Dead Man

Black Magic Outlaw Book One

Waking up dead is the worst. Trust me. I know these things.

The last time I woke up this hungover I was naked, soaking wet, and wrapped in a Cuban flag.

This time, at least, I had clothes on. I couldn't see them in the pitch black, but I could feel them. I could feel other things too. Raw pounding in my head. Enough tightness in my chest to make every breath a chore. I was in ten kinds of pain. Apparently that wasn't enough because my leg was asleep too.

There was more. Cold, wet, grimy more. Flies buzzed around my face, circling the stench of death. My arm was slimy. I shifted my weight and something crunched beneath me. My hands and feet pressed against the tight confines of a box.

Smell of death and decay. Check. Some kind of giant coffin. Check. I'm no mathematician but things were starting to add up.

Despite the evidence of my apparent death, I didn't panic. You see, I'm a necromancer (among other things) so I know a little about the subject. I couldn't tell you where I was or what happened the day before to get me here, but I had an inkling I was still alive. Even if just barely.

I tried to sit up. A stabbing pain pulsed through my body until I relaxed again. Request denied.

Okay, deep breath time. I focused inward to calm myself, then reopened my eyes. A thin sliver of light crept through the seam of my crypt overhead, but it was too weak to illuminate the interior.

Good thing I knew a trick or two.

I stared into the darkness, more deeply than before. Not into the box or any physical place, but into a place within me. The pupils of my eyes leaked and my green irises filled with black, and with a blink I could see.

And you thought the necromancer thing was all about wearing black and growing your hair long. I hate to burst your bubble but I'm not a walking death metal stereotype. I don't wear a trench coat and I have a crew cut. I live in Miami, for fuck's sake. It's hot and humid *in the winter*. No sense getting a heatstroke to appeal to northern sensibilities.

Not only that but Cisco Suarez (that's me) isn't just a necromancer. He's a shadow charmer too. That's the magic I just called on. The darkness all around me, it was still there—I could just see through it now.

The thin razorblade of light now stung my eyes. I avoided looking directly at it and checked the rest of the tomb. Crushed cardboard boxes. Stuffed plastic bags. My accommodations weren't as morbid as I'd feared. This wasn't a coffin but a dumpster.

Maybe I wasn't dead after all. Just down for a nap. A bed made of beer bottles. My pillow? A dead sewer rat.

That would've made most men jump, but remember: necromancer. I scrunched my nose and reached for it.

The simple act of limberness was a battle of pain. My muscles were sore. Dry and withered like the old husks of a toppled tree. My bones creaked and my joints were half-dried cement. I stirred up more dust than the Mummy. But I pushed through the agony until I dangled the dead rat by its tail.

It had been decapitated. A tribute. Sacrificial magic, and not mine. That spelled trouble.

I checked for other signs of ritual or binding. Charms. Runes. Burnt sacraments. Scanning the contents of the dumpster, I spied a couple of dark-red cowboy boots on my feet and literally hopped in place. (I almost knocked my head on the dumpster lid.) You see, the rat I could handle. My wearing a bona fide pair of alligator boots was unacceptable.

Don't get me wrong. There was nothing magic or cursed about them. It's just that the modern Cuban doesn't wear cowboy boots. Cisco Suarez doesn't wear cowboy boots.

That's me again, by the way. Shorter and catchier than Francisco, it always reminded me of a comic book name. What kid didn't want to be a superhero? I liked the sound of it so much I picked up referring to myself in the third person. My fatal flaw.

Enough about my name. Let's talk spellcraft. I'm what you call an animist: an everyday human who happens to tap into spirits for magical energy. Wild, huh?

I know what you're thinking: A cleric deals with gods and a wizard with books, right? Well, put the Player's Handbook away and forget everything you think you know. Gods and books have plenty of overlap. (The most famous book in all history is a notable example.)

Fact is, magic is a universal force in the world, pure energies known as the Intrinsics. They're the building blocks of all creation. People like you or me can only manipulate them through spirits. That makes us animists.

Everything else is just a title. Wizard. Cleric. Learned men like to use mage (it's more sophisticated). You see shaman or witch doctor applied to primitive peoples. Or if you wanna vilify animists, call them witches and warlocks. You get the idea. I'm sure some academic somewhere compiled a list of unofficial "official" definitions—but you'd have a hard time running into that terminology on the street. And the street is where the real stuff happens.

Case in point: the dumpster I was lying in.

Some alarm in my head screamed that I was hurt. Maybe fatally. The thing was, besides stiffness, there wasn't anything wrong with me. I wasn't dying, anyway. I kinda felt like a homeless vampire more than anything else. Which would be a lot funnier if I didn't know vampires actually existed. After all, right now I had a hangover from hell—maybe hell was where I came from.

You're probably bored by now, right? Sorry. I think too

much. It's a problem I'm trying to address.

With a strained kick of an alligator boot, the lid of the dumpster flew open. Blinding light engulfed me and seared my senses. I literally hissed and uselessly threw my hands up in defense. Maybe I was a vampire after all.

But I didn't burst into flames. After I took another second to get my head on straight, I realized I was still drawing upon my shadow sight. I drained the darkness from my eyes, my lids pushing out black tears, until it was safe to look.

A blue sky. Fluffy clouds. Palm trees.

I was in South Beach.

Not the pretty coastline with white sand they show on TV during football games. That was never far in Miami Beach, of course, but the back alleys were far less picturesque. I was just off Washington Avenue somewhere, outside a dive bar. The alley was empty. I heaved myself over the dumpster wall and landed on the concrete with a thud. I wouldn't win any vaulting medals but it got the job done. Standing and walking involved entirely new kinds of pain, but either it was wearing off or I was getting used to it.

Normally I'd assume this predicament was my doing—it wouldn't be me if I didn't go big—but the dead rat was a bit much. It was also a dead giveaway that someone else was involved.

I padded at my jean pockets. I had a cell phone but no wallet. Was I robbed? It seemed unlikely given the evidence of spellcraft. A beatdown, then?

I frowned. I'd annoyed people, sure. I'd had minor run-ins with gang tough guys and stirred up the local talent, but that was life as a small-time hustler. I was too young for real enemies. No reason anyone should wish me dead.

The preternatural fog in my head wasn't going away. I couldn't think clearly. No amount of head-scratching helped.

With my head on a swivel for danger, I staggered to the pink sidewalk. (Miami Beach, remember?) I was ready for anything. What I didn't expect was to be ignored.

Small groups of shoppers strolled up and down Washington Avenue. Horns honked and cars inched forward and came to a stop at the light. I got a few odd looks but nobody confronted me or threw any blood curses my way. It was just your average whatever-day-it-was in South Beach.

A man strolled by and held his hand out to me. While trying (and failing) to make eye contact, I accepted his offering. A nickel and two pennies. He avoided my puzzled expression and continued on his way.

That was random, but I couldn't be accountable for the South Beach crazies. Cisco Suarez needed to stay on task. Since everything appeared normal outside, I considered pumping the bar employees for information.

The car that was stopped on the road in front of me clicked its doors locked. I looked and the woman in the passenger seat averted her eyes. Bitch. Then I got a glimpse of myself in the window reflection.

I would've locked the doors too.

Besides my healthy tan, nothing of my disheveled appearance was recognizable. My usually close-cropped hair hung over my shoulders in a wild mane. My eyes were permanently frantic, sporting the raised-by-wolves look. The full-on homeless beard didn't help. And my clothes. Besides my jeans and red cowboy boots, of all things I wore a yellowed and bloodied tank top.

Tank tops were never really my look but, to my surprise, I actually filled this one out. My chest strained against the thin fabric and my bare arms looked carved from marble. Still in disbelief, I flexed a bicep at my reflection. Maybe the car windows were made from magic fun-house mirrors.

This warrants an explanation. I may be a little cocky and reckless at times, but one thing I'm not is a gym rat. I was always that scrappy skinny kid who was too stupid to stay down. Yes, that means I lost a lot of fights. I wanted to be a superhero but lacked the dedication. What animist would spend time working out anyway? The power of the world at your fingertips, wasted by repeatedly picking up and putting down heavy things.

No, I was never out of shape, but I was supposed to be thin. Now I suddenly felt like Peter Parker after running into that radioactive spider. I was straight buff, is what I'm saying.

My jaw glued to the floor, I stared like a lunatic. The driver floored the gas at his first opportunity. In their place, a matte-black jeep slammed on its brakes. Which was weird since the light was green and the cars behind it honked. I snapped out of my shock as the group of Haitians in the jeep focused on me, anger in their eyes.

They yelled, "Dead man!" and dismounted, brandishing light automatic weapons.

I threw seven cents at them.

Also by Domino Finn

About the Author

Domino Finn is an award-winning game industry veteran, a media rebel, and a werewolf junkie. As a grizzled author of urban fantasy and litRPG, his stories are equal parts spit, beer, and blood, and are notable for treating weighty issues with a supernatural veneer. If Domino has one rallying cry for the world, it's that fantasy is serious business.

Take a stand at DominoFinn.com